THE
CH

MW00938520

BOOK ONE

NOVUS

by

CRYSTAL MARCOS

Cat Marcs Publishing

Silverdale, Washington

ACKNOWLEDGMENTS

First and foremost, I would like to thank God. There is no way I could have written this book on my own.

I express my deepest gratitude for my editor, Jim Whiting, and his expertise in helping me make my novel print ready. From the beginning, Jim wanted to know who I was as a person. That means a lot to me.

Many thanks to my dearest mother-in-law Ruthie. Who, even after seeing the book in its raw state, still calls me her daughter. Besides myself, she was the first person to read this book.

And a special thanks to my creative little cupcake, Kaylee, who gave me some of the unique names in this book.

Cat Marcs Publishing
PO Box 54
Silverdale, WA 98383

www.CatMarcs.com

Printed in the United States of America

Library of Congress Control Number: 2015944605
Cat Marcs Publishing, Silverdale, WA

ISBN 978-0-9843899-8-8

To my husband for repeatedly asking,
"Is that book ready yet? I'd really like to read it."

NOVUS

PROLOGUE: LIFE

~~Their fate was to be no one's son or daughter, no one's brother or sister, no one's father or mother, no one's kin.~~

NATURAL DISASTERS. Disease. Climate change. War. In the last three centuries, the world's population has been on a drastic decline. In an attempt to combat these issues and preserve themselves, Humans created those they call Cresecren. The name stems from the Latin word *crescere*, which means to grow something, to cultivate. Although not Human, they were created in the likeness of Humans. However, they do not share the same privileges. They are prohibited from choosing a life of their own but instead are assigned a set path to serve Humans.

Cresecrens were originally developed for the military to decrease the number of Human casualties, for scientific studies conducted to prolong Human life, and for high-risk jobs such as hazardous material disposal and underground construction to decrease the number of Human deaths. In more recent years, privileged Humans who were motivated by greed or an increased sense of entitlement began using Cresecrens as domestic servants.

Cresecrens were designed to be distinguishable from Humans. Their eyes were genetically engineered to be a striking deep violet, unlike those of any Human. In later years, they were also given plainly visible permanent markings on their jawlines so there is no mistaking or confusing who they are. These markings are codes the color of coal that show their birthdate down to the exact second.

Humans implemented a lethal plan to discourage Cresecrens from removing their markings. If that should happen, either accidently or intentionally, the Cresecren would suffer an untimely and agonizing death. Additionally, this plan insured that Cresecrens would never forget who they were.

All Cresecrens follow the same twelve-year developmental process. They spend the first five years of their lives in a life-sustaining cocoon. This coma-like state is referred to as "Limbo." While in Limbo, they develop physically in the same way as any Human. Feeding tubes provide sufficient nutrients, and electrodes attached to the brain feed them knowledge of their own existence. In addition to basic life needs, they develop motor skills and speech during these important Limbo years.

At the end of the fifth year, Cresecrens are released from Limbo to a secure facility and allowed to interact with Human researchers and scientists. This is when they first eat solid food and learn to balance themselves. These years are also vitally important because they learn all that is necessary to prepare them to be released into the real world to their assigned placement. In their eleventh year, Cresecrens learn the identity of the Human organization or family they will serve. The next twelve months are dedicated to studying all there is to know about being a valuable Cresecren to this particular organization or family.

Then they receive their birthday markings and become a permanent part of the organization or family. By this time, they should be fully aware of their sole purpose for existence: to spend their lives serving Humans by doing what Humans could not or would not do.

Cresecrens who did not fulfill their purpose—by becoming too old or maimed to continue to be of service or too stubborn to mind who they were meant to serve—are cast out into Cresecren camps where they will remain until they die. These camps are self-governing and are periodically monitored externally by Humans via surveillance cameras. In the remnants of the Northwest region of North America, those camps are Gavaron and Solitare.

ANTICIPATION

IT WAS my birthday—the anniversary of the day I was made, of the day I was given life, of the very moment I was created to serve—and Alecander was late. Alecander is twice my age and we share the same dark hair. We bonded, although bonding is not normal Cresecren behavior. He took me under his wing the moment I stepped on the beach of Gavaron over two years ago. Alecander was the closest thing I had to a father.

I eagerly awaited my visit to the Conservatory but I had promised Alecander I would wait for him before I entered the ship. Going to the Conservatory is a birthday tradition in Gavaron. When we lived among Humans, our birthdays were never celebrated. In Gavaron, the elders decided we should have something to look forward to and celebrate. Every year on our birthday, we trade one of our items for a new one at the Conservatory. The object is to find something more useful than the one claimed the year before.

I thought about the Rawnetts, the Human family I had served and how I endured yearly ridicule from the twins. They teased me relentlessly about how I spent the beginning years of my life. I was particularly relieved at that moment, knowing I did not have to hear their taunts again.

I caressed the weathered hard cover of the book I had read over and over in the last three hundred and sixty-five days. I recited the first passages by heart while I waited. Some might have thought it a foolish choice. However, it had proved itself useful in many ways: entertainment, survival, and research. I would miss it.

I grew antsy and began to study my home by the sea. There was not much to admire. It was once a land full of foliage and rich in resources. At first glance, someone who looked at the main entrance to the underground quarters of Gavaron might have mistaken it for an ancient shipwreck, but in reality it was once a pirate-themed restaurant. I stood on the deck, my preferred entrance to our underground housing. I thought about when the first Cresecrens were banished here and had to make do with what was already present on the land. I imagined the mostly elderly Cresecrens who were no longer able to work trying to build a suitable place to live. Because of an overseas tsunami, they reaped some fortune out of others' misfortunes by using items washed up on shore. Eventually, the federal government did lend a hand in making Gavaron more habitable. We had since encountered aftereffects from other tsunamis and continued to collect useful items that claim our beach.

I saw how seventy-eight years of over-utilization and a growing population of my people had taken their toll on my surroundings. I recalled hearing about the disasters such as the

Great Fire which destroyed seventy percent of our orchards and the Great Flood of '99 that almost obliterated our homes. I wondered where I would have ended up if it had destroyed everything. There were close to three hundred of us in Gavaron and we were only allowed to inhabit certain areas.

My mind wandered for a while until it returned to thoughts of Dahsie and the Conservatory. Dahsie was one of the many Appointeds in charge of different sections of Gavaron. She was the Conservatory Appointed and took her position very serious-ly. I do not believe she ever left the undergrounds of Gavaron since the death of the previous Appointed just before my arri-val. No doubt she would be disappointed I was tardy. Courtesy of Alecander, I would probably have to listen to a scolding be-fore she let me enter.

I peered down into the hull, but the weathered crimson couch was empty. *Where are you, Alecander?* As I took a step back to leap down onto it, I heard my name from behind. I recognized the voice instantly. Alecander's.

"You're late," I said.

He smiled. "You waited."

"Of course. I said I would. Now get on with your speech about what you think I should and should not do today. Dahsie awaits," I said, knowing full well I would have entered the ship had Alecander been one more second late.

"Yes, we mustn't keep her waiting." Alecander reached into his russet satchel and handed me a brown paper bag.

"A present?"

"Yes."

"No one has ever given me a present," I said, as if he did not know.

"Open it."

Whatever was inside was light. I unfolded the bag gently, trying not to crumple it.

"You won't break it," Alecander said with a sly smile.

It was a Supply Appointed Assistant's neck flag, deep purple and soft. I immediately recognized it as a symbol of freedom. Well, as far as freedom could extend its hand to me. The deep purple represented the color of Cresecren eyes. The neck flag was a pass to the outside world for Cresecrens from the camps. Alecander and I were to wear them like necklaces while we traveled to gather supplies. Before we were allowed to enter the Supply Depot, we were to hang them on the end of a flagpole. This informed others of our presence.

I loosened my grasp to allow it to slide down my fingers, draping into a rectangle.

"Where did you get this? Is this why you were late?"

"You are welcome, and yes." Alecander's smile engulfed his face.

I asked what I already knew. "You were chosen to be the Supply Appointed?"

"Yes, last night. I was summoned to the Supply Depot. I received my own neck flag and one for the assistant of my choosing."

"You chose me," I said, more as a statement rather than a

question, suddenly comprehending that the flag would allow me to enter forbidden terrain, the land outside these invisible walls, the land of the Humans!

"There is no better person."

"Thank you." I gasped the words I had used before but rarely meant. This time I truly felt their meaning.

"You're welcome. Blynn and Phillip, the old Supply Appointed and her assistant, have been transferred. I didn't get all the information but I gathered that yet another Cresecren ground is being built down south. We leave tomorrow at 4AM for the Supply Depot. It would be wise if you go to bed early tonight."

Go to bed early? I did not think I would sleep a wink as I eagerly awaited the morning to come. The excitement almost kept me away from my thoughts of the Conservatory. I gently placed the neck flag in my satchel. I did not see Alecander's flag but I trusted it was safely in his own satchel.

"Alecander, give me your speech. I wish to enter the ship," I reminded him. Each year, he told me about how much I had grown both physically and mentally. He also felt the need to remind me about what he thought was a good birthday choice.

FREEDOM

CHOOSE WISELY. Use your head not your eyes. Alecander's words echoed in my mind as I jumped down into the ship onto the tattered couch. I have long since perfected this art. I do not get bruises nor roll off the couch onto the floorboards any more. I peered down and saw that the ladders were empty. However, Famous was working his way up the rope pull. Famous is not his real name. He used to serve the rich and famous Quinso Vardo, giving him a never-ending supply of outlandish stories of lavish parties and the endless flow of seductive women. There was outrage in the common knowledge that Quinso wanted to put his mark on anything the world had to offer regardless of the consequences. He was willing to dabble in any business, including pharmaceuticals, despite having no formal experience in the field. Quinso began receiving death threats when one of the drugs he developed had irreversible adverse effects. Unfortunately, Famous was the Cresecren selected to open all packages, check all vehicles. Anything and everything passed through him first. That is how Famous ended up in Gavaron without lower legs and an incredible story about how he lost them.

"How's it going, Cayden?" Famous called up.

"I'm late for the Conservatory," I answered quickly before Famous began another of his tales.

"Excellent! Is it that time already?" he said, reaching my eye level and reading the codes on my jawline. "You're late. Dahsie has probably already rubbed the fur off of her mangy cat's head."

"Probably," I said, grinning to myself as I realized Alecander would receive payback for making me late. *He* would have to listen to one of Famous' outlandish tales. "Alecander is outside. If you hurry you can catch him," I said.

"Don't choose anything I would choose," he said to me, winking.

I leapt down the last few steps to the gritty ground. Sprinting to the Conservatory stairs, I recalled my first birthday selection after arriving in Gavaron. I had searched for over two hours for the perfect present. I nearly drove Dahsie mad with the cast-iron rod I lugged around, poking and prodding the precious commodities. There were many things to choose from, like cloth material, baskets, and tools. Afterwards, I left with that very rod, thinking I could choose no better. It was not the best choice I could have made but I still used the rod on a regular basis. For example, I entertained myself by either swatting rocks into the sea or at targets in the forest. I also tied a line to it and used it to fish.

The Conservatory was the most illuminated area of

Gavaron. It was located above the walkways of our living quarters, lighting most of its surroundings. The walls, doors, and floors of the Conservatory consisted of heavy-duty shatterproof glass. I entered the doors and was greeted by Dahsie's shaming eyes, partly hidden beneath her wild gray locks. I could see her assistant Kayella shaking her head and giving me a playful but timid grin. Kayella is a half-year younger than me but she looks older. Working beside Dahsie will do that.

Lucky for me, my scolding was short-lived. Dahsie had an appointment to get to. She scooped up her cat Elza and left.

"You shouldn't have been late," Kayella shyly giggled, shaking her auburn hair over her violet eyes and then sweeping it back into place.

"I have Alecander to thank for that," I answered.

"You should be thankful Dahsie's scolding wasn't long-winded," Kayella said.

"Yes, I am SO thankful that Elza had an appointment," I said. Dahsie took her to the veterinarian who was not really a veterinarian. He had worked with many animals on the farm of the Humans he served. It eased Dahsie's mind to refer to him that way.

I handed Kayella my book and she looked at it expectantly. "You chose a book last time?" She checked her records to confirm.

"Well, I can read," I stated as though she did not know that all Cresecrens could read as part of our training for service.

Although books were rare, they still existed. Among the Humans, some are immensely valuable.

Kayella pointed to a shelf where a couple of books were lying and asked, "Will you choose another?"

"Maybe. It is as good a place as any to start," I said as I scanned the vast Conservatory and clutched my book for the last time. I thought about Alecander's practicality in choosing a flashlight on his last birthday. He spent many nights wandering the beach and sleeping above ground. I doubted that my choice would be as practical.

On my way out, nearly three hours later, I felt I made a foolish choice. In fact, I was sure of it. I glanced down at my satchel and sighed. *Alecander will surely speak his mind.* My thoughts were interrupted as I passed Dahsie holding her prized kitten and someone I did not recognize, a newcomer I felt sure. My eyes caught sight of his jaw markings. His creation date did not match the current day. Curious, I paused and looked back over my shoulder as I exited the Conservatory. He reached Dahsie's counter and pulled something out of his satchel. Dahsie examined it closely. She nodded and gestured toward the array of objects. Whatever he offered Dahsie, she wanted. I had heard of this kind of trading but had never attempted it myself. I did not think I had anything Dahsie would want and could not think of anything to give up.

I braced myself for Alecander's didactic words as I received my meal of oatmeal with apples and a glass of watered-down milk in the Cafeteria. There were several schedules for eating.

Each of us was allowed two meals every day. Alecander and I ate mid-morning and mid-evening. If we had any success hunting, our stomachs rejoiced. Chances were we would be eating at the Cafeteria most of the time since the food supply in the vicinity was scarce. We hunted more for entertainment and fresh air rather than the game. There was also fishing but the areas where we were permitted to fish had a low supply of edible sea creatures. We were not starving but from time to time we would find ourselves hungry.

I was thankful the food shortage happened the year before my arrival. For two months, President Zantham, a Human, decided to make an example out of my people for the growing number of rejected Cresecrens entering the camps. He feared Cresecrens were purposely acting out to escape from their duties. He wanted to ensure that we did not evade the purpose for which we were created. An independent group of peace activists who call themselves The Truce fought for our rights to receive food. The supply was regenerated but not without subtle reminders that the government was in control.

I found Alecander at our usual table with Bentum and Aurora. Bentum and Aurora are an older couple, one of the few mates in Gavaron. Aurora cannot see and Bentum cannot hear, so naturally they found each other. As I sat down, the table wobbled and I realized this time I would not be leveling it with my book. I immediately put my glass of milk to my lips to avoid talking. The last thing I wanted was the inevitable conversation with Alecander. I did not want to be made to feel like a child in front of the others.

Alecander lowered his eyebrows and looked at me, but Aurora spoke first. "What did you choose?" I was always impressed by how she knew I was there, no matter how quietly I approached.

I cleared my throat and tried to think how I would explain my decision. I still could not think of a convincing answer. "A map."

"A map?" Alecander asked.

"Of Gavaron? What would you need one of those for? You know this place like a baby knows his mother," Aurora said.

Alecander's eyes told me he knew the map was not of Gavaron. I shifted in my seat uncomfortably.

"He has a map of the Den," Alecander told Aurora.

The Den is the world we can no longer enter without being an Appointed or summoned. It became its name by definition and reality: the lair of a wild, usually predatory animal.

Aurora's hand was as white as our reconstituted milk as she took Bentum's ebony hand. She wanted to be sure he caught everything. He had almost perfected the art of lipreading. Bentum had lost his hearing a little over a year ago after being exposed to toxins while working with developers of a new kind of fuel. He was no longer fit for his duties working for a researcher or able enough to be put back into the Cresecren training pool. Thus, he was placed in Gavaron. Once Aurora had Bentum's attention, she began signing. Through watching them, I have learned to recognize many signs. When she signed "map," I looked at Alecander.

"Why would you want a map of the Den? Becoming my assistant does not suddenly give you free rein of the outside world. You know we are to follow the strict route. Foolishness!" Alecander said scornfully.

I answered truthfully. "I wanted it. I felt compelled to take it, or perhaps it fascinates me. I do not know exactly why I chose it."

"You *guess* it fascinates you? Did you miss your mark and hit your head this morning when you leapt into the hull of the ship?" Alecander asked, irritated. "Anything else in the Conservatory would have been more useful!"

I could see Aurora's hands moving quickly to relay the conversation to Bentum, who expressed amusement. Despite her faulty vision, there was a twinkle in Aurora's eyes. It seemed as if she could see right into my brain and dissect my thoughts.

Aurora is quite stunning with her fiery, wavy red hair. She wears it long past her shoulders even though it would be easier to care for it if it were short. Bentum keeps her well-manicured and as clean as one could be, living in those quarters. Their relationship is the closest thing I had ever seen to love in Gavaron. Aurora arrived here mere months before Bentum. She had worked for one of the many scientists who tried to find the fountain of youth in the form of a pill. Aurora was a test subject. She is grateful she was only blinded as a result of the testing and did not meet the same end as the scientist. Most of the world believes he died after taking the drug voluntarily.

However, he actually died by the hands of The Truce, the small group of Humans who advocated for Cresecren rights. They helped the scientist to "test out" the drugs on himself. Aurora was questioned but she answered truthfully when she said she saw nothing.

After all that Aurora has been through, her greatest fear in life is that she would live forever.

"There has been talk of our being able to go wherever we wish in the future," I said, my voice unsteady.

"This talk you speak of has been going on for decades. Look at my lips as I say this. It is *never* going to happen! Besides, even if there were a chance, you know very well that those maps are not complete," Alecander replied.

"Oh, let him have his fun!" Aurora laughed. Bentum's broad shoulders rode up and down as he chuckled along with her.

"I will eat the rest of my breakfast with the sane!" Alecander growled as he got up and stalked away. I watched the table wobble as he exited the Cafeteria.

DEATH

THAT NIGHT in my chamber, I lay in my rest pod, impatient about the next day. I scanned the room for something to entertain my mind, using only the dim light shining under my chamber door. The Conservatory stayed lit all through the night in case someone was created during those hours. I climbed out of my pod and pulled it down into a sitting position in front of my desk. My chamber was very small, and I never got used to the confined area. I wished then that I had a mate so I would have had a larger area to pace. Or, if nothing else, someone with whom to share my thoughts. There were rare occasions when a Cresecren took a mate but it was based on survival, not love. Bentum and Aurora were lucky to have one of the few mate chambers. Mine was simple: a crate in the corner for visitors or more likely for Alecander to sit when we played chess. Those games filled many of our nights. We used the hefty storage trunk as a table. I would pull my pod next to it and we took turns sitting on the crate and pod. The trunk stored my meager clothing, some hunting tools, and Human remains—in the sense they were the remnants of Human civilization on Gavaron soil. I could get a drink of water or clean up in the sink nestled into the stone wall. Above the sink was a shelf and a small mirror above that. A hook for my satchel hung above the crate and completed the eclectic design. *Ah, home sweet home.*

I fumbled with the map on the desk. I was surprised that such a seemingly insignificant item had caused such a stir. I pushed it aside, pulled the chessboard off the shelf and set up the pieces. I remember the week Alecander and I spent making the game. We carved the pieces and board from an old fallen pine. I cringed, remembering the splinters I had gotten. Before I could place the pawns on the board, I heard banging on my door which caused me to knock over my king. *Of course! Alecander is not even playing and he wins!* He almost always did. On those few times he lost, I thought he was just letting me win. I assumed he must be at my door because he wanted to play a game. He must not have been able to sleep either.

I slid the door open to find Kayella standing wide-eyed. She looked shaken, beads of sweat covering her forehead. Her arms were crossed in a protective position, and one finger twisted a lock of her auburn hair.

"Kayella? What happened? Are you hurt?" I asked as I pulled her inside and glanced both ways down the seemingly deserted corridors. I slid the door shut.

"What is it, Kayella? Did Dahsie do something to you?"

"No!"

I waited patiently and offered her my rest pod. She

remained standing, staring ahead.

She swallowed. "You have no reason to believe me. None at all. Ever since I can remember, my dreams have reflected reality. They are jumbled and I never remember the entire dream but something always stands out and I see it come true."

"Why has this brought you here?"

"You can't go into the Den to the Supply Depot. At least, I feel you shouldn't go." Kayella rubbed her forehead with the sleeve of her blouse.

"Let me get you a drink." I pulled down a metal can and filled it with water.

Before I turned around, Kayella's hand was on my arm. Her footsteps were so silent that she startled me. I pivoted to look at her as she spoke a single word hauntingly. "Death." Kayella looked so serious that I did not speak my initial thought of "nonsense." Instead, I handed her the can and asked her to tell me about her dream.

"It won't make any sense to you. How can I explain something I don't understand? They are bits and pieces of a puzzle." Kayella became flustered, her hand began to tremble, and water sloshed to the floor. "I came because I felt I needed to warn you not to go tomorrow." She grabbed my arm tightly. "Have someone go in your place. I have to go and warn Alecander." She dropped the can into the sink, splashing water along the wall. Before I could stop her, she ran out the door and down the corridor. I stood there, taken aback. The Kayella I knew was timid and sweet. I knew nothing of this Kayella.

Death. Such an ominous word. Is it that I might die? Or Alecander? What exactly had Kayella seen? Did it even matter? It was probably a nightmare and she was feeling the aftereffects, perhaps even sleepwalking and talking. I had no idea how Kayella came to be in Gavaron. Perhaps the reason was disturbing the Humans she served in the middle of the night. I decided to let Alecander deal with Kayella when she shared her dream with him. I was not going to give him an excuse to keep me from going into the Den. I returned to my pod and I lay awake another hour before falling asleep.

Outside the Vehicle Grotto where the cargo vehicle was kept and which also contained the only other entrance to the underground living quarters, I again arrived before Alecander. It made two days in a row that I had beaten him. *I had better not make a habit of it or he will expect it.* I felt surprisingly refreshed, despite having only slept a few hours. I grew antsy as I waited. It was nearly 4AM and the early-morning heat was beginning to replace the night chill. The day before was nearly ninety-five degrees and I wondered if it would top one-hundred on this day. Spring had finally ended. I never looked forward to the scorching summer months. This was one of the reasons we Cresecrens decided to build underground, mimicking the Human movement. The sun also aided us in our transportation for without it we would have had to figure out another way to receive our food rations. Our cargo vehicle is mainly powered by the sun. The night before, the vehicle was loaded with items to trade at the Underground Market. It was a place where anyone could buy, trade, or sell items to or from vendors. Trades were made with handmade items or found possessions for items some of us needed desperately or desired greatly. For some Cresecrens, it was all they thought about. Famous traded hand-crafted wooden bullets for cheap bottles of wine. He said the wine reminded him of the good old days. He may have forgotten that he used to drink fine wine from Quinso Vardo's private reserve, not the cheap wine he gets from the Underground Market.

Supply Appointeds are only allowed in the Underground Market one day a month, after they gather food rations, basic toiletries, and medical provisions at the Supply Depot. Anything from the Underground Market would have to be traded for since Cresecrens had no money. Before we left, Alecander would have made a list of those things desired from the Market. I have never made anything to trade or traded anything I owned because I have never needed anything more than what I already had. I thought about making another chess set but I could not think of anything I really wanted. However, this day I rummaged through my storage trunk and took out a shark's tooth, which I found on the shore over a year ago. I always meant to do something with it but never made the effort before. My stomach quivered with excitement, as I had not left Gavaron for so long. I had not seen a Human in a long time. I needed to keep myself in line as my freedom one day a month was at stake.

"Early, are we?" Alecander said.

"I will not make a habit of it!" I cracked a smile, noticing that he had a bulky handwoven backpack in addition to his satchel. I had heard that the Supply Appointeds were fed well on their travels. I was certain that food was inside the backpack. I made a mental note that Alecander did not mention the map of the Den and patted my satchel as I entered the cargo vehicle.

SUPPLY AND DEMAND

OUR SOLAR POWERED vehicle could go just twenty-five MPH. It almost felt as if jogging would be faster. Apart from eating and staring out the window at the mostly barren land, I slept most of the way. Our conversation about Kayella had been brief. Alecander never saw her the night before because he had chosen to sleep under the stars. When Alecander inquired what Kayella had wanted, I did not tell him the whole story. He passed it off as a vivid nightmare. Remembering her wild eyes made me briefly question my decision to enter the Den.

Five hours after setting out, we finally neared the Depot. Alecander began poking me to make sure I was awake. About a mile from the gates, we exited our vehicle and were met with a blast of heat. There were three flagpoles: one for Gavaron, one for Solitare, and one for the new site being built down south. From the middle pole, two neck flags already dangled with little wind to cause any movement. The Appointeds from Solitare, up north, were already there. After hoisting our flags, we got back in our vehicle and drove to the gates.

The flags signaled the Supply Depot we were there for our

monthly visit. They had extra precautions to make sure we were in fact expected guests. The Supply Depot had issues in the past with riots from the hungry. Guards at two towers stood steady with their guns fixed on us. Devices came down on either side of the vehicle, scanning our violet eyes and our bar-coded faces.

"The government takes food supply very seriously," I said.

"Hush boy, stay still. If they can't confirm who you are, they'll shoot you and then ask who you were," Alecander replied.

I remained silent, afraid to breathe until they confirmed our identities. We parked in our designated spot. We were approached by two armed guards whose weapons were not drawn. They escorted us into the building, which was essentially an enormous warehouse. Its white walls were so different from the dusty walls of Gavaron and reminded me just how far away from home I was.

"Thank you, gentlemen. I've got it from here," Alecander said when he reached the desk of a shaggy-haired man.

The guards walked off without as much as a shrug.

"Gavaronians?" The man did not look up from his chair.

"Yes," Alecander answered.

"Let me just sign you in and you can start collecting your handouts." The man's tone was insulting as he looked up at us with a sneer.

My nails dug into the underside of the desktop and I bit my lower lip. I grew warm despite the air-conditioned room. *Do NOT screw this up! Remember this is freedom.*

"We are grateful for what we are given," Alecander replied graciously. If he was aggravated, he gave no indication of it.

"Seems to me like we give YOU people enough. A portion of my pay goes to taxes that fund the likes of you. I can't even afford to pay for one of you to work for me part-time yet I still have to pay to keep you alive." A vein pulsed between his eyes.

I bit down harder on my lip. Alecander remained composed. "May we go on now?"

"Sure, sure. Can't stand to look at you any longer anyway!" the man said, turning his back to us.

I imagined myself hurtling over the desk and ensuring that he could not look at the likes of my kind again.

We found most of our supplies ready to load. Someone said that our medicine was behind schedule because some items needed to be cleared. Probably Famous' potent painkillers, I thought. The Cresecrens from Solitare had almost finished loading their vehicle. They were a lanky older woman and a young man with curly red hair, probably no older than me.

They seemed all business and did not look in our direction until they were finished. The young man walked over to us while the woman watched. He said condescendingly, "We'll have first pick again at the Underground Market. Gavaron should at least try to give us a run. Only the best for Solitare!" He scurried back to the woman and shared a chuckle with her. They jumped into their cargo vehicle and headed for the Underground Market.

"I did not know it was a race," I grumbled.

"It's not. However, they are right. They will have first pick," Alecander replied.

I will see about that next month!

One of the Humans caught my eye because she was so much younger than the others. She was much more enthusiastic and energetic about her duties. She demanded attention like a lone wildflower in spring among a field of lifeless grass. Even her attire was out of place. Everyone else wore matching ill-fitting black and brown uniforms. She wore lemon-colored shorts and a pale blue tank top which flattered her crystal blue eyes. Her golden tresses were pulled back loosely into a ponytail.

I must have been watching her closely for the better part of an hour. Finally, she walked up to me with the container of medical supplies and said, "If you are going to stare at me, we should at least be on a first-name basis. My name is Linnayah." She smiled.

My face and neck grew hot. "My name is Cayden. I apologize if I am making you uncomfortable. I am just curious. You do not seem to mesh with your current surroundings."

"Oh, you mean those drab uniforms?"

"And the fact that you are less than half the age of everyone else working here. And there are other noticeable differences."

Alecander called over to me and said he would be back in a few minutes. I nodded and watched Linnayah watch Alecander exit. Not surprisingly, Alecander would draw this response from a female. He was created to have the appearance of an Adonis. I surprised myself when I wished at that moment Alecander would trip.

"I don't work here. I am volunteering," Linnayah said.

"Volunteering?" I repeated.

"Yes, some of us still attend school regardless of the majority of the world's view, and we have reports to do. My report is titled 'Supply Day.' I know, it's not very creative. Anyway, I want to be educated. It still has meaning to me, unlike some of my generation who choose to work or those who take things that aren't theirs to survive."

"Are you referring to Pillagers?" I asked. She shifted her weight on her feet but did not reply.

Pillagers are the lowest form of Humans. They prey on others even though their victims are in no better position than themselves. They take as much as possible as fast as possible, wrecking anything or anyone standing in their way. They manage to elude the law, very careful to cover up their tracks.

"Thanks for the help," I said, trying to be polite.

"No problem." As she leaned in a little closer, my toes dug into my soles. Her whisper caressed my ear. "I slipped in a couple extra bags of oats and a jug of milk." She winked. "Don't tell."

I was not used to a Human being that close or that generous before. I just stood there, staring back at her.

"There you go again, staring! If I wasn't a confident person you would give me a complex." Linnayah bent down, lifted up a box and handed it to me. I took it and loaded the last of the boxes into our cargo vehicle.

For the remainder of our time in the Supply Depot, I tried hard not to look for Linnayah but failed miserably. I could not help it, she fascinated me. *Why would she give us anything extra to eat? Why risk getting in trouble? Where does she live? What is her family like? Where does she go to school? I would like to read her school report sometime. Would she get high marks for it? Will I see her again?*

Alecander went to see the shaggy-haired man to sign us out of the Supply Depot. He left me behind to spare my fingernails and the man's well-being. I did not see Linnayah anywhere, as I had lost track of her. *Where did she go? Will I see her once more before I leave? What is the matter with me? What am I doing? Caring about what a HUMAN is doing. Maybe Alecander is right in calling me ridiculous yesterday.* I climbed into the cargo vehicle and did not permit myself to look back.

DESIRES

WE TRAVELED NORTH for about an hour to the Underground Market. All the lifting and loading at the Supply Depot had made us ravenous. So before we descended for business, we shared a loaf of rye bread and cured ham slices. I tugged on my neck flag before exiting the vehicle to allow for breathing room. We would not be hanging our neck flags here. Instead, we were to display them draped around our necks to let everyone know we were there on official business. In the Den, we are known as rebels, rejects, or maimed but at the Underground Market we were known only as traders with potential business opportunities. I was anxious to see what the Underground Market was all about. I tapped my satchel, thinking about what I might trade for my shark's tooth. Alecander retrieved the list of what everyone was hoping to get from his satchel and we took two rolling carts full of merchandise to trade. My pace quickened as we neared the entrance to the Market.

We passed a woman with a young child leaving the Market. The two so closely resembled each other that I was certain they were mother and daughter. The woman ignored us; however, the little girl could not keep her eyes off of us. The woman tugged at the girl's hand to pull her along. I could not resist looking over my shoulder and I saw the child's mother whispering something in the girl's ear. The woman caught my gaze and smiled tenderly. I returned the smile and they continued on with the child giving me one more long look over her shoulder. I had not seen a child in a long time. There are no children in Gavaron. No innocent laughter fills the air nor do their cries pierce the night. I will never know what it is like to have a child of my own. Cresecrens are cursed or blessed—depending on one's opinion—with being infertile.

The main entrances to the Market were three elevators as wide and long as my chamber, big enough to accommodate large groups of people with a plethora of merchandise. We watched as a group of people entered an elevator and the doors closed. We entered the next elevator with our items for trading in hopes that they would be someone else's treasure.

When the doors opened again, the air was thick with a combination of savory and sweet scents mixed with a musty underlining odor. The area ahead of us stretched ahead as far as I could see. I was overwhelmed by excitement with so much to see and hear.

"Where do we start?" I tried to keep my voice steady. *Who would have thought I would be so ecstatic to go shopping?* The Conservatory was one thing but this, this was so much more. I had only seen Markets on television. I had never been allowed to leave the premises of the Humans I served, the Rawnetts.

"We need to find a man named Jinjo. Or rather I was told he would find us. I'm not sure how easily he will find us as this place is quite crowded. He will know which vendors are interested in what we have and who carries what we want," Alecander said.

"I will!" The voice came from behind us. We turned to discover a man dressed in a canary yellow floor-length short-sleeved robe and a golden wide-brimmed sun hat. Long chains draped from his earlobes with keys dangling from them. His feet were bare and weathered. His robe was open, revealing his bare chest with strands of coarse dark hair. I shuddered to think if the rest of him was also bare under his robe.

"Jinjo?" Alecander asked.

"As I live and breathe." His arms stretched out to both sides as if he were royalty. I felt that maybe I should bow or salute.

"I am Alec—"

"You are Alecander and you are young Cayden," Jinjo interrupted. "May I call you Alec? Alecander seems such a long and formal name. May I have your shopping list?" Alecander handed Jinjo the piece of paper in his satchel. "Um, I see. Nice. None of those here. Lovely." He removed his sun hat from his bald head, placed the list inside it and then put the hat back. He remembered everything on it.

"Thank you for assisting us," Alecander said.

"My pleasure, but before we get down to business come let us drink!" Jinjo said, leading us toward a little bar. I looked at Alecander and he shrugged. I did not know what I wanted to trade my shark's tooth for or if anyone would even be interested. I did know I was not interested in a trade for a drink. Neither Alecander nor I had any money. As if Jinjo knew what I was thinking, he said, "Don't worry! This one is on me!" He sat down on a bar stool and waved away the two men sitting on the stools next to him. "Leave the ordering to me," Jinjo said.

As we sat down, a voluptuous bar maiden wiped off the counter in front of Jinjo. She did not clear the counter in front of Alecander and me even though there were half-empty glasses that obviously did not belong to us.

"Vhat vill it be, gentlemen?" She spoke with a strange accent I had not heard before. It was strongest with words that contained w and th.

"My Love, surprise us," Jinjo said, taking her hand and kissing it.

"Oh, you are still in zee dog house after last night," she said, turning away to get our drinks.

"This is my beautiful wife, Zira. Together for fourteen years and she is still as feisty as the day we met. The day she dumped a beer in my lap. God, I love her!" Jinjo said as he pretended to clutch his heart.

"Shut it, Old Man," she said, handing Jinjo his ale, "or I vill repeat vhat I did zee day I met you!" She glared at him, tucking a loose black strand of hair behind her ear.

"You can't stay mad at me forever, My Love," Jinjo sing-songed.

"Vanna bet?" she said, handing an ale to Alecander.

I found it all a bit humorous. I never understood why Humans took husbands and wives. They seem to forget why they had fallen in love. *Love. Such a curious word.* I half-expected her to place a pint of ale in front of me but instead she gave me a tall glass of milk. That was fine by me as I had seen what drinking did to Famous.

"Thank you," I said.

"You're velcome, sweetheart," she purred.

Jinjo raised his voice. "Oh, now you're just trying to make me jealous, woman!"

"I vas going more for aggravated," she said, turning her back on him and walking over to another customer.

"Alec, do you have those wooden bullets?" Jinjo asked.

"Depends on what you are going to do with them," Alecander answered, glancing over at Zira.

Jinjo laughed. "Don't be silly. It isn't like that with us. We fight like fierce warriors and make up like wild rabbits."

Alecander handed the bullets to Jinjo. They were wrapped in a frayed handkerchief. Famous had told me that wooden bullets were used mainly for target practice.

"My Love, I have something for you!" Jinjo called.

"Vhatever it is vill not be good enough," she answered, walking back to him.

Jinjo held up the handkerchief and Zira's face lit up as she recognized the handkerchief. I put the pieces of the puzzle together: Famous was Zira's bullet supplier and she paid him with cheap wine.

"I had almost forgotten," she said, taking the handkerchief and laying it on the counter. A smile slowly spread across her face.

"If you weren't so busy being angry with me . . . " Jinjo began.

"Don't spoil zis moment too, Jinjo!" she scolded.

"Yes, My Love."

Zira scooped up the bullets and handed the handkerchief back to Alecander.

"Famous vill need it again for next time. Tell him Zira sends her regards." She grabbed two bottles of inexpensive wine from under the counter and handed them to Alecander. Then she stepped onto a stool and reached above a shelf of bottles to retrieve a gun.

"I'm going on break," she said, leaning in to kiss Jinjo on his forehead.

Jinjo walked around to the other side of the counter and grabbed his wife's bottom as she left. She squealed. He reached under the counter and pulled up a sign reading *BE BACK LATER* on the counter.

I finished my rich and creamy glass of milk. It was nothing like the weak milk of Gavaron. Alecander hardly touched his beer. Jinjo asked if he could finish it for him and Alecander pushed the drink toward him. Jinjo tossed back his head, keeping his sun hat in place and guzzling down the amber liquid.

"On to business then," Jinjo said. "I don't recall seeing your requests on the list. What do you two desire?" Jinjo asked as he stretched out his arms dramatically.

"My items are the paper and pen," Alecander answered. *Paper and pen?* I never pictured Alecander as much of a writer and he had no one to send a letter to. None of us did. I figured he probably wanted it for the shopping list every month. *What was he trading?* Before I could inquire, Jinjo turned to me.

"I really have no idea what I am after," I answered honestly, again touching my satchel instinctively.

"Oh, there is so much here. I am sure what you are looking for will find you," Jinjo said, touching my neck flag with the end of his extended finger.

I never thought I would have such a grand time shopping. Jinjo knew who carried what and who would most likely trade for specific items. He was like a Human filing system. I saw several things of interest but wanted to weigh my options before I asked for a trade. After Jinjo discovered what I was carrying in my satchel, every time he saw me eying anything he would say "Willing, not willing, most likely." That helped narrow it down a little. This place was better than the Conservatory on its best-stocked day!

There were things I had never seen before and things I had only seen on television. There was even a used television salesman selling ancient models.

"What is that booth offering?" I said, walking toward a booth that housed about a dozen women and one man.

"Look closer, Cayden," Alecander replied.

As we approached, some of the women began posing. One

crossed her legs and flipped her hair, and another—who looked the youngest of the flock—blew me a kiss.

As we passed, the young male reached out. "Perhaps you would prefer me?" he said almost desperately.

"No, thank you," I said politely.

"Please!" he said, grabbing my arm. I caught a glimpse of deep scars as his jacket slid back to reveal his arms. Tears welled up in his eyes. In just those few seconds, I could read the pain and sorrow that seemed to consume him. His frail body was quivering.

"Let him go, Graundrew! Desperation is unbecoming," Jinjo ordered. He retreated back to his chair with his eyes downcast.

I secretly thanked my creators for sparing me from this profession. The law forbade Cresecrens from prostitution because we were not created for carnal desires.

I looked away and hoped I would not have to pass that booth again. I caught sight of someone familiar. It was Linnayah. *What was she doing here?* I smiled at the anticipation of talking to her again and straightened my shoulders as she approached. Linnayah was so determined to get where she was going that she did not look my way. She had changed into a flowing almond-colored dress but something else was different about her. Her face was troubled. Nothing like her playfulness back at the Supply Depot. She bounded toward the prostitutes and my chest tightened at their recognition of her. She entered the booth and passed several of the young women. I could hear

Alecander and Jinjo behind me in a heavy barter discussion with a merchant. I stared at Linnayah's booth. Every second she spent in it made it almost impossible to move. Linnayah grabbed the shoulder of the young lady who had blown me a kiss and interrupted what I assumed to be negotiations with a man at least three times her age. The girl turned toward Linnayah. She looked annoyed. *Is that foul man Linnayah's regular customer? Is Linnayah angry the girl is taking her income?* I could not hear anything through the bustle of the Market.

The other prostitutes took a step away from Linnayah and the young lady, anticipating a confrontation. They argued and Linnayah tugged on the young lady's arm. The girl pulled away, shaking her head. The man grew agitated and looked as though he might walk off. I could hear Linnayah saying, "Please, please."

Suddenly the girl looked back at the man and said something that made him relax. He turned to face the Market, giving me a clear view as he picked his rotting mangled teeth. The young lady took Linnayah's head in her hands and said something to her and hugged her. Linnayah's head turned in my direction and I could see agony and tears welling in her eyes. She half-heartedly returned the hug and watched as the girl walked away with her customer. To add insult to injury, the man grabbed the young lady's hair and sniffed, proceeding to bury his lips under her dark curls before they walked out of sight. I did not know what happened. I wanted to console Linnayah, but I did not have the slightest idea how.

Linnayah brushed past all the remaining prostitutes and hurried from the booth. They watched her exit and returned to business as a group of young, obviously wealthy men approached. Linnayah walked away with her head hanging low. It was obvious she was not upset about the girl stealing her customer. If she were a prostitute, she would not be walking away from the group of potential new customers. It had to be something else that caused her pain. Linnayah was trying to get the young girl to leave with her.

"Alec," I said. Alecander gave me a cross look and I continued. "Sorry! Alecander, do you mind if I explore the Market for a few minutes by myself?"

"I don't know. Depends on if you plan on using that map of yours," he answered with a hint of sarcasm.

"You know me better than that."

"Do I?"

As I broke away from Jinjo and Alecander, I lost sight of Linnayah. I moved in the direction I had last seen her and pretended to be checking out what the vendors had to offer. I found her leaning against a wall. Her nose was crimson from crying. *Now what do I do?*

I gave myself a moment to think. I focused in on the flower vendor ahead of me. I crossed over without a moment's hesitation. His supply was low, most likely because he began the day with a small stock. Flowers had grown more scarce over the years and those who could afford them were few and far between. I opened my satchel as the elderly vendor stepped towards me.

"Hello there. Is it that time already?" he said, gesturing toward my neck flag.

"Yes, sir," I said politely and with as much enthusiasm as I could muster, hoping he would accept the deal I was about to present.

"I am eager to see your offering," the old man said.

I handed him the shark's tooth. He held it up to admire it.

Glancing back toward Linnayah, I could see that she had not moved. When I returned my gaze to the old man, he was holding out a yellow tulip. "This is the flower you want. A symbol of friendship and certain to bring sunshine into one's heart."

"Thank you," I said, taking the tulip and finding myself for the second time in two days meaning what I said.

"No, thank you," the old man said, coveting his prize.

As I approached Linnayah, she snapped her head up and took a defensive stance. When she recognized me and saw the tulip outstretched toward her, she softened.

"You look like you could use some cheering up," I said apprehensively.

"You bought me a flower?" she said, surprised.

"I traded for it."

"I don't know what to say. You could have probably traded for anything in this place, yet you chose to give me a flower," she said, holding her hand over her heart.

"I can still probably trade this for something else if you do not want it," I said, hoping she would not take me up on that offer. My arm began to ache from holding the flower out to her.

"No," she said taking the tulip and caressing it. "Thank you."

There were many things at the Market I would have loved to have but seeing Linnayah smile made the trade worth it.

"Would you like to tell me what is troubling you?" I asked in a more relaxed tone.

"A friend. She is what is troubling me," she began.

"The girl back at the booth?"

"You saw what happened?" Linnayah asked. My eyes told her I did. "Her name is Kiara. She's my best friend. Well, WAS my best friend. We don't talk as much as we used to. Not since she took to her new . . . " Linnayah choked out the next word. " . . . profession. I tried to talk some sense into her. Kiara used to go to school with me, then dropped out when things got really bad at home. She is a great girl who got involved with the wrong people. I still can't believe it. I came here today to invite her to move in with my family. My parents can afford one more mouth to feed and she could go back to school. Kiara said she couldn't do it. She couldn't leave her family. Not much of a family if you ask me. Her dad knows what she is doing and lets her leave the house every day. Her mother convinced herself that every morning Kiara is going to school. I actually thought Kiara would come with me. I was foolish."

"You are not foolish. You are a true friend. Most people do

not bother with making friends anymore. For you to have considered Kiara a best friend, she must also have a good heart. Perhaps she needs time to think it over. Maybe she will come around," I said, trying to be encouraging.

"You don't know Kiara like I do. She is exceptionally stubborn and strong-willed. She would rather risk her life than take a handout from anyone."

"But you are not just anyone."

"Why are you being so nice to me?" Linnayah's lips curled up into a soft smile.

I did not have the chance to answer that question.

CONSEQUENCES

THE BUSTLING NOISE of the Market grew louder. I could hear shouting from the direction I had come. Alecander or Jinjo were nowhere to be seen. People were frantically gathering their belongings and attempting to flee. Someone ran toward me. Linnayah gasped at his sudden approach. I instinctively held my arms up in defense, then recognized the charger to be of my own kind. His coded jawline and neck flag indicated he was at the Market on official business. I had never seen him before so I thought that maybe he came from the new camp down south. The Cresecren held out his satchel to me but I did not take it.

"Don't act like you don't know me, brother!" he said, dropping it at my feet.

"But I do not!" I cried as he sprinted away. Before I could bend down to retrieve the satchel, Linnayah picked it up and opened it.

"What is this?" she said, pulling out a small chrome remote. I took it from her.

"There! The young Cresecren has it! Stop him!" I heard. Before I could turn around, a deafening sound behind me blasted with such force that it slammed me into Linnayah's small frame and knocked us to the floor. My heart beat frantically as if trying to free itself from my chest and for a moment it was the only sound I could hear. After a quick check of my own body and finding I was all right, I worried that I had crushed Linnayah. I quickly climbed off. I felt the blood rush from my face as Linnayah lay there with her eyes closed and her arms outstretched. She still clutched the tulip in one hand and the satchel in the other. Smoke surrounded us. I could barely see anything around us. I only heard the wailing, screams, and cries from behind me through ringing ears.

"Cayden, Cayden!" I heard a barely audible voice. I did not want to look away from Linnayah's face. I felt an arm on my shoulder and I broke from my stare. It was Alecander, who seemed to be all right although he was covered in ash and had a few scrapes on his arms and neck. Jinjo stood behind him and had blood gushing from under the rim of his hat down between his eyes. One bare foot was badly mutilated. It looked like a piece of raw meat I had seen earlier in the butcher's booth.

"We have to go!" Alecander said urgently. "Now!"

"I cannot leave her," I said, feeling weak. I squeezed my hands into fists and realized I was still holding the remote. Pieces began to fit together. A man who dared to call me brother had delivered a remote to me, followed by a blast. *Did this very remote cause the explosion?* I quickly surveyed my surroundings. It was a bloodbath, a burning inferno. Kayella's warning word from last night echoed in my mind. The word found its way to my lips as I turned to face Linnayah and spoke, "*DEATH.*"

"Hurry! We don't have much time," Jinjo said, pointing to a nearby door. He pulled a key off one of his ears and headed to the door, dragging his injured foot behind him.

"Now, Cayden!" Alecander ordered.

Alecander's tone was forceful and his eyes were more serious and scared than I had ever seen beneath his calm exterior. I felt a gentle grasp on my arm holding me in place. My heart leapt. Something I had never remembered feeling but knew instinctively what the sensation must be. I turned to see Linnayah's blue eyes questioning me.

"Are you all right?" I asked, gently taking her hand from my arm.

Before Linnayah could answer, Jinjo called to us from the doorway. "We must go now!"

I saw the urgency on his face so I carefully lifted Linnayah and carried her through the open door. I could feel the warmth of her body lying limp in my arms. I was the first out, and then I heard Alecander tell Jinjo to go ahead of him. We were in a corridor wide enough to accommodate merchandise being carried into the building. It was long and gradually sloped upwards toward the outside world. The sun warmed the corridor and was almost blinding. Another blast from inside moved us forward and I held Linnayah tightly. I was not going to let her fall. *Did Alecander make it through the door?*

I swung around. Alecander was examining Jinjo, who was

trying to stand up.

"Leave me," Jinjo said.

"We will not!" Alecander insisted, pulling Jinjo to his feet and bracing his arm around Jinjo's waist. The blood from Jinjo's face streamed down the bridge of his nose. It took everything I had to keep from becoming ill.

"Damn door!" Jinjo said. "Maybe I should have taken the offer to go ahead of you," he said jokingly to Alecander. "Slammed my backside on the way out and knocked me to the ground."

"Let us move, Jinjo," Alecander encouraged. They took a few painful steps and I turned to continue up the corridor.

"Jinjo! Jinjo! Jinjo!" A piercing scream shrilled down the corridor.

"Alec, you should have left me for dead. My wife will surely kill me now!" Even in the severity of the situation Jinjo still joked.

We struggled our way up the corridor as Zira sprinted toward us, holding her gun. In her bar maiden attire, she was unmistakable. I looked at Linnayah to see how she was doing. Surprisingly, I still held the remote. My body tensed. *Had I detonated the second blast?* I was sure the first blast was not my doing. *Or was it?*

Zira reached us and tucked her gun in the belt of her dress. She hurriedly looked over Linnayah and me, then moved on to Alecander and Jinjo.

"Give me your arm, Old Man," Zira said to her husband.

"Do you have any bullets left, My Love?"

"No, vhy do you ask?"

"Just making sure you were not thinking of using them to finish me off."

"And let you have it so easy?"

Once we were outside, the heat pressing into our lungs made breathing difficult. Linnayah reassured me she was going to be all right as she patted my cheek softly. I set her upright on a boulder until she insisted she was fine. I put the remote into my satchel, unsure of what else to do with it. From where we were standing, there was no view of the main entrance. *Would anyone else make it out?* I turned to Alecander.

"Are you all right?" Alecander asked me before I could ask him.

"Yes. And you?"

"I'm fine." He looked toward Jinjo and Zira. "It's him I am worried about."

Zira was trying unsuccessfully to stop the bleeding on her husband's head. She had removed his hat and his robe. Thankfully he was wearing a pair of sequined silver shorts. Zira pressed the robe against Jinjo's head and cursed when it would not stop bleeding. She pulled the gun from her belt and dropped it on the ground.

"Our Market, Jinjo! Vhat vill ve do? Vhy vould anyone do zis?" Zira cried.

"My Love," Jinjo said weakly. "You mustn't worry about that now. I need to know that you are going to be okay without me." He pulled her hand down from pressing on his wound.

"Jinjo, stop trying to annoy me! Head vounds bleed a lot. You're going to be fine." Zira wiggled her hand out of his grasp.

Jinjo's voice quivered. "It isn't the head wound I am worried about, My Love."

"Where else are you hurt, Jinjo?" Alecander asked, rushing over to him. I instinctively followed.

Jinjo did not answer. His face had paled and his breathing grew shallow.

"Let us lay him down," Zira said.

"No," Jinjo whispered.

Alecander and I saw the wound at the same time. I do not know how we managed to miss it before but there was a big sharp piece of metal protruding from his back, right behind his heart.

"Vhat is it?" Zira said at the sight of our somber faces. We did not respond.

Zira tried to see what we were looking at when her husband said softly, "My Love, I need to know."

"Vhat, Jinjo? Vhat?" Zira replied, agitated.

"I need to know if you will be all right without me. Please, Zira," Jinjo persisted.

She took Jinjo's face in her hands and looked him deep in the eyes. "I vould be fine vithout you, Old Man. But you are not going anyvhere. Do you hear me?"

Jinjo did not answer. He did not blink. He never moved

again.

Zira shook her husband. "I said you veren't going anyvhere! Don't you ever lis—" Her voice broke off.

Jinjo's body was limp in Zira's arms. Tears streamed down her rouged cheeks. She cradled Jinjo's body tightly against her chest. Alecander and I moved away to allow Zira time with her grief.

I walked over to Linnayah, who still sat on the boulder. Tears clouded her crystal blue eyes. Our eyes met and she leaned toward me, burying her head in my chest. I held her tightly.

I could hear Zira telling her husband, "I love you, Old Man." For the first time, my heart ached for another person's sorrow. I do not know exactly how long I held Linnayah but I knew I did not want to let her go when she finally loosened her grip on me.

"You are still holding the flower I gave you," I said, surprised. I removed my neck flag and stuffed it inside my satchel. I instantly felt cooler as the soft wind reached my neck.

"No one has ever given me one before. I wasn't going to leave it back there."

We turned our attention to Zira and watched as she laid Jinjo carefully on his side, kissed him on his lips, removed the remaining key from his ear, picked up her gun, and faced us.

"Vho has done zis?" she said, looking as though she was ready to rip apart anything in her path.

"I do not know," I answered truthfully.

"Nor I," said Alecander.

"I . . . I'm not sure," Linnayah stuttered.

"Vhat do you mean you're not sure?" Zira demanded.

Linnayah did not answer.

"Leave her be, Zira! She is as shocked as any of us," Alecander said cautiously.

Zira's eyes were filled with rage and her chest heaved heavily as she moved toward Alecander. He tensed as she approached him. Instead of attacking him, she walked past and bent down on one knee. She flipped a faux rock on its side and placed her hand on a small screen as the ground softly rumbled. A section of browning grass began breaking way and rose before us to reveal a garage that housed an antique car. It was a pristine cobalt-blue Ford Mustang. Very few people could afford to own cars like this one, which ran on gasoline alone. The only other time I saw one was outside the Rawnetts' home when a very wealthy uncle had paid a visit.

Zira opened the car door and climbed inside, starting it with the key from Jinjo's ear. She pulled the car forward a few yards, shut it off, and got back out.

Zira faced us and asked with a face that had aged ten years in mere minutes, "Vill you help me carry Jinjo into zee garage? It is vhere he vould vant to be. He loved his Market almost as much as he loved me."

We placed him in the center of the garage. As I touched Jinjo's body, it was strange to feel lifelessness where just moments ago there had been such an abundance of life. Before we covered Jinjo with a tarp, Linnayah took the tulip I had given her and placed it on Jinjo's chest. Zira covered her quivering lips with her fingers and her eyes spoke a thousand thank-yous. I vowed silently that I would replace Linnayah's flower. A flower she held onto so dearly and now so easily gave to another.

Before leaving, Zira dumped a box of bullets onto the counter and sighed at the few that came out. She loaded her gun and tucked it back in her belt.

We walked toward the Mustang and watched the lift slowly close. Zira took the butt of her gun, bent down, and smashed it against the screen that unlocked the lift. She covered the shards with the faux rock. As she moved toward the car and climbed into it, we stood there not knowing what to do.

"Get in," Zira ordered. "I'll drive you all to your vehicle. No sense in you valking in zis heat." I realized then that Alecander and I had nothing but our satchels. In all the commotion we left the bags that held our trading offers inside the Market. Something that seemed so important minutes ago was trivial under the new circumstances. We got into the Mustang. The car leapt forward.

As the parking lot came into view, a huge explosion blasted our cargo vehicle and everything around it into the air. I could not see if there were people caught in the blast. Zira whipped the car around and kept her foot on the gas pedal. It was apparent she was getting us out of there, using speeds I had never experienced. I felt a burning sensation in my cheeks and a tightening in my stomach as the world went whizzing by my window. The fastest I had ever traveled before was the maximum speed of the cargo vehicle. This was three or four times as fast.

I glanced at Linnayah, which did not relieve any of my fear. Her face had lost its color as she dug her nails into the edge of the seat.

"Linnayah, are you all right?" I gasped. She did not respond. I watched her for a minute and when she seemed to stop breathing I slowly reached over to cover her hand with my own. Linnayah released her grip on the seat only to dig her nails into my flesh. I was relieved but also in pain. Soon after, Zira began to slow.

"Vhat the hell is going on?" Zira said. No one answered. "Vhere zee hell am I going? Zat is my home. Zat is all I had left. Damn it! Everyzing is gone! Ve vorked so hard for so long and zis, zis is vhat ve get? Vho did zis to us? Jinjo, your death vill be avenged!" She stopped, jumped out, and ran until she grasped a lone tree with one arm, flung her head back, and screamed at the top of her lungs before collapsing against it. Linnayah released her grasp on my hand and the circulation returned.

I may never know what it feels like to lose a mate. As I watched Zira rock back and forth moaning, I wondered if love was worth what she felt.

VISITORS

"SHE NEEDS to be alone for a while," Alecander said. He drove the car behind a thicket while we waited for Zira.

"I did not know you could drive one of these," I said.

"It has been a long time but you never really forget. I drove for the woman I served, Valarie, when I was among the Humans. She preferred her vintage cars."

Valarie's father was a wealthy inventor who passed away when she was a teenager. He left her all his fortune and life's work. However, with no mother to watch over her, Valarie did as she pleased. Many people had high hopes that she would follow in her father's footsteps as an inventor, but nothing ever came of that. Instead, Valarie became one of the few Socialites known for her everyday over-the-top lifestyle. She was famous among those who stayed connected with the outside world.

Many handsome Cresecren males worked for Valarie: security guards, personal bodyguards, a chef who specializes in healthy cuisine/personal trainer, someone to do high-risk tasks about her properties, and Alecander, her chauffeur. She fancied Alecander and held on to him as long as she possibly could.

However, she felt she had standards to uphold as a woman always in the public eye. Valarie was growing older. Despite many alterations to her appearance, she feared having Alecander nearby would reveal her true age. She let him go the day he turned twenty-eight. She had not kept another Cresecren man past the ripe age of twenty-one. Alecander asked her respectfully not to put him back into the Cresecren training pool but rather let him go to Gavaron for all his faithful service. Valarie granted him his wish.

A man carrying a basket ran by, I assumed on his way to the Market. I wondered what he would do once he reached it and saw what had taken place. Soon after Zira joined us at the car. Alecander offered to drive but Zira insisted she would be fine. I could see her eyes in the rearview mirror. They were dark, sorrowful, and reddened.

"I vill take you home, back to Gavaron, but I vant one zing from you," Zira said turning her head toward Alecander. "I vant to stay zere for a vhile. I can't go back to zee Market, probably ever." Alecander did not answer right away. "Please," Zira pleaded.

"You may make your home where you please. You are Human. Why do you give me the courtesy of asking?" Alecander replied.

"Zank you," Zira said without answering the question.

"I want to go too!" Linnayah said earnestly. "And you HAVE to take me."

"Why would you want to go with us? Your family will

surely worry," I said.

"I want more information on my report for school." I had forgotten all about it. "Plus my mom and dad work at the hospital. I think they will be very busy over the next few days. They won't even notice I am not there. I have gone days before without seeing or hearing from them when a catastrophe has kept them busy. It isn't a big deal. I'll get in touch with them as soon as I can."

"She comes," Zira answered before anyone could reply. Perhaps she wanted Human companionship. Either way, Alecander and I had no say.

The drive to Gavaron took us a fraction of the time it took to get to the Supply Depot. We became accustomed to the Mustang's speed and Linnayah no longer dug her nails into anything. The remote in my satchel occupied my mind. Our conversation was mostly robotic. When I brought up the subject of the Market, Alecander gave me a stern look and swept his eyes toward Zira. There were long stretches of silence and one stop so we could stretch our legs and relieve ourselves. Most of our conversation was about Gavaron. What was it like? What was there to do in Gavaron? How were we going to live the next month without our food and supply rations? In light of the situation, we wondered if the government would supply more goods for our people.

Upon arrival at the Gavaron line, the dryness of the land cleared up and became greener. The forest trees thickened before becoming more sparse and revealing our world.

"It's amazing!" Linnayah exclaimed.

"Not vhat I imagined," Zira said.

"Did you picture darkness and ghouls?" Alecander replied.

The ladies giggled. Even if it was only temporary, it was nice to see a smile on Zira's face.

I watched Linnayah as she scanned our small corner of the world: the beach, the ship entrance to the main quarters, the Vehicle Grotto, the orchards, and everything else. Perhaps home really was not as appalling as I had thought.

It had been a long time since a Human had stepped on Gavaron soil. The last one was over four years ago, a drifter who stayed a night on our beach before moving on. Linnayah and Zira would certainly be an amusement for my people. No doubt, they would become the talk of Gavaron for years to come.

"We will hold a meeting tonight on the beach. Everyone should be informed of what has happened. Cayden, take Linnayah and go see Dahsie and tell her we will need the microphone. Zira will come with me to make arrangements for a chamber for Linnayah and her to share," Alecander told us.

Linnayah and I went to my chamber and cleaned up. We did not want to draw any extra attention to ourselves.

"Gavaron is not as dreadful as they make it seem," Linnayah said as she sat down on the crate.

"It is inhabitable," I agreed.

"Inhabitable? This is glorious compared to some of the ways others live!"

"You are not going to write that in your report, are you? You would not want to start a wave of Human movement within the Cresecren walls! There would not be enough provisions for us all." Linnayah rolled her eyes. "Don't worry about my report. I promise it won't bring you more unwanted guests."

"I did not say I did not want you. Uh . . . I mean, I didn't say you were unwanted here . . . I mean you are Human, you can go wherever you please," I said, mortified at my choice of words.

"You must be flustered because you used a contraction in your speech. Why do you sound so formal all the time? And will you stop with the 'you are Human' bit?" She pointed to her chest. "I am Linnayah," she said as her finger moved to my chest, "and you are Cayden." She looked directly into my eyes. "And WE are both beings on this earth. For the remainder of my stay, I want you to pretend I am no different from you."

"But you are different."

"Uh, uh, uh, I said pretend." She winked at me.

"Okay, Your Highness," I said as I opened my chamber door, but I could not see how that would be possible.

"'Your Highness' would imply I have a higher status than you," she said.

"And implying we are different," I said through a grin as we left my chamber.

I planned on continuing this dispute but Linnayah lost interest as she saw Famous. *Did the man have radar?*

"Hello, Cayden!" Famous called as he approached. *Why*

could it not have been a time he had to recharge his wheelchair? He was so active that he needed to do that about every other day.

"Famous." I nodded acknowledgement.

"What could you have possibly traded for this lovely Human woman?"

"This is Linnayah. She is accompanied by Zira. Alecander is calling a meeting on the beach tonight and you will learn of our first trip to the Den as Supply Appointed and Assistant. I am on my way to Dahsie to get the microphone." I grabbed Linnayah and ushered her hurriedly toward the Conservatory. I knew Famous could hold us for hours if we let him start telling stories. It was definitely not the time for a famous Famous conversation.

"I know of a broad named Zira! What about my wine?" Famous called after us.

"I would not worry about that," I called back over my shoulder.

"Hey, what does that mean?" Famous shouted.

"Famous seems to be an intriguing character. I would like to learn more about him sometime," Linnayah said.

"I am sure he will happily oblige."

We passed a few people on the way to see Dahsie. Linnayah smiled, waved, and said hello. Sometimes she received a favorable response, and other times a blank stare. When we arrived at the Conservatory and I explained why it existed, Dahsie appeared. She acted as though she did not even see Linnayah.

"What are you doing here? Did you not like your birthday choice? You know there are no returns for another three-hundred and sixty-four days," Dahsie said.

"There is nothing wrong with my choice. Alecander is calling a meeting tonight. I am here for the microphone." I had all but forgotten about the map in my satchel. Remembering it made me think about not wanting to enter the Den anytime soon, or even never.

"I see," Dahsie said, her eyes narrowing. "Kayella," she called over her shoulder, "bring me the microphone!"

Kayella, her warning, Death.

Dahsie went about her business and logged in that we were checking out the microphone. Elza ran across the counter and startled us, then jumped down and curled her tail around Linnayah's ankle.

"Friendly kitty, aren't you?" Linnayah said, bending down to pet the feline. Elza purred and her calico tail wagged back and forth.

A moment later, Kayella emerged with the small square microphone. As I took it, our eyes met and I knew she knew what I had seen. *DEATH*. I watched her curious eyes travel over to Linnayah. She handed me the microphone but her eyes never wavered from Linnayah. She turned and walked away without uttering a word. Kayella would be at the meeting tonight and would get all the information about what she seemed to already know.

Alecander arranged for Linnayah and Zira to stay in a mate

chamber. I imagine Zira was not fond of its name since she had tragically just lost hers. Linnayah did have one question.

"Your mates don't sleep in the same pod with you?" Linnayah asked.

"No," I answered.

Zira said, "It's best. I did not vant to share." A small sliver of a smile graced her lips.

"Everyone else has eaten, but I will talk to Leric to see about meals for us," Alecander said. No doubt Leric would have questions too. I was not sure how he would like having to feed two unexpected guests. He took his duties as Cafeteria Appointed almost as seriously as Dahsie did for her Conservatory.

I had not thought of it before that moment, but I was hungry and surely everyone else was too. By now, the whole of Gavaron was more than buzzing with the news that the cargo vehicle had not returned.

Zira, Linnayah, and I returned to my chamber to wait for Alecander. He arrived with beans and roasted potatoes accompanied by glasses of the well-known watery milk. These were meals I was sure these ladies were not accustomed to. Zira and Linnayah sat in the pod while Alecander sat on the storage trunk and I chose the floor. We decided it was best if we stuck together and stayed out of sight until the meeting. Alecander had had a tough time avoiding others when he went to find Leric. Bentum and Aurora were the only ones who managed to stop him. Alecander did not give them many details. Bentum kept pressing for answers but Aurora convinced him to wait until the meeting.

Zira did not touch her food, except to move it around her plate, and the milk never made it to her lips.

Alecander told her, "Zira, you should eat something."

"I am not hungry."

"At least drink, Zira, and avoid dehydration."

She lifted the glass to her lips and took one small swallow.

"I'll be fine. I don't zink I vill be eating tonight. I promise I vill try to finish zee milk. You eat it. Zere is no sense in it going to vaste," Zira said, holding out her plate to Alecander. Alecander did not take it. "I von't eat it. It VILL go to vaste," she insisted.

"You're sure?" Alecander asked. Zira nodded.

Alecander took the plate from Zira and offered it to Linnayah. She held up a hand in refusal. "No thank you. I've had enough. You can share it with Cayden."

Alecander and I were grateful to share the extra helping. He left us shortly after finishing his meal. We knew we would see him on the beach soon. Zira was somber. Linnayah tried to make small talk without disturbing Zira. I tried to follow Linnayah's conversation but could not stop thinking about the remote in my satchel. I was uncertain why Linnayah had not brought it up yet. I was certain that I did not detonate the blast. *Well, almost certain.*

Out on the beach, the air was cooling slightly. Dusk gave a little relief from the smoldering daytime sun. Every inhabitant of Gavaron showed up for the meeting. There were murmurs as we walked past toward the stone slab Alecander stood on. If Linnayah or Zira were intimidated they showed no such sign. I passed Dahsie and Kayella. Dahsie was holding Elza. The poor cat looked as though it wanted to be set free. Her nose was wildly sniffing the air. I tried to meet Kayella's eyes but I sensed she did not want to meet mine.

We did not have to push our way to the front. Those with curious eyes stepped back and cleared a path to Alecander, who had just raised his hand to his neck to adhere the microphone to his throat. He cleared his throat and raised his hands. The crowd hushed.

"I gathered you all here to discuss today's events," Alecander began. The crowd shifted restlessly.

"Where are our supplies?" someone shouted.

"Where is my wine?" thundered Famous' unmistakable voice.

"Shut up about your wine!" someone else replied. "What about my medicine? I'll go blind without my medicine!"

"Was it a mistake of the Humans to put you in charge, Alecander?" still another shouted. "Or perhaps it was the decision to take the boy that was a mistake!"

Linnayah gave my arm a gentle squeeze and I held my tongue.

"Peace, my people! We must work together to get through this!" Alecander commanded.

"Get through *what*? You haven't told us anything," bellowed Bentum. He stood by a torch, where the light gave

Aurora the chance to interpret what was being said for him.

"If you spare me a moment, I can tell you what I know. Otherwise, I will say nothing and you will learn nothing," Alecander answered.

Everyone fell silent.

They listened as Alecander explained what he knew. Neither Linnayah nor I shared the knowledge of my possible obliteration of the Underground Market. When Alecander spoke of the devastation, I could not keep myself from looking in Kayella's direction. Her knees buckled. I took a step towards Kayella but she regained her footing. I watched as she continued to listen with her head bowed. I kept my eyes on Kayella to be sure she was okay and let my ears focus on what Alecander was saying. He said that Linnayah and Zira would be staying with us temporarily and gave no real explanation. Alecander added we would have to wait. Wait until we heard word from the outside world about what would be done for us. I had already decided that I would go fishing and see if I could catch something. I had little confidence in any provisions coming soon from the Den.

Late that night, I found myself creeping like a thief toward Alecander's chamber with my satchel. I hoped Alecander was still awake. Thankfully, he was. I hurriedly stepped in and he closed the door behind me.

He stood there waiting for an explanation.

I said nothing. I walked past him in the dimly lit room and gently pulled out the remote. I gingerly placed it on the desk.

"What is this?"

"It is from today."

"This is what you traded your shark's tooth for?" he asked.

"No," I answered. He looked up and met my eyes. "This is what someone who called himself a brother handed me at the Market moments before the first explosion."

"Why did you not tell me this before?" Alecander turned his attention back to the remote.

"I am not sure. I guess . . . because I feel I may have been responsible for the blast. I did not mean to detonate it."

Alecander examined the remote more closely. He flipped it over and lifted a flap with a gritty fingernail to reveal a compartment.

"It is hollow. Did you remove its power source?"

"No. I have not taken it out of my satchel since we left the Market."

Alecander breathed out in relief. "Then you could NOT have detonated anything."

I let out my own breath and plopped down onto his storage trunk, pushing my fingers through my thick strands of hair.

"Someone was trying to make it look as though you caused the murders," Alecander said.

Murders! I did not think about it like that before.

"Why? I am no one."

"Not you in particular. It could have been any one of us. You just happened to be the chosen one."

"Why have I not been summoned? Why has not anyone

come for me?" I said.

"With the number of people they have working the scene of the crime, it could take days—even a week—before they realize we were not in the cargo vehicle when it exploded. We would be the last to be searched for. If they suspect you of any crime, surely you would be hunted but they are in no fear of your getting away. Where would you go? It isn't as though you can roam the Den undetected," Alecander reminded me.

"What should I do?" I asked desperately, thinking of what the punishment for murder would mean.

"Nothing, Cayden, you do nothing. Your worrying about the outcome will not help the situation. You tell the truth when they do come and hope for the best. I will do the same. Now, go and get some rest. I'm going to try. We have had a very long and eventful day."

Before the door closed, I heard Alecander say, "You are not alone."

Although I was exhausted and my eyes burned, I did not go directly back to my room. Instead, I headed toward the mate chambers. Every door was closed. I could hear only my own hushed footsteps. I told myself I was just going to check to see if the ladies were all right. I did not plan to disturb them. I passed Bentum and Aurora's chamber. The sun and the moon symbol on their door seemed to glow in the faint light. The chambers looked alike from the outside, so symbols made it easy to identify whose was whose. Two chambers down I found Zira and Linnayah's temporary housing. The symbols on their door seemed to fit their personalities: fire and wood. Zira seemed to be like fire, while Linnayah seemed to possess characteristics of wood—natural and strong. I thought about the bear symbol on my door and I wondered if I shared any characteristics.

"Don't you think it is a little creepy to be spying at this time of night?" came a soft whisper from behind.

I gasped and spun around to find Linnayah. "I was not spying!"

"Looks like it to me," she whispered. She tried unsuccessfully to mask a smile.

"I . . . I was just checking on you . . . I mean you and Zira. What are you doing out here anyway and how did you sneak up on me undetected?"

"Shhh! I think Zira finally fell asleep," she said, pressing her ear against the door. "It would be a shame for you to wake her just because you were curious."

"I—"

Linnayah cut my words off. "Goodnight," she said, leaning in so close that my toes dug into my shoes. She opened the door and disappeared into the chamber.

"Strange girl," I whispered to the door. Then I realized I was the one acting strange. I was the one standing in the corridor in front of a Human girl's chamber in the middle of the night. *What was I doing?* I gathered my thoughts and was suddenly overtaken by drowsiness.

NEW MORNING

I WOULD HAVE slept past my assigned meal time if I had not heard the tail end of the first chimes. I hurried out, stopping only to put the map from my satchel into my pocket. I just made it to the Cafeteria before the meal time bells rang. Linnayah and Zira were already seated at our table. Alecander, along with everyone else, was still in line. Leric must have insisted on making everybody wait while he made sure our Human guests were served first. The aroma of cinnamon and apples tickled my nose as I entered the Cafeteria. I was positive the delicacy would be oatmeal.

There was an open seat across from Linnayah. I interrupted a conversation between her and Aurora. Aurora was admiring Linnayah's decision to remain in school when so many others had not.

"You almost missed meal time. Were you up late last night?" Linnayah asked casually.

"I had trouble sleeping," I answered. "How well did you sleep?"

"Once I laid down in my pod, I had no problem."

Linnayah looked tired but still very beautiful. I looked down at my murky milk. I thought about how just yesterday Linnayah had put extra containers in our supplies and I had loaded it into our truck. That truck was now just a pile of shattered metal. I imagined the milk splattered over the metal pieces. I wanted to strangle whoever had robbed us of our precious gift. I reached into my pocket and pulled out the map. Alecander cleared his throat. I did not bother to look up at him. Instead of opening the map like everyone was most likely expecting me to, I folded it and refolded it. When I thought it was the right size, I slipped it under the uneven table leg. At least there it would serve a useful purpose.

It was silent for a moment before Aurora spoke to Linnayah. "If you want, I can take you to meet Kayella after breakfast. She is about your age. I think it might be nice if you met a young Cresecren woman and observe what she does in her daily tasks. It might help with your research."

"That is a great idea! I'd love that!"

I was not sure how that would go over with Kayella. I had not had a chance to speak with her since before we went to the Market. I certainly was not going to try to talk to her with Linnayah present. I would have to wait. Kayella's warning haunted my mind once more: *DEATH!*

Linnayah's voice brought me out of my deep thought. "What are you going to do today?"

"I am going to take a boat out and go fishing after the next meal time. It will be cooling down by then." I turned to

Alecander. "Did you want to join me?"

"I would, but I am headed out with Bentum to the woods. We hope to bring something back. It has been a while since we hunted. We might actually find something edible this time."

"Not if you don't improve your aim!" Bentum teased.

"One time! One time, I missed a rabbit darting through the brush and he never stops talking about it!" Alecander shook his head and smiled.

"By going separate ways, we have more of a chance at catching something," I said.

"May I come with you? It might be great research for my paper to see how you provide food," Linnayah asked me.

"I . . . I guess so," I stammered. The thought of us alone in the boat for hours made me uncomfortable.

Zira spoke up. "I am not staying here alone vith my zoughts. I vill be going hunting too. I do have a gun."

"You don't have to threaten us. We could use the extra eyes," Bentum joked.

"If you go again soon, may I come?" Linnayah asked. "I think it would be fascinating to watch. I'll be very quiet. The animals won't even know I am there. I promise!"

"You think that watching a deaf person hunt would be fascinating? Just wait until you see Aurora hunt." Bentum took his mate's hand. "Next time we go, you will come with us. You'll watch Aurora hunt. What I can do is nothing compared to her!" Bentum beamed.

Linnayah smiled broadly. "Wonderful!"

THE HUNTED

Early that evening, after we feasted on cured ham, potatoes, and freeze-dried tomatoes, Linnayah followed me to the docks. Her hair looked lighter in the sunlight and her golden locks blew freely in the breeze. We were thankful for the wind. The boats were built to provide areas of shade. This would help protect us from the heat until the sun went down. The fishing gear was stored under a bench on deck.

We had two fishing boats the previous summer but lost one due to an unfortunate accident that took the lives of an elderly and his mate. I kept that information to myself, knowing the chamber that Zira and Linnayah shared had belonged to them.

"This is amazing work. Did you help build it?" Linnayah asked.

"No, but Alecander did," I answered.

"Impressive!" she said, running her hand lightly along the railing of the boat. *Great! One more reason she should be impressed with Alecander.*

"I can make chess pieces," I said, knowing full well it was not as impressive as building a boat. Alecander had helped me with the chess pieces and board but I chose not to share that information.

"Really?" was Linnayah's only response, which deflated my ego. I bet if she had known Alecander made them she would have said it was impressive. *What is wrong with me? I sound as if I am jealous!* I decided I did not like the feeling of jealousy and would try hard not to let it get the best of me.

Linnayah watched as I cast off the lines, pushed the bow away from the dock, and jumped back onto the boat. Instead of watching my footing, I was busy watching her admiring the sea. I nearly missed the boat with my second foot and had to grab onto the side. Thankfully, she missed my awkwardness and I regained my composure swiftly.

"I haven't gone fishing before. In fact, I have never been on a boat," Linnayah said.

"Never? Really?"

"My dad has this fear of water and my mom is a vegan so she wouldn't go fishing. I just never had the opportunity."

"I certainly hope you do not get seasick."

"Let's hope I don't." She moved closer to me. I found myself once again digging my toes into the bottom of my shoes. She reached behind me to grab a fishing pole. "Will you show me how to use this thing?"

We had a decent evening and caught one large trout. Even though I offered to let Linnayah reel it in, she insisted that I do it. She did not want to ruin the chance for extra food. She squealed when I flopped it onto the deck and it floundered next to her feet. I unhooked it and placed it in the bench hold. We admired our catch for a moment before I closed the panel.

"I never asked how your day was. Did you find hanging out in the Conservatory interesting?" I asked.

"I found Dahsie, Kayella, and especially Elza very entertaining."

"I could see how you might find Elza or even Kayella entertaining, but Dahsie? She is a bit . . . brazen," I said, casting the line back into the sea.

"She's really not that bad. She's actually quite fascinating. Did you know she once rode a horse? Can you imagine? A horse? There must only be a few hundred thousand left in the whole world. It is hard to believe there was once over sixty million!"

"I know there was a workhorse here in Gavaron that died about ten years ago. Maybe that is the horse she rode. It has a grave behind the Vehicle Grotto in the cemetery. I am surprised the old woman surfaced above ground to ride it."

"Be nice, Cayden. Dahsie told me the horse brought her joy for the first time in her life. Her cat Elza is the only one who does that now. Perhaps that is why she doesn't surface very often. Maybe it hurts too much," Linnayah said, as she shed a tear.

To change the subject, I asked, "What do you think of Kayella? She is usually very pleasant but she has been acting . . . different lately." I chose my words carefully.

"Oh, Cayden, you are no different from any other boy, are

you?"

"What do you mean?" I wished she had referred to me as a man. I was seventeen, after all.

"I think Kayella was hoping to occupy the mate chamber instead of Zira and me."

"But they would never give her a mate chamber without a mate."

"Kayella knows that, silly! She was planning to propose a new arrangement to you sooner or later. She said you both get along well and even though you haven't spoken much lately, she believes you would both benefit from the arrangement. Kayella was working up the nerve to ask Dahsie if you could trade working with her part of the time. In exchange, you would have access to anything you wanted at any time in the Conservatory. She wants to be free!"

I was dumbfounded. "Free?"

Linnayah continued, "Yeah, she is in her youth, you know. She wants to go fishing, hunting, swimming . . . " Linnayah leaned a bit closer. "Did you know she loves to sing? Dahsie won't let her do that in the dingy Conservatory. She's just like any girl. She wants to experience life! She didn't ask to be the Conservatory Appointed Assistant. She was just given the job." Linnayah leaned in even closer for dramatic effect and it worked. "Kayella DOESN'T want to become Dahsie. If you help her, you could both benefit. I think she is very smart and adorable, too. She would make a great mate for someone. You should at least consider it."

"Why are you telling me all this and not her?" I was curious and unsure of my own thoughts about the situation Linnayah had just presented.

"She said she couldn't do it."

"Could not do what?"

"Ask Dahsie. Kayella is terrified she would say no and then her dream would be crushed. She would rather hold on to the dream of a happier life than know she could never have one."

"So, when Dahsie dies, Kayella takes her place, having to spend even more time in the Conservatory?"

"Exactly! You have to help her," Linnayah said, looking at me intently.

"I . . ."

"Listen, you would both benefit. You would have a bigger chamber and access to everything in the Conservatory without having to wait until your birthday. PLUS you would help a friend avoid becoming another Dahsie. The world only needs one Dahsie." Linnayah smiled. "She is your friend, isn't she? You do get along, don't you?"

"Well, yes. I guess so. I mean I do not really have any friends."

"Nonsense. You have Alecander, Bentum, Aurora, Kayella, and me. I am your friend." Linnayah reached over and laid her hand on my arm. "Just because no one ever said the word 'friend' doesn't mean they are not."

I was not sure what I felt at that moment but looking into Linnayah's eyes, I wanted to make her happy.

"I will do it!"

"Do what?" she said excitedly.

"I will propose the arrangement to Dahsie myself. That way, if Dahsie does not allow it, Kayella will never have to know I asked."

"Wonderful!" Linnayah leaned in to kiss my cheek. She stood up to retrieve water out of the bench. I was glad she was not looking at me as I felt my face flush. I turned away to hide it from her.

We were silent for a little while. Linnayah stared at the ocean and I stared at her. I thought about sharing a mate chamber with Kayella and working for Dahsie. Besides the obvious negative of working alongside Dahsie, I could not think of any other downside. I would have my free time, as Kayella and I would work alternating shifts. I would have about twice the room size. And maybe during a late restless night I would want to talk to someone. Kayella would be there to listen.

As my thoughts filled with the new possibilities, I lost track of time and night fell. Linnayah whistled tunes I had not heard before as she watched the fishing line. The melodies were lulling me to sleep. I wondered if the others had made it back yet and if they had brought something for Leric to skin. He would gladly cook it for us, knowing he would get a share of the tasty morsel.

"Maybe we should head back now," I said.

"Let's give it a few more minutes. I have a good feeling we are going to catch another one." Linnayah looked over her shoulder at me. Her soft smile warmed my heart. I granted her those last minutes, knowing full well we would not catch anything else. I was amazed we had caught anything at all.

Just as we were about to head in, Linnayah said, "Look! Look! I knew it! I had a feeling!"

I laughed. "This one is all yours. You reel it in."

"No, Cayden, what if it gets away?" she squealed.

"If you do not hurry it will! Here, I will help." I handed her the pole and stood behind her. Her hair whipped in my face as I tried to get my head at a good angle to see. This was a hefty catch! We pulled back on the pole and slowly reeled it toward the boat. Linnayah giggled while I burst out laughing. I could not remember the last time I laughed that hard. Suddenly lights on the shore caught my eye. Unfamiliar lights. I stopped helping Linnayah.

"Cayden, I can't do this by myself!" Linnayah cried nervously. I loosened my grasp on the fishing pole and stepped to the rear of the boat. I leaned over to see if I could make out what the lights were attached to.

"Darn it, Cayden, the line broke! I told you I couldn't do it alone," she said, disappointed and angry. I kept concentrating on the shore. My intuition told me something was wrong about those lights.

"What are you looking—"

A deafening sound pierced our ears as the pirate ship exploded and pieces splashed into the water close to us. Another set of lights appeared in front of the Vehicle Grotto and started across the beach toward the first set. I checked on Linnayah. She stood frozen with her hands over her mouth. I hurried to the motor and started it, knowing it would still be several minutes before we reached shore.

A second explosion sent the Vehicle Grotto tumbling down onto the sand. A scream, my own, shook the darkness. The lights were headed across the beach toward the edge of Gavaron. One cast its lights upon the other and provided me with a clear view of the attackers.

They were gideons, small aircraft that glided a few feet off the ground. They had two pilots and could carry up to six heavily armed fighters. A gideon's weaponry consisted of miniguns but the ammunition was not always easily acquired because it was scarce. The real weapons to fear were the ones carried by the fighters. I had seen models of these vehicles in a school project the Rawnett twins had done. They went as far as building a miniature of my living quarters and then blasting it to smithereens to demonstrate the gideon's destructive abilities.

The gideons disappeared as we approached the shore. I was not sure what I would do once I reached the shore. I only knew that I had to get there as fast as I could. Alecander, Aurora, Bentum, Kayella, Zira . . . Linnayah was right. They were all my friends. *Were they inside? Did they make it back from hunting? Why is this happening?*

"Who would do this?" Linnayah gasped.

"I do not know. However, I will find out." My jaw trembled. "I will not let my friends die and my home be ripped away without knowing who is responsible. If the coward strikes a blow, he should at least have the decency to show his face!"

I leapt onto the dock. Linnayah followed right behind me. We raced toward the ruins. I heard nothing—no voices, no screams.

"Bentum!" I heard Linnayah call in relief. I saw him, too, along the edge of the woods. Zira and Alecander appeared beside him. Alecander was limping. Zira paused to wait as he climbed through brush and Bentum sprinted toward us. I slowed as he approached. He grabbed me by the shoulders and lifted me effortlessly.

He spat in my face as he yelled, "What happened? Who did this?" My shoulders burned as he watched my lips.

"I do not know!" I shouted back.

Bentum did not budge. His eyes remained steady on my lips.

"What happened?" Bentum asked again, his voice lowered as he loosened his grip on my shoulders.

"We were on the boat when it happened. We don't know," Linnayah said softly as she touched Bentum's arm to get his attention. He turned to look at her and released his grip, dropping me to my feet.

"You! You!" He approached her. "What have you done?"

Linnayah backed up. "I don't know what you mean."

"Who have you brought to us?" he demanded. Linnayah continued to back up. He lunged toward her. She stumbled and fell onto the sand. Before I could react, Zira jumped in front of me.

"Don't even go zere, big boy!" Zira put the end of her pistol into the side of Bentum's neck.

Bentum stood still as he clenched his fists in frustration. Linnayah sat up. Alecander hobbled into Bentum's sight and said calmly, "No need to cast blame now. Our thoughts should be on survivors."

"Survivors," Bentum repeated with a hint of hope in his voice.

"There aren't any survivors down there," a voice called from behind us. Famous' statement captured everyone's attention. Zira lowered her gun and Bentum turned his attention from Linnayah to Famous. I wasted no time getting Linnayah to her feet. She brushed the sand from her hands, hair, and dress. I barely felt the grains as they hit my skin. *No survivors! DEATH!*

Famous was in his wheelchair as he approached us. "It's all right, Kayella! Come on out!" he shouted. *Kayella! She was okay! Another friend had survived!*

Kayella slowly emerged from behind an evergreen tree. Alecander flashed his light in her direction.

"Is there anyone else?" Bentum asked desperately.

"I'm sorry, I don't believe there is," Kayella answered, exaggerating her head movement to signify 'no' for Bentum. He fell to his knees as he tried to understand what that meant. I laid a hand softly on his shoulder.

"We barely made it out alive," Famous added.

"How did you get out?" Alecander asked.

"That crazy old witch had a splendid idea, pardon my choice of words, I shouldn't speak ill of the dead." Alecander aimed the flashlight at Famous' lips for Bentum's benefit. "Dahsie built a third exit out of Gavaron from the Conservatory. The only ones aware of it were Kayella and Dahsie herself. The old bat built it so she could have easy access to the outside to check out the stars at night. She was an amateur astronomer, if you will. The night air probably did her some good. It wasn't good for her to be in that stuffy Conservatory all the time," Famous said.

Kayella took over and Alecander turned his light in her direction. "I never would have known of its existence if I hadn't backtracked one day. I returned after my shift for something I had left behind. Dahsie wasn't expecting anyone so she probably thought it was a good time to go out. I was quiet as a mouse as I didn't want a scolding about my forgetfulness. I heard rustling in the back and out of curiosity I peeked out. It was then that I discovered Dahsie's secret. I always wondered why she would never let me touch a certain shelf, always claiming that the items on it were special. I never saw anything special about them. Dahsie shifted two of the items to the right. Then she placed the item furthest to the right onto the empty space on the left. The shelf slid over enough to let Dahsie pass through and closed right behind her. It was weeks before I had a chance to investigate. Along the walls and ceiling Dahsie—and who knows who else—made maps of stars. I assumed that place was her escape from reality."

"Could Aurora still be alive?" Bentum said, part question and part statement.

"No, she didn't make it. I am sorry, no one else could have made it," Kayella said, choking on her words.

"How . . . how do you know?"

Neither Kayella nor Famous answered right away. It was as though they were searching for the right words or maybe they were hoping the other would speak first.

"How do you know!" Bentum said again, this time with growing agitation.

"Because I watched her die!" Kayella blurted out through her tears.

Famous took over for Kayella, who began to cry uncontrollably. Linnayah walked over to the sobbing girl and put her arm around her. "They came in just as I entered the Conservatory. The corner of my eye caught sudden movement. At first, I thought it was that darn cat, Elza. She is always darting around, sneaking up on me. It definitely was NOT Elza because I saw her peering at me from Dahsie's desk. It was a man dressed in all graphite and what made me certain something was wrong was the fact he was wearing a gas mask. Soon there were more of them, all wearing the same attire. I knew better than to sit there like a dumbass. I locked that Conservatory door from the inside faster than Elza could pounce on my wheelchair."

"Famous, stop embellishing." Alecander reminded him this was no time for one of his legendary tales.

Famous continued, "Kayella didn't have a clue what I was

doing. She tried to shove me aside and unlock the door. I grabbed her and sat her on my lap. She probably thought I was trying to be fresh. She must have seen them too because she became perfectly still. I rolled away from the door but one of them was already making his way up the stairs. I knew he wasn't getting in. Dahsie kept that place under lockdown when she wasn't expecting anyone. I turned away so I could see what was going on down below. Then I saw Aurora."

"Aurora," Bentum repeated. I was sure he was not catching everything being said but maybe that was best.

Famous nodded. "Are you sure you want to know what happens next?" Bentum paused before nodding. "Okay, but I am just the messenger. Please keep that in mind, buddy." Famous sat up straighter, as if positioning his chair to wheel away just in case Bentum decided they were not buddies. "Aurora was there because she was waiting for you to come back from hunting. I know because I stopped to chat before I went up to the Conservatory." *Of course, he stopped to chat.* "Aurora said she could sense you would be back soon. I wish I could have sensed those bastards were coming. I would have taken Aurora to the Conservatory with me. One of those men walked right past her and she could hear another trying to break the glass of the Conservatory with the end of a gas tank. Aurora took off running down the corridor but it was too late. One of the men had already released a purple haze of gas into the air. We watched as it caught her and she stopped dead in her tracks, flung her arms back and fell right to the ground. It was as if someone had grabbed her by the back of her neck and threw her to the ground. She rolled over and . . . "

Kayella cried into Linnayah's shoulder, "I wish I could have done something to help her. But I couldn't. I just couldn't."

Famous continued, "Her face, her beautiful perfect face, it wasn't there any more. It was replaced by something monstrous. She was screaming and clawing at her own flesh." Bentum had dropped his head. "I was thankful for the thick glass at that moment. Then I noticed the man clad in graphite who had been battling with the door was no longer making a ruckus. We turned our attention towards him and discovered he was releasing gas. The gas seemed to be searching for a way in. We knew the glass would only temporarily hold it back. It WOULD eventually get through. Kayella grabbed me and said 'Come with me!' I didn't know where she was going but at that moment anywhere else was fine by me. She grabbed Elza off the desk and threw her on my lap, commanding me to hold on to her." Famous gave a quick glance at Kayella, noting that she was quiet. If it was not for Kayella, Famous would have left Elza. He was not really an Elza person. The cat was fascinated with his wheelchair and was always pawing, scratching, or leaping onto it.

Kayella continued where Famous had left off. "He did as I asked. Elza is around here somewhere." We all glanced around but she was not within sight.

"We should build a fire. This is the only light we have," Alecander said.

"I've got gasoline . . . " Zira stopped short and we watched as a look of horror crossed her exhausted face. "Zee Mustang!" she cried. She turned towards the rubble that now covered her beloved vehicle. Alecander had moved it into the Vehicle Grotto to shield it from the sun and keep wondering eyes and hands away.

"I vote we move toward the orchards. Away from . . . this," Linnayah suggested.

When we reached the orchards, I plucked an apple from a tree and tossed it to Linnayah. "With all the destruction, I am surprised they did not touch the orchards," I said.

"They wouldn't destroy a source of food, boy. Hey, toss me one of those, will you?" Famous called.

The evening was silent. I did, however, find out what happened to the hunting crew and why they were slow in returning. Zira and Alecander had bet who would catch the first prey. Alecander had guessed if they spotted anything it would be a rabbit. He was right. Alecander steadied himself on a fallen tree trunk readying his spear when Zira fired from behind him. Alecander swore the bullet whizzed by his ear. He lost his balance, fell on his spear and broke it, and twisted his ankle. Minutes later, they heard the first blast and headed toward the beach.

Everyone settled down for the night. We decided it was best to move on in the early morning. We were unsure where we could go or how we would get there. We only knew we were not willing to stay and find out if the attackers would be returning. Bentum was quiet and sat by himself. Zira finally joined us before we turned in, carrying the rabbit she had shot. Elza was still nowhere to be found. I studied Linnayah, who was sitting by a sleeping Kayella. Linnayah was perfectly still and her eyes were closed. I recalled our conversation about Kayella, Dahsie, and the Conservatory. I realized that with Dahsie's death, Kayella was free.

MOVING ON

I WOKE to the smell of cooking rabbit and steaming trout.

"Good morning, lazy-bones." Linnayah smiled as she picked apples and placed them in someone's satchel.

I was the only one still lying down. It was hard to realize that nearly three hundred people would not wake this day. I could hardly believe only five Cresecrens survived: Alecander, Bentum, Famous, Kayella, and myself. It did not seem right to say good morning. "Morning," I said as I sat up, feeling quite groggy.

"Nice of you to join us," Alecander called as he removed the fish from the fire.

Linnayah crouched down. "We are going to eat and then head over to the cemetery to pay homage to those who were lost last night. Afterwards, we will gather anything useful. Then we leave Gavaron."

"Leave Gavaron," I murmured.

The smell of cooking fish must have lured Elza out of her hiding place, as she was pouncing at Famous' wheels. Famous kept shooing her away but each time she returned. We ate hurriedly and decided it was best to go, just in case anyone came looking for survivors.

As we walked towards the cemetery, Linnayah carried Elza. She reminded me of a mother cradling a child.

"What about your family? You should get back to them," I said.

"My family?" Linnayah said, sounding surprised. "They are very busy with their work. They are practically living at the hospital. I am not in a hurry to be home alone."

"We should probably take you home," I said, thinking that we never really decided where we were going. There was talk of heading north to Solitare or south to the new Cresecren grounds. I had voted for the south even though the grounds were not fully developed. I was not interested in seeing the lanky woman and curly-headed boy from Solitare I'd met at the Supply Depot again. Plus, down south they should be happy to receive the extra hands to help build, which hopefully would make up for the extra mouths to feed.

We gathered around the weather-beaten graves. Three freshly dug small holes were in the ground before us. It was the best we could do under the circumstances. We stood motionless and in silence. Kayella took the first steps toward the mini-graves. "This was a gift from Dahsie." She removed a necklace. I had seen it before. It was woven out of tan braided rope and a star hung at the end. She dropped it into the fresh soil and threw a clump of dirt over it.

Bentum stepped forward. He kneeled down and opened a

clenched fist, releasing sand into the hole next to Dahsie's. "Aurora loved the sand. She loved its feel between her toes. She sat with me many times on the beach and had me describe the ocean and Gavaron to her. She wanted to know every detail. Aurora, you need not worry any more whether your physical being shall live forever, but you will live on to those who knew your beauty within."

Tears streamed down Linnayah's face and dropped onto Elza's fur. She attempted to wipe them off. Bentum bent down to toss a handful of dirt over the sand. Alecander stepped forward and placed a hand on Bentum's shoulder. He then dropped a piece of wood representing the other victims into the last tiny grave.

"This is a piece of the ship at the entrance of Gavaron. My brethren, you will all be missed," Alecander said. As the wood gently fell to the earth, the sound of fast-approaching aircraft sent a warning to us. Famous turned and headed toward the noise, either as a reflex from his days protecting Quinso Vardo or just being plain stupid.

Alecander ordered the rest of us to head for the woods. I grabbed Bentum's arm. The intensity of my grip told him to follow without my having to speak a single word. When we reached the trees, I looked back to make sure everyone was with us. Unfortunately, not everyone was. Alecander was limping after Famous. I took one step out of the woods when Bentum raised his husky arm to block my path. I watched as Famous whipped his wheelchair around and headed straight toward

Alecander at top speed. *Famous was going to ram right into him!* A gideon headed toward Alecander and Famous. Alecander, who was frantically trying to get out of the way, spun around. The wheelchair rammed into Alecander's legs, knocking him lopsidedly into Famous' lap. If this had not been a life-or-death situation, it would have been humorous.

I watched in horror. The gideon raced forward, knocking over anything in its path. Bentum turned to us and yelled frantically, "Run!" I could not leave Alecander. The gideon grazed the back of Famous' chair. This propelled my friends toward me. A weapon-wielding man dressed in the graphite clothing Famous had described emerged from the top of the craft. The gideon could not enter the orchard because the trees would not allow clear passage. If the marksman was accurate, it would not matter. He raised his rifle to eye level and I was certain he would hit his mark. Suddenly a large chunk of rubble rocketed towards him. He fired as it hit him in the side of the head. The shot went wide. I stepped out of the woods, wondering who had thrown the rock. It was Bentum. He nodded at me and disappeared into the woods.

Famous and Alecander had just reached the trees when another man jumped from the vehicle to the ground. He reached overhead to grab the rifle from the marksman as another gideon approached at top speed. I turned and joined Alecander and Famous as they rode through the woods dodging trees, bushes, and branches.

Gunshots whizzed through the woods. A sizzling sound

zipped by my left ear and gouged a hole the size of my fist in a nearby tree. I had heard of the "Bleeding Heart" but never witnessed it in action. It was designed to take out an enemy's heart. I quickly decided to run in a zig-zag pattern through the forest to make it more of a challenge to hit me. This was not easy to do as I had to avoid trees and foliage. I knew they would pursue us until they killed us. My only concern was how long I could elude them. *Why did they want us dead?*

I did not see Famous or Alecander. I wanted to look around for them but dared not slow down. I wondered about the others. I took solace in the fact that they had additional time to head away from the chaos.

I do not think I had run so fast in all my life. I prided myself in being a fast runner but feared I was not fast enough to outrun their weapons. I wanted to look back to see how close my pursuers were but could not spare even a moment. The heat was oppressive and sweat dripped into my eyes. I felt a burning sensation in my side and suspected a side stitch. A small tree fell in the distance as a result of a Bleeding Heart.

The woods thickened as I approached the center. They would soon thin out again and break open past the Gavaron boundary line. *Then what?* We would be exposed, just waiting to die. It was not until I reached the edge of the woods that I realized I had not heard another gunshot or seen any more damage from a Bleeding Heart. My side still burned.

As I stepped into the open, swatting a tree branch off my face, I stopped in my tracks. I did not see anyone. I scanned the area quickly as I walked further into the open. I heard movement behind me. Then I heard Famous' unmistakable voice whining about something.

"Shut up, Famous! If we haven't lost those hunting us, they will surely find us by your bellowing!" Alecander said, as Famous shoved him off his lap.

"I can't feel my legs!" Famous cried.

"There is a good explanation for that: you don't have any!" Alecander growled.

"You know what I mean. Your riding all that way on my lap was crushing me! How much do you weigh anyway?"

"Never mind that. Where is everyone else?" Alecander asked, looking at me.

Something hot wrapped around my ankle. I prepared to stomp at it with my other foot when I saw that it was a familiar dark hand. Bentum peeked out below a clump of grass and tugged my ankle toward him. We lifted the layer of brown grass above his head. Alecander jumped down while Bentum tried to support him to take some of the pressure off Alecander's ankle before he hit the ground. I lowered Famous, looking over my shoulder periodically to make sure we did not have any unwanted company. I lowered Famous' wheelchair and then it was my turn. I reached for the latch of the entrance as I heard movement in the woods. I lowered it as fast as I could. It was so dark in the underground area that I could not even see the whites of anyone's eyes.

I heard a soft sizzling noise followed by a spark of light.

Bentum was holding an illumination orb. He ignited it by twisting the bottom and top halves of the clear ball in opposite directions. Bentum placed it on a small ledge. The ball slowly grew brighter, providing enough light to illuminate the walls around us. We were in an underground passageway.

Bentum said, "Kayella found this illumination orb before I sent them on ahead."

We jogged along the corridor. Famous wheeled first so he would not ram into anyone. Bentum was Alecander's crutch and I followed closely behind. It would be tough for the enemy to find us here. The entrance was well-hidden. *Why was I not aware of it?* I probably would have explored it a long time ago if I had known of its existence. *Where did it lead?* As soon as the thought entered my mind, I knew why I was not privileged to know this information. I WOULD have explored it. I struck the dirt beneath my feet in one heavy step.

"Are you all right, Cayden?" Alecander asked.

"I will be fine."

"It does not look like it penetrated your skin," Alecander said.

"What?" I said. I immediately realized he was referring to the burning sensation I had felt in my side. I looked down and saw a burnt area of skin through a hole in my shirt. An enemy marksman had hit his target after all. It was red and looked inflamed, but thankfully it was not deep or bleeding.

We moved forward until we came to a fork. One branch continued on straight while the other veered off to the left. We watched as the illumination orb continued straight ahead.

"Which way, Captain?" Famous asked.

Bentum shook his head. "I can't remember what Kayella told me. Give me a second."

Alecander unhooked his arm from Bentum's shoulders, hobbled over to the other tunnel entrance, and crossed to the far wall. Without hesitation, he slid a piece of the wall to the side, took out another illumination orb, and ignited it. I studied the wall. There was no possible way anyone would know that piece of the wall slid open without being informed of it. I realized Alecander had known of this place but never once mentioned it to me. *All those nights playing chess and he could not have brought it up just once?* I struck the ground again with my foot as we headed down the new tunnel. We continued through the tunnel to the left until the tunnel split again. *Which path do we take now?*

"Follow on," Alecander said.

We trudged on for a few more minutes in silence. "When does this thing end? I'm starting to get tunnel vision!" Famous asked in an awkward attempt to be funny.

"Soon," Alecander answered.

"Who the hell built this thing anyway and why wasn't I privileged to know of its existence?" Famous demanded.

"There weren't many who knew," Alecander answered.

"You knew?" I replied, feeling slighted.

"Luckily, I did know or we might have taken the wrong path," he reminded me. "The tunnels began being built a few years after Gavaron's construction."

We came to another fork in the tunnels but this time it was a three-way split. Bentum recalled the information given to him by Kayella and took us down the one furthest to the left. Alecander continued, "Humans helped with its construction."

"Humans?" I answered. "They barely aided in the construction of Gavaron itself. Why would they aid in a tunnel?"

"Need," Alecander replied. Bentum let out a frustrated sigh, letting us know he wished to be a part of the conversation.

Alecander slowed his pace and unhooked his arm from Bentum's. He walked over to the left wall as the orb traveled on straight ahead. He ran his fingers along the wall.

"We are going to be lolling around in the dark here any second now if you don't keep moving," Famous said, driving his wheelchair close to Alecander's heels.

"I believe it is here somewhere," Alecander said.

"What?" Famous anxiously followed the dimming light with his eyes.

Alecander pushed the surface of the wall with his palm but nothing happened. I could barely see what he was doing and I shifted uncomfortably, wondering what he was up to.

"I'm going on ahead. You can gallivant on your own," Famous said, wedging his wheelchair between Bentum and Alecander. Before he could make any progress, light streamed in as the wall slid wide open to reveal an exit.

My hand shielded my eyes as I adjusted to the blinding sun. I cautiously stepped out. It took only seconds before I could see my surroundings clearly.

Alecander had walked ahead of us. He was inches from a cliff. It must have taken his eyes longer to adjust. He took another step.

"NOOOOOO!" I yelled and lunged forward to try to grab him but it was too late. I could not bear to see or hear him fall. I swung around and instinctively grabbed my ears and pulled my head down hard. I felt a crushing pain in my chest like I had never felt. Everything around me began to spin as I heard the others gasp.

A KEEPER

I WANTED to run, run faster than I had ever run before. *But to where?* I wanted to scream but no sound came from my lips.

"Now, that's what I call amazing!" Famous hooted.

I turned to see Alecander standing with both feet on the open air. He smirked at me and lifted an eyebrow. I wanted to embrace him and push him off the cliff at the same time. I was still taking it all in when Bentum joined Alecander. My heart skipped a beat as Bentum's foot crossed from the cliff edge off into what should have been certain death. Instead, he turned around to face Famous and me and he let out a hearty chuckle. I gingerly walked forward as I heard the door behind us close completely. Alecander and Bentum laughed at me as I approached. Famous whirled by me, nearly making me lose my balance, as he joined the others. Again, my heart skipped a beat, anticipating a fall.

"I heard of this type of camouflage but this is the first time I've seen it!" Famous said. He joined in the laughter.

I had never heard of this type of camouflage. Alecander had never mentioned it. My stomach began to clench as I wondered about what else he had not shared with me. All those nights we played chess and he never mentioned the secret tunnels or the camouflage? I took my first step from the ground I was certain of and planted my foot down on that which I was not. I was truly bewildered. I stretched out my arms toward the trees and a ledge on the other side of what appeared to be a small valley between two cliffs.

"Incredible," Bentum said, as he bent down to run his fingers over the ground.

"It is only temporary," Alecander explained. "This scene was triggered to display once the tunnel door began to open. It is a deterrent for further exploration and meant to drive others back through the tunnel. If we stand here long enough, we will see it turn back to its original form. Just be careful where you step. A rock or a tree may be disguised. Also, it is always guarded by a Keeper."

As if on cue, a petite woman with olive skin and long jet-black hair appeared. Her hair partially covered tattoos on her arms. A short tan vest hugged her body. She was Human. Her dark doe eyes and appearance gave no warning of danger.

"I am the Keeper, "she said with a high-pitched voice that matched her daintiness.

Famous snorted. "You? A guard?"

The Keeper took three quick strides. She leapt and twisted her body in midair. Her feet hit an invisible solid surface and she twisted her body again, landing on Famous' shoulders as her muscular legs squeezed his neck mercilessly. Famous struggled to free himself.

The woman bent down to murmur in Famous' ear, "My name is Lace, and I AM the Keeper!"

Before any of us could react, she released him and was back on her own two feet. Her ebony hair had rearranged itself, allowing me to see her tribal tattoos and the strength in her arms. Both arms were adorned with the scripted letter K. This woman who had seemed demure moments ago was now a protective lioness. Famous struggled to regain his composure.

"We mean you no disrespect," Alecander said, stepping forward. "We are just trying to reunite with our friends and hope you have already seen them."

"Watch where you step. She probably finished them off!" Famous spat out.

Lace toyed with Famous. "Maybe I should have squeezed a little harder!"

Bentum chuckled. This seemed to lighten Lace's mood and she relaxed.

"I have seen the others. They are safe and with my family. I will take you to them," Lace said. She sprinted toward where we came in. She stopped short, reached into her vest pocket and threw an iridescent sphere against the wall. The sphere flattened and within a few seconds covered the entire area where the door had been. Pleased with herself, she said, "Sealed!"

Just then, the camouflage began to give glimpses of the true world: specks of dirt, edges of stones, the tree trunk where Lace had planted her feet to propel herself toward Famous began to appear. We followed Lace. She stopped at a makeshift shelter where she gathered up a half-eaten apple, flask of water, and small backpack. I wondered if one of the others had given her the apple. She ate it and in between bites she said, "It has been a long outing, I am ready to go home. Follow close behind and when we come to the markings, follow in my footsteps or you will no longer be with us."

"What markings? What do you mean, 'no longer be with us'?" Famous spluttered.

Lace did not answer and took off like a gazelle toward a meadow. She called back over her shoulder, "The injured one should ride with the maimed one to keep up."

"Not again!" Famous whined.

"You heard the woman!" Alecander responded. I know he did not want to sit on Famous' lap any more than Famous wanted him to, but he sat down with a hard thump and a small grin out of spite. I was certain his ankle was bothering him tremendously for him to follow Lace's suggestion so willingly.

"Now, don't get us killed," Alecander warned.

"Humph!"

We took off behind Lace. I looked back over my shoulder to make sure Bentum got the message. He was right behind me. I prided myself on being a fast runner. It was one thing I was really good at doing. I ran very fast earlier but not for sport—it was to save my life. Lace was also fast, incredibly fast. I do not know why but I felt the need to catch her. I pulled away from the others. I knew Famous could pass me at top speed in his chair if he had been alone. However, Alecander was weighing him down. I was gaining on Lace and I ignored the pain in my side. No matter how fast she ran, I stayed on her heels. I hoped she would tire faster and I would have more endurance. *That is it! She has lost her fuel.* When she finally slowed down, I saw the chance to overtake her and I took it. As soon as I caught up to her, she turned, looked at me, and gave me a sheepish smile.

I did not see the marking because I was too busy looking back at Lace to notice. *Great, my arrogance is going to get me killed!* The flash of black and the burning pain in my chest knocked me onto my backside. The impact left me stunned. I could hear the others approaching but I could not comprehend what they were saying. Something weighted down my chest, then Bentum bent down and lifted Lace off me. She had fallen across my chest. She dusted off her pant legs and glared at me. Her eyes looked like a wild boar's.

"Perhaps I should have let you proceed," she said, looking at her skinned and bleeding arm. Leaves fell from her hair and dirt was ground into her left cheek.

"Are you all right?" Bentum reached out his hand to help me up.

I nodded, though my pride would not let me take Bentum's hand. I insisted on getting up myself.

"She saved your life, Dimwit!" Famous said.

"Saved my life," I whispered as I saw four hatchets lined up along the path. One of those surely would have split my head open had Lace not knocked me out of the way. The black flash must have been her black boots. I recognized the marking, a $\mathcal{K}$ carved into a tree. It was a larger version of the ones on Lace's arms. Thankfully, Linnayah had not been here to see me make a fool out of myself.

"I am sorry, I . . . I do not know what came over me," I stammered. Lace did not reply. "Thank you . . . for saving my life."

"We will see soon enough if it was worth saving," Lace replied, straightening her backpack. Over her shoulder, she called back, "Now, let us try this again. Follow me closely. Do not stray or YOU WILL DIE!"

Instead of following the obvious path ahead, Lace went to the right of the tree into a thicker part of the woods. We walked some time and my eyes continually searched for more hatchets or poison darts flying out from nowhere. Lace and I were a little ahead of the others. Famous, still with Alecander on his lap, had to fight off foliage. I noticed Lace had not tended to her wound. I tore a piece of my shirt and tapped her on the shoulder. I jumped back when she swung around with her right arm raised.

"Sorry, I just wanted to give this to you," I said.

She looked at the cloth curiously.

"It is for your arm . . . to help it stop bleeding." She ignored it.

"If anyone is following us, you might be leaving a trail," I explained, referring to the droplets of blood that occasionally fell to the ground.

Lace raised an eyebrow and took the cloth. She managed to walk and tie the cloth around the wound, as if she had done it a thousand times before. She stopped next to a boulder to wait for everyone to catch up. Famous was still cursing in Alecander's ear about anything in the way of his wheelchair. He veered off the main path and stopped abruptly. He shoved Alecander off his lap.

"You could have just asked me to get off!" Alecander exclaimed.

Famous did not reply. Instead he began hysterically swiping at his legs and arms and screaming, "Get them off! Help! Get them off of me!" I sprinted over to him. He kept ferociously slapping his thighs and swinging his arms in true terror. He reached for something in his mouth, and began choking on his own fingers. I grabbed his hand. I saw it then, a vile fist-sized black, brown, and orange spotted bug working its way into Famous' mouth. I was in shock by the number of identical bugs crawling all over his body. They seemed to have appeared out of nowhere. I pulled the bug out of his mouth and flung it into a bush. Before I could do anything further, I felt little legs crawling up my own leg. I looked down. Hundreds of them headed for us along the ground. I began stomping my feet and screaming.

Lace swooped in and grabbed the back of Famous' wheelchair, pulling him sideways toward her. I could hear her screaming at him but I could not hear what she was saying. I heard a loud slap and then there was absolute silence.

"Famous!" I screamed. I could no longer see anything as the bugs were crawling over my face, trying to burrow into it. I was clawing at my face when I felt my arms being pulled away. I fought against the pull. *I have to get these bugs off of my face!* The pull on my arm was violent and I lost my footing. I was being dragged backward. Suddenly, the pressure on my forearms released and I fell forward, landing on my knees. *Was this some giant insect?* Pain shot through my left cheek. I felt the first blow to my face, the same sound before Famous was silenced. *This is it. It is over for me.* I felt another blow to my face and I expected the end of my existence.

"Cayden?" Are you all right?" I heard Alecander say. I opened my eyes to see Lace's open hand swinging toward my face. Bentum grabbed her by the wrist. She looked furious. Her eyes burned with anger. I looked around anxiously for the wicked insects. I saw none.

My eyes fixed on Famous. "You are all right!" I said, stunned.

"Yeah, she slapped me a good one too. Not so sure that was really necessary though," Famous muttered, rubbing his cheek.

"I told you not to venture from my path!" Lace scolded.

"What the hell happened to us?" Famous demanded.

"The Visions is what the hell happened to you!" she answered.

"The Visions?" Alecander asked.

"The Visions were first developed by the government to promote safe sex with the hope of battling some of the rampant diseases, but never released to the general public. Then it was changed into a weapon. You should be honored to have seen it firsthand and survived. Nothing of what you saw or felt was real, but your mind knew no difference. The longer you are in the Visions, the more it takes over and tricks your mind into believing it is real," Lace explained.

"Not real?" I said. "I still feel stinging near my eyes!"

Lace smirked. "From your own self-induced injuries since you were clawing at your face."

"Glad to be of amusement to you," I grumbled.

"We better get moving," Lace said.

This time we all made exaggerated steps to follow her as closely as possible. We came to a boulder marked with a 𝒦. "Gather close to me and do not move," she said. Lace pushed her palm down onto the 𝒦, which lifted from the rock and embraced her hand. A soft rumbling at our feet began and we descended.

I grew anxious as I knew I would see Linnayah and the others soon. I wanted to be sure everyone was okay.

Lace's face lit up. "Welcome to my humble home!" The view was astonishing. "Humble" was not how I would describe it. Lovely colored scarves hung from the ceiling like little hammocks. Pristine ivory tiles with golden trim covered the floor. Two elaborate massive carved wooden doors adorned with giant carved 𝒦s stretched from floor to ceiling. I could see the necessity of keeping a place like this secret and protected.

"This reminds me of my old stomping grounds, the days

with Quinso Vardo," Famous said.

Bentum said, "It's beautiful!"

"Glad you like it," Lace said as she leapt down the last few feet as graceful as a cat. As soon as the last of us stepped off the platform, it started to ascend. "You haven't seen anything yet," Lace said, heading toward the great doors.

"They really honor you here," I said to Lace as I noticed the ruby-red 𝒦s inside the clear crystal doorknobs.

"Honor me?"

"Yes, the 𝒦s displayed everywhere. They honor you, the Keeper."

She laughed as if I had just told her a hilarious joke. Lace turned a doorknob and a much smaller portion of the wood opened, allowing enough room for a person to enter.

"May I present to you—Kenosis," Lace said, stretching out her arm. "*This* is what is being honored."

As soon as the door opened, I smelled burning sandalwood and vanilla incense. The smell triggered memories of my past life serving the Rawnetts. Mr. Rawnett would become intoxicated every Friday night after work and spend the entire weekend in a drunken state. He was a weekend alcoholic . . . a weekend bastard. In an effort to mask her husband's weekend cigarettes, Mrs. Rawnett lit candles to try to disguise the smells from her sons. The twins knew about his love of tobacco. I often caught them smoking their father's cigarettes in the backyard. Seeing the wooden, intricately detailed furniture, lush fabric couches, fantastic glass furnishings, and grand paintings that filled the room interrupted those unpleasant memories. It was like nothing I had ever seen before.

The remainder of my crew and a handful of people I did not know were sitting at a long table and eating. The table's golden top was almost blinding. At the sight of us, Linnayah, Kayella, and Zira stopped feasting and leaped up to greet us. Their eyes lit up, relieved to see us. Linnayah ran over to hug us and saved me for last. It seemed odd for someone to want to embrace people she barely knew. I had to admit I did enjoy feeling her arms wrapped around my back.

"I am not happy to see you," she said, squeezing me tightly. I thought I had heard her wrong until she let go, looked me in the eyes, and said softly, "I am ecstatic!"

I smiled and fought the urge to pull her close to me again.

Lace sat Alecander in a chair at the end of the table next to Kayella, who smiled wide when our eyes met and straightened a strand of loose hair. Seated next to Zira was a younger man with the same coloring and features as Lace. Without speaking a word, he got up, pushed an ottoman over from the living area, and placed it under Alecander's foot. He left momentarily and returned with a bottle half-filled with a plum liquid that looked like a thickened wine. Lace prepared a plate for Alecander while the young man tended to his foot. With little coaxing needed, I sat down. There were foods I had never seen before and they smelled so delicious that my mouth watered. I filled a plate. As we ate, Lace introduced the others.

"This is my brother Amil," she said, pointing to the young

man who placed a splint and the mysterious ointment on Alecander's ankle. "This is dear Desmin," she said of an elderly Asian man with salt-and-pepper hair who had not stopped smiling since I first laid eyes on him. "And this is my Aunt Secora who prepared the food before you." I had all but forgotten about Elza, Dahsie's cat, until she appeared in the arms of a small boy. He had come from behind the kitchen area, where I assumed the sleeping quarters were.

His wide eyes were filled with curiosity. Lace got up and stepped behind him to coax him towards the table.

We all fell silent as we admired the boy. His large doe eyes were the same as Lace's.

"This is my son Bonjú. He is my reason for living," Lace said, her usual commanding nature softening as she bent down to kiss him on his forehead. Zira also softened at the sight of him. I think we all felt his warming presence and his innocence affected us. He joined us at the table and sat between Zira and his mother. We chatted and entertained the little one as his mother explained to us that very few visitors passed through and surely never this many at once. Bonjú had many questions for us. Zira had the toughest time relating to his questions. She seemed awkward in her answers, shifting back and forth in her chair.

"All this space for so few of you?" Famous stated.

"It wasn't always so," Lace answered.

"And who is this?" Famous asked, gesturing toward a portrait of a young man, his thick hair pulled back behind his ears.

"My husband," Lace answered.

"Where is he?" Famous inquired.

"He is with God," Lace said.

Bonjú got up from the table and wanted to play hide-and-seek. He tugged on Zira's leg but she jerked her leg away from him. Lace grabbed Bonjú and spun him away. "Okay, Honey Bear, go and hide. I will find you." The little one ran off giggling and called back over his shoulder, "Don't forget to find me!"

Lace answered cheerfully, "I never do!" She turned sharply to Zira and under her breath said, "Give it to me!" Her expression reminded me of a protective mother bear.

"Give you vhat?" Zira asked.

"You can have it back when you leave but you may not keep it here in the open, not around my son!"

Zira slid back from the table. I expected further confrontation. I was worried she would underestimate what Lace was capable of doing. Zira had size but would be no match for Lace. Zira paused for a moment before lifting up her skirt and revealing the gun attached to her thigh. She handed it to Lace and said, "You VILL give it back!"

Lace took the gun and nodded. "I will give it back to you tomorrow when you leave." She turned and disappeared down the hall to search for her son.

SIGHT

THAT NIGHT Bonjú wore us all out with each of us taking turns finding his hiding place. He reluctantly retired to bed with Lace and Secora. I was disappointed when Linnayah said goodnight. I could not blame her for taking Lace's offer of a nice warm bath before settling in for the night. I remained in the living area, sipping Secora's delightful warm tea. It was quite refreshing with a hint of lemon and an undertone of mint. Alecander had just told me goodnight, which left me alone with Desmin and his perpetual smile. I felt as though he was staring at me and I grew uncomfortable. I realized that he had not uttered a single word since we arrived. This realization made me even leerier. I decided then was a good time to go to bed, so I rose from the couch.

"I know you can see," Desmin said. I froze and looked at him.

"See what?"

"Please sit down," Desmin said.

I contemplated ignoring the old man's request, but he had my curiosity. I sat down. "Why do you smile so? What could bring a man so much joy that he would never stop smiling?" I asked.

"I smile because I pretend. I pretend all is well in Kenosis. We all pretend for the sake of Bonjú, but he too sees when his mind is tired or he is not well. Just like I know you can see," Desmin said.

"You are not making sense!" I stated, frustrated after such a long day. I rose again. I wanted nothing more to do with the conversation.

"Sit!" the old man said. Before I saw him move, he was on the couch next to me. He placed his arm across my chest and gently coaxed me back down. I was stunned at how swiftly he moved.

"How . . . How did you get here so fast?" I asked stupefied.

Desmin chuckled. "Look around you." Desmin said, moving his head slowly from left to right. "Do you see?"

"Sure, I see," I said, growing more agitated.

"What do you see?" Desmin asked.

"Beauty, richness, luxury, expense . . . " I answered, looking around the room and then straight into Desmin's eyes, "and peculiar."

"Try again," Desmin urged. "Look within."

"Desmin, you seem harmless enough, and I am tired. I think I will turn in. You can play this game by yourself."

I began to rise again. This time Desmin's efforts to keep me seated were much more forceful. He pushed me down and did not let go. I struggled under his hand. He had surprising strength. I relaxed. Looking at me intently and no longer smiling, he said, "Look harder."

"Okay, okay! Get your hand off of me!"

"Look first," Desmin said, slowly releasing his palm.

I did as Desmin asked. I closed my eyes a second longer than I normally would. I opened them to a strange place. My eyes darted around, taking in as much as they could before the vision disappeared and I returned to my comfortable surroundings. What I saw in those few seconds was Kenosis—not as I had always seen it, but in a state of despair. I shut my eyes a little longer this time and reopened them. This time the vision lasted longer. The wooden doors were dilapidated. The couch I sat on was torn and dull gray, not luxurious green. The floors were compacted dirt, not graced with pristine tiles. A handful of furniture and household items were newer and respectable. Remembering the painting of Lace's husband, I turned to face it. Though the portrait was as impressive as I remembered, the frame was not fine wood with a gold finish but plastic. In those moments, I held my breath. And in seconds, the Kenosis I knew returned.

"What the hell!" I said.

"No, you are not in hell. You are blessed! Blessed to have the opportunity to see things the way they really are."

"You see things as they really are too?"

"No, but I have seen Kenosis in its original state, before the technology we call The Mask was installed." I tried to grasp the idea of technology that could make a person see things differently than they actually were. Desmin asked, "Now that you have seen Kenosis in its true form, which do you prefer?" I did not answer. It was obvious. "So, I smile," Desmin said, standing up and retiring for the night.

I sat there for a minute not knowing what to do with my newfound information. In a house full of people, I suddenly felt alone.

"Hey there! I got up to go to the bathroom and I heard voices," Linnayah said from behind me. "Did you see that bathroom? Secora lit lavender incense and filled the bath with Epsom salts and warm water. Can you believe the tub is made of porcelain and has golden knobs? I wonder if they are real gold?" she said, taking a seat beside me. I barely looked at her. "I haven't felt so relaxed in years!"

I shuddered as I thought about what the bathtub truly might look like. I doubted Linnayah would have been so willing to climb in if she knew.

"I doubt it," I answered in reference to the golden knobs.

"Surely you weren't talking to yourself, were you?"

"No, I was talking to Desmin."

"Desmin. I didn't know he spoke. What did he say?"

"Not much."

"He really isn't a man of words, is he?"

I turned to look at Linnayah. My breath escaped me. Her blond hair was out of the ponytail and flowed down around her shoulders. She was wearing a soft blue nightgown that hung just above her knees with thin straps that caressed her shoulders. The color accentuated her eyes. She crossed her legs and I noticed that she was barefoot. I kept my mind focused on the Kenosis I had grown to enjoy. I did not let myself see what I now knew to be true. I did not want to think about how filthy her feet were becoming from the compacted-dirt floor. I liked this vision of Linnayah and did not want to see that she was actually wearing weathered rags. Though she would have been just as breathtaking.

She tweaked the nightgown. "Lace was kind enough to let me borrow this."

I tried not to stare. "It is lovely."

"She had one for Kayella, too. You should see her. She looks gorgeous!" Linnayah said, attempting once again to play matchmaker.

"I am sure she does," I said. *Kayella would make a good mate . . . for somebody else.*

"I wish we could stay here. They all seem so very nice. Plus it is so wonderfully gorgeous here!" *If she only knew.*

"What about your family? Have you even contacted them?" I asked.

"My family? Oh, I . . . um . . . Yes, I messaged with my parents earlier today before you got here. I told them I was staying with a friend. They are still so busy with patients from the Market that they are just glad I am not at home alone. Besides, this is an adventure, isn't it? My report will be the talk of the whole school!"

"You are risking your life! You have no idea who we are and

yet you came with us without a second thought. You could have fled and gone home but instead you came here with us," I said.

"I guess you could say I like living on the edge."

"You are quite the mystery, Linnayah. I know you do not have to tell me anything. But if you ever decide you would like to, I would love to listen."

"How about we talk about you?"

"Okay, what do you want to know? I am an open book!"

"For starters, I would be interested in hearing how you ended up in Gavaron. My mind is full of ways you could have gotten there."

"Really? Do tell."

"Well, I knew it wasn't because you couldn't work any more. You seem to be quite healthy and physically fit. You also don't SEEM like the type to steal or do anything unlawful."

"Thank you for the noble thoughts."

"Well, your people do have an extremely low crime rate."

"I will spare you from guessing any further."

She scooted closer. I could smell the lavender in her clothes and hair, sweet and calming.

"So, where do I begin?" I said.

"At the beginning," Linnayah giggled, smiling and encouraging me to tell my tale.

"Right. Well, the Human family I served was the Rawnetts. There were two young twin boys, and Mr. and Mrs. Rawnett. The twins were relentless in trying to find ways to mistreat me.

Mr. Rawnett was pleasant enough during the week, but during the weekend no one could stand to be around him. He was a weekend binger on cigarettes and spirits." Linnayah scrunched her brows together. "He was often unkind to Mrs. Rawnett during those times. He would say things that would burn your ears if I told you. Mrs. Rawnett was hurt and I think she felt lonely. She wanted him to appreciate her but he never did. He treated her like she was not even there most times.

"Mrs. Rawnett began being friendlier to me. She would leave school materials on the table for me to read after her sons were done studying. I figured it out when she caught me reading them. Instead of punishing me, she would continue on about her business. She also gave me chores to do in the kitchen when she was there teaching her boys so I could overhear what she was saying. She watched learning channels and called me in the room to polish shoes."

"She let you learn! Learn things other than what you were meant to know?" Linnayah asked, surprised.

"Yes. As time went on, my knowledge increased. I learned about so many things. We never spoke about anything other than business to be done about the house, but I let her know I appreciated what she was doing. I would do extra things around the house. I think, in a way, she was doing it for herself. She needed to feel needed. The twins were losing respect for her as they witnessed their father belittling her. Her world was crushing her. Surprisingly, one day, she started reading her Bible and praying in the room I was in."

"Really?"

I nodded. "She noticed I stopped changing a light fixture and began watching her read. I was interested in this God she spoke of, a divine being whose one commandment for mankind is to love thy neighbor. Love thy neighbor? It is hard for me to grasp. People do not speak to their neighbors. Most do not even have neighbors. People rarely smile anymore unless they want something from you."

Linnayah frowned. I wondered if the frown was because she agreed or disagreed. "I would not have the chance to overhear more about her God. One particularly long weekend, Mr. Rawnett began his love affair early with his weekend mistress, Bourbon."

I paused and felt exposed for the first time. Linnayah placed her hand above my knee and patted it encouragingly three times. I continued and her hand remained on my leg.

"The twins had gone to bed and Mrs. Rawnett turned on music in their room. She always played classical music to drown out any outburst by her husband. She tried to avoid him. This night she could not. I had finished late working on labeling where items go in the refrigerator. This job was the result of a drunken request by Mr. Rawnett, who could not find a lemon for his whiskey sour. I used to make his drinks, but he was convinced that I was making them weaker by adding water to them. Well, he could not find a lemon and began throwing things from the refrigerator. He accused me of stealing his lemon. I saw slices of lemon next to a knife on a cutting board where he had already used them for previous drinks. I pointed it out to him and he grew angrier. Needless to say, he ordered me to begin labeling the refrigerator.

"I finished up my task, stepped away from the refrigerator, and bumped into Mrs. Rawnett. I was not aware she had even entered the kitchen. She lost her balance, but I grabbed for her before her head could hit the stone countertop. I was about to ask her if she was okay when the next thing I knew, Mr. Rawnett was yelling at me to get my hands off of his wife! I was speechless. I immediately let go of her. Mrs. Rawnett was trying to tell her husband to calm down. His only reply was, 'Shut up, you whore! Don't tell me to calm down!'

"Mrs. Rawnett snapped. She walked up to him and slapped him across the face hard and yelled, 'You can call me many things, but THE one thing you cannot call me is a whore!' She stood her ground, shaking fiercely with rage. Mr. Rawnett was dumbfounded. He turned his attention toward me with eyes full of fury. He charged at me like a raging bull, but his unsteady fist whizzed past my chin."

Linnayah squeezed my leg again. "I shoved him away from me. I wanted to swing back at him. I wanted to make him suffer for what he was doing to his own family. Then I heard Mrs. Rawnett pleading, 'Please don't hurt him, please stop!' He came at me swinging and missing again, this time striking the countertop. He yelped in pain. I asked if he wanted some ice to soothe it. He looked at me like he was going to eat me alive and lunged past me toward the other counter.

"He turned around, clutching the knife he had used to cut his precious lemons and now intending to use it on me. I swallowed hard and held my hands up defensively. Mrs. Rawnett stood behind me, still pleading with me not to hurt her husband. I could see her out of the corner of my eye. She grabbed something off the table and ran around to the other side of the counter toward her husband. Mr. Rawnett was too busy glaring at me to notice her. He saw Mrs. Rawnett about a millisecond before she swung whatever was in her hand toward her husband's knife-wielding hand. It flew out of his hand and stuck into the wall behind them. Mrs. Rawnett said in a low and powerful voice, 'That will be enough, Richard!' He looked back at the knife, then at his wife and suddenly he looked tired and defeated. He turned toward the cabinet, pulled down a glass, picked up a lemon wedge and threw it into the glass before he overfilled the glass with bourbon. He staggered out of the room, the whiskey sloshing out onto the floor with every step.

"I looked at Mrs. Rawnett and saw she had used her Bible to defend me. She said, 'I intended to read this tonight in hopes of saving someone's life. I didn't know it would be yours. Please clean up the mess before you turn in for the night.'"

"You didn't do anything wrong! It still doesn't make sense. Why would you be sent to Gavaron?" Linnayah asked.

"I was guilty of watering down his spirits," I said jokingly.

"Ha! Ha!" Linnayah said. "Now, tell me the real reason."

"The next day, I was sent to Gavaron for two reasons: fighting with a Human with intent to inflict serious harm, and sexual misconduct with a Human," I said.

She gasped. "What? But you didn't do either of those things!"

"I know, but it was Mr. Rawnett's word against mine."

"What about Mrs. Rawnett? What did she do?" Linnayah's head shook slightly back and forth, her brows furled.

"She did not do anything."

"What do you mean? She didn't say *anything*?" Linnayah took her hand off my leg and crossed her arms.

"I am not sure why people do the things they do. Perhaps she thought I was better off in Gavaron. Maybe she was trying to protect me. Maybe she was trying to punish herself. Or perhaps she did not need to be needed any more."

"Do you miss it?"

"Not even a little!"

"Were you better off in Gavaron?"

"I would not say better off, but I would say I felt freer."

"How could you feel freer? You couldn't leave Gavaron!"

"But I could be *me*. Well, as close to being me as a Crescren can be." I laughed as I realized I had just made a rhyme.

Linnayah smiled. "You aren't the only one who doesn't know who they are, Cayden. We all feel like that sometimes. Perhaps you are more like us Humans than you think." She leaned back into the cushion, staring up at the ceiling.

"What about you, Linnayah?"

"What *about* me?" she answered, eyes still on the ceiling.

"Tell me more about your family."

"I will, Cayden, but some other time," she said, closing her eyes. "It's late and that story could take a very long time."

I sat there and watched her fall asleep while I wondered what her family might be like. Her beauty was distracting my thoughts. Her mouth hung slightly open while she slept. I thought about the warm kiss she gave me on my cheek when we had gone fishing. I shook my head and stood up. I took a blanket from another chair, draped it across her lap and gently laid her down while pulling the cover up over her shoulders. I sat in the chair Desmin had used earlier and pulled over the ottoman Amil had used to secure Alecander's foot. I tried desperately not to stare at Linnayah while she slept. My own exhaustion soon claimed me. I woke only once during the night when I heard Bonjú screaming. I imagined Lace telling her little boy to close his eyes and everything would be all right.

The next morning I woke to smells of breakfast and one of Famous' elaborate Quinso Vardo stories. The couch was empty and the blanket neatly folded back on the chair where I had originally found it. I stretched the kink out of my neck and joined the others. Linnayah had her dress on and I noticed it had been cleaned. The feast looked even more delectable than the one the night before. Everyone looked refreshed so I glanced down at my own dirty clothes and skin.

As if on cue, Secora said, "Cayden, after breakfast if you would like to bathe and give me your clothes I can clean them."

"Thank you," I said.

I heaped food onto my plate and shoved my fork into a

piece of stewed potato. Before taking a bite, I paused when I noticed Desmin smiling and watching me. My thoughts flashed to our conversation last night. He must have seen the concern on my face. *What is wrong with this food?* Desmin laughed. I closed my eyes briefly. Reopening them, I surveyed the table. It was dilapidated and the dishes were not porcelain-white but the food was perfect. I blinked again. Desmin had stopped laughing and was now enjoying his own meal. I began eating, giving him a lopsided smile to let him know he had fooled me.

After breakfast, I took advantage of the offer to clean up. The bathroom was every bit as lovely as Linnayah had described. The floors sparkled and the towels were plush. I climbed eagerly into the tub. Secora had lit lavender incense. It reminded me of Linnayah. I pictured her at the Supply Depot, which seemed a lifetime ago. I relaxed and dipped my head under the water. It was warm and revitalizing. I could still see Linnayah's face. When I emerged, I heard laughter that seemed to pause right outside the door and continued down the hall, taking the images of Linnayah with it. *Desmin*! I glared at the door. I reflected for a moment. I liked the gleaming whiteness of the tub and the shimmering knobs and fixtures. This room would stay as I always had seen it. I would not try to see Kenosis in its truest form again.

TRAINING

AFTER DRESSING, I heard voices down the hall. Alecander poked his head out and motioned for me to enter. Inside, I found Lace, Amil, and the overly jovial Desmin along with my companions. Everyone turned to look at me.

"Your ankle!" I exclaimed to Alecander.

"Yeah?" he answered, grinning.

"You are not limping!"

He hopped. "It feels better than before I injured it!"

I thought about the plum-colored ointment Amil had applied to Alecander's ankle and wished he had offered me a small dab for my bullet wound. After thinking about it, I came to the same conclusion: it really was not a life-threatening wound.

"What's this?" I asked as my eyes widened. The mahogany floor began to part and an enormous round container that housed a plethora of weapons appeared. Some I recognized, some I had no idea how to even hold. A few empty spots indicated that some were missing.

"Desmin has advised me to give you weapons," Lace said.

"And when Desmin advises, you do as he says," Amil

added.

I looked at Desmin for further explanation. He stood next to Lace with his hands interlaced, smiling and silent as usual.

"Of course," I muttered under my breath. The old man was growing more and more mysterious.

The plan was for Lace to give us weapons based on her observations during the time we had been with her. We would receive brief tutorials, practice for a few hours, eat again, then be on our way.

Lace began by handing Zira her confiscated pistol and a small box of bullets.

Bentum received what at first seemed to be a mallet but was much more. Amil motioned for Bentum to watch. He swung the mallet above his head. The head abruptly released itself from the handle and crushed a dummy about thirty feet away. The handle also released a blade, so Amil was not defenseless while he retrieved the head. Lace tossed another practice dummy toward Amil and he punctured it in mid-flight. Amil retrieved the head, slid the blade into it and lifted it up, then handed the restored mallet to Bentum.

Lace handed Famous a set of handcuffs. "Handcuffs? You're joking, right? You do have a sense of humor, Lace!" he said.

"Close combat is your best chance for survival," she replied. "Naively, people don't see you as a threat so in the line of fire you will be the last to be confronted. Your upper body is stronger than an average man. What an enemy might see as a weakness blinds them to what I know to be strength."

Lace took back the handcuffs. She tapped them together and pulled them apart, stretching her hands to reveal a long chain. Blunt spikes rose out of the cuffs. She gripped the cuffs and began boxing a training dummy. She swung the chain around its neck and pulled back. Lace released her victim and tapped the cuffs back together to return them to their original state.

"They function as handcuffs too. We will program them with your fingerprints later for locking and opening them."

"Well, okay then!" Famous willingly took his weapon.

Kayella was up next.

She shook her head. "I can't take anything."

"Yes, you can," Lace said, pulling a small dagger out of an ornate crimson sleeve and pushing the handle in Kayella's direction.

"I won't!" Kayella cried.

"That IS a different story," Lace said. Kayella sat close to a wall, looking like a small child as she watched us with wide eyes.

Lace turned to Linnayah, offering her the dagger Kayella had refused. Linnayah reached past Lace's hand and grabbed another weapon.

"I think this one will suit me better."

"I see," said Lace, sizing Linnayah up. "Very well." Lace put the small dagger back in its sleeve.

Linnayah eyed the weapon she had chosen. It was a chrome rod with grooves for a firm grip. I almost told her to take the

CRYSTAL MARCOS

knife instead but soon found out there was more to this rod than at first appeared.

Linnayah twisted the rod and blades rose up from each end. I was dumbfounded at how she had known it would do this. I was also perplexed by the pleased look on her face. This weapon looked surprisingly natural in her hands, which made me feel uncomfortable.

"Thanks," Linnayah said.

Lace handed Alecander an onyx pistol crossbow. It was small enough to be aimed with one hand. I hoped she would hand me the same weapon. It seemed like it would be simple enough that even I could handle it. I had never received any kind of training with weapons. I knew very little about them. I wondered how I really felt about possibly killing someone. I could defend myself, I was certain of that. I was not certain I could inflict pain upon another living being. I glanced over to Kayella and suddenly felt like joining her against the wall.

Amil had just finished demonstrating a few moves to Linnayah. She took the bladed staff from him confidently. Amil walked over to the dummy and lifted its right arm up to reveal a fake dagger. Once Amil was clear, Linnayah ran toward it. With a flawless, forceful stroke downward, she disabled the dummy's knife hand. She then kicked it where no man ever wants to be kicked and it dropped to the floor. She did not hesitate to kick its head back so that it hit the floor with a thud. She pounced on it like a cougar, bent down to pick up the head, and held a blade to its neck. Her eyes were unfamiliar.

Amil stood still, open-mouthed in surprise. I imagine my mouth was also gaping. *Who is this woman?*

"That isn't what I showed you," Amil said to her.

"I know," Linnayah answered with a smirk. The blade she had been holding retracted into the staff.

"Cayden, your weapon," Lace said, drawing my eyes away from Linnayah.

Lace held a strange gun out to me. I took it carefully. It was surprisingly light and not too difficult to hold with one hand. It appeared very powerful.

"Thank you," I said. I was starting to get comfortable using those particular words, having said them so many times over the last few days.

"Come, I will show you both how to use your weapons," Lace said to Alecander and me. She led us to the training area, across from where Bentum and Linnayah were practicing. Zira did not need to practice. She knew her pistol well and chose not to waste any precious bullets. She also seemed content with not receiving a new weapon.

Each of us faced a target, a black board with white full-body silhouettes. Inside the silhouettes were oval rings covering most of the torso. Lace demonstrated Alecander's crossbow.

"You only brought one arrow," I said.

"That is all he will need," Lace said.

Lace took the bow with her right hand and loaded it with her left. She aimed at the target, pulled the trigger, and hit it in the middle of its forehead. "Retract!" she commanded. The arrow came whizzing back to the gun and returned to its chamber.

"Amazing!" I gasped.

"It recognizes my voice and only comes back when I tell it to," Lace told Alecander. "We will have to reprogram it with your voice."

"What about the blood?" Alecander asked as his face paled.

"Don't worry about that. Blood barely sticks to the arrow no matter how gory the outcome," she teased.

I looked at my weapon, wondering what special properties it might have. Its sleek silver exterior indicated its exquisite craftsmanship. I could not help looking up from my gun to see what Linnayah was doing. She and Bentum were teaming up against a band of hoodlum dummies and holding up very well. Amil stood off to the side controlling the dummies as Zira cheered them on and Desmin smiled. Even Kayella had risen to her feet to watch the action.

Lace helped Alecander reprogram his crossbow. Shortly after, I heard the crossbow fire and looked at the target to see if he had hit it. He hit a target all right . . . mine.

"Sorry!" Alecander apologized.

"You can't afford to be sorry, Alecander," Lace said.

"Retract!" Alecander commanded. After the arrow obeyed, he fired again. This time at least he hit his target, though along the very edge. I gave him an encouraging smile.

"Tell me, Lace, what is in my possession?" I asked.

"A laser gun with kill or taze mode. Kill . . . is obvious.

Taze disables your target for an ample amount of time," she said.

"A what?" I asked, trying to comprehend what she said.

"Or as we call it, Mercy," Lace added.

"Mercy," I repeated.

Lace showed me the taze and kill switch on the topside of the gun. It was activated by simply rolling a finger over it. Holding a finger over the selected mode for a few seconds locked it in place. I was relieved to receive a weapon where I could choose to spare someone's life. I was determined to always keep the weapon in taze mode. Regardless of Lace's advice to try the kill mode, I did not see the point if I would never use it.

Lace said, "What if it isn't a person you needed to destroy? What if it was an object you needed to disable or better yet, what if it was dinner getting away?"

She did have a point there. "I will try one practice shot in kill mode."

Lace grinned.

"I think I will practice first in taze mode, though, if you do not mind," I said.

"As you desire," Lace said, showing me how to use the gun.

As Lace stepped aside to let me practice, I stole a look back in Linnayah's direction. She was no longer practicing with her weapon but was instead sparring with Bentum. *Sparring with Bentum!*

My immediate reaction was to run over and make sure Bentum read my lips as I blasted, "What the hell are you thinking?" But Linnayah seemed to be handling him just fine.

Lace spoke quietly to me. "Concentrate or she may be the death of you."

I refocused. I nervously checked the mode of the gun once more to make sure it was on the taze setting. I gripped it firmly, right hand on the trigger and left on the foregrip, the handle in front. I nestled the back end of the gun against my shoulder and aimed it at the target. I had never held a gun before and grew uncomfortable as I prepared to shoot. I prayed no one besides Lace was watching. The pulse in the gun seemed to move through my body as I fired. There was a low static noise and an indigo ray streamed out. I missed hitting the target between the legs. I tried several more times, missing every single time. I began to draw an audience. Desmin, Zira, and even Alecander, who had hit his target, stopped to watch me.

"You can do it, Cayden!" Kayella's meek voice sounded from behind me. I did not look toward Bentum and Linnayah, but I was sure they were watching me too.

"Switch to kill mode!" Lace ordered.

"Why? I have not even hit my target yet."

"You will hit it," Lace said confidently.

I shrugged and decided I might as well. I had already shamed myself so another miss would not hurt. I reluctantly switched to kill mode. I swallowed hard and suddenly felt extremely thirsty. I felt everyone's eyes watching me. *Kill mode.*

I pulled my finger inward, pausing for a moment. I decided

this time to aim for the head instead of the torso. I took a deep breath, parted my lips, and pulled the trigger as I released my breath. This time, the afterpulse through my body went deeper into my core. I stepped back to steady myself. When the ray reached the target, a red circle beamed from the center of the silhouette's head.

"I hit the mark?" I gasped in disbelief. "I hit the mark!"

I looked over at Lace for approval. She nodded and looked around to see if the others had noticed. They did and were all smiling, clapping, and cheering me on. Desmin maintained his usual silent demeanor.

"How did you know I would hit it?" I asked Lace.

"In kill mode you feel the will to survive," Lace answered.

QUIET

Wᴵᵀᴴ ʜɪs ᴍᴏᴛʜᴇʀ's permission, Kayella decided to give Bonjú Dahsie's prized cat, Elza, as we prepared to depart. He beamed and looked over at his mother for affirmation. Lace nodded and Bonjú jumped off the couch, spinning around with his new feline friend in his arms.

"Thank you! Thank you! I will love her always!" Bonjú squealed.

I will actually miss you Elza, I thought as I rubbed the back of her head.

Famous was not as tactful. "Good riddance!" he spat, wheeling toward the exit. I knew he would have danced a jig if he had legs.

Once we were outside of Kenosis, Lace continued to lead us toward our destination. This time each of us heeded her warning and stayed on the path. It was a bit challenging but we managed. No one felt like losing a limb or dying that day.

"You are safely out of my domain beyond that tree. This is as far as I go," Lace informed us.

We said our farewells and thanked Lace for her hospitality.

She did not invite us back to Kenosis and we understood that what she had done for us was a one-time occurrence.

"Onward through the Den to Solitare!" Famous said with mock authority.

"We have not decided that is our destination," I replied.

"Well, we have to head somewhere, now don't we," Famous said. "Besides, I quite like the name. Sounds like people will leave us alone there."

I searched for some marking that would tell us we were exiting Kenosis' territory. I finally found it on a decomposing tree stump: the weather-beaten beautifully carved 𝒦. I smiled as we passed it. I looked over my shoulder for one last look at Kenosis and saw that the scenery was already changing into unrecognizable terrain.

We traveled for some time as discreetly as possible. Famous was in our group so silence was virtually impossible. When we were certain there was no one around, we would have short conversations.

"How do we know we are going in the right direction?" Linnayah asked Alecander.

"We don't. Cayden's map sure would have come in helpful. We have to trust Lace to have given us correct information," Alecander answered. *Of course, the map would be of use now! Why did I have to make that symbolic point of leaving it under the table leg?*

We finally began to relax and our hands were no longer hovering over our weapons. Linnayah managed to get Kayella up next to me and we shared some small talk. Every once in a while, Linnayah would look back over her shoulder to see if her matchmaking was successful. Every time she turned, her staff would swing toward her back to remind me of her killer abilities. I had not had the chance to ask her where she had learned to fight. I was not even sure if I wanted to know. I felt my gun against my back and thought about how little I still knew about using it.

"We need transportation," Kayella said.

"I know, but the question is how do we get some, and from where—or better yet—whom do we get it from?" I asked.

I scanned the rest of our group. I wondered what each one was thinking. Why luck would have it that each of us had survived after so many of our kind were lost? I wondered if Bentum was thinking of Aurora. I wondered if Zira was mourning Jinjo. I wondered if Famous would always be irritating no matter the situation. I wondered if Alecander felt any remorse, knowing that I now knew he had withheld information of the Den from me. I wondered what Kayella looked like in her gown the night before. I wondered if Linnayah would ever know how I felt about her.

Zira jabbed at Famous. "Vhat's a matter, Famous? You've been quiet for longer zan usual. Are you feeling okay?"

I smiled to myself as I realized how calming the silence was. I stopped smiling when Famous did not have a snide comment in response to Zira's question. I swung around and reached for my gun. To my horror, Zira stood before me, enveloped by a behemoth arm with a gun pressed against her temple. Famous' empty wheelchair was behind her. I could not get my own gun off my shoulder smoothly but it did not matter: someone had already beaten me to it and knocked me over the back of my head. I fell to my knees hoping I would not lose consciousness. My vision blurred and I struggled to focus. Kayella screamed before she was grabbed by a woman. The woman was strangely familiar. She held a knife to Kayella's throat. I turned on my knees toward her. Linnayah had her weapon drawn and Alecander had his hand on his bow. Bentum continued walking forward, not noticing the scuffle.

"Put your weapons down!" the woman commanded. *Bentum! Notice that Alecander is not beside you!* If he could get to his mallet undetected, he might do something to help. Linnayah did not drop her weapon but Alecander did. A large thud and the ground shook as I turned to look toward Bentum. Another man much smaller than the one who held Zira had pinned Bentum to the ground and had his arm twisted behind his back. Bentum struggled to get up and I sensed the terror he must have felt, not knowing what was going on. I wished he could see my face so he would know I was here with him.

Focus! My vision began to clear and I saw that the woman was growing angry with Linnayah for not dropping her weapon.

"Linnayah, please, put your weapon down," Alecander told her calmly but firmly.

Linnayah reluctantly obeyed.

"Kick it to me!" the woman demanded.

Then I saw it, the marking between the woman's knuckles.

"Kenosis!" I gasped. The woman turned. "You look so much like Lace."

She swept her eyes over our group. "The weapons? Lace gave them to you?"

"Yes." I said rubbing the back of my head. "Are you her sister?" I asked.

"Her aunt."

"Secora's sister?" I asked.

"Yes," she said, releasing Kayella, who ran over to stand between Linnayah and Alecander. The burly arm released Zira and she helped me to my feet.

"I am Concora," the woman said, extending her hand. I shook it firmly, relieved we would not be killed this day. "Before we let your very large friend up, please tell him everything is okay. I would not want anyone to get hurt."

I walked over to Bentum. I slowly bent down and gave him a reassuring smile even though my head was throbbing.

"Everything is okay!" I flashed him the universal sign meaning okay. Bentum relaxed. The man on Bentum's back let him up.

Concora informed us, "We have been watching you for a while. Sorry about this, but we had to be sure you were not a threat to Kenosis."

"We understand," I answered, still rubbing the back of my head. I thought about Bonjú, Lace, and Kenosis and knew what she meant. *If only we had had someone like Concora and these men to protect Gavaron.*

"Forgive us."

"I understand you were just trying to protect what is yours. You are forgiven. Though I SHOULD probably ask one thing of you."

"Anything."

"Although I have enjoyed his silence, where is Famous?" I said, pointing at his empty wheelchair.

"Are you *sure* you want me to return your loquacious friend?"

Alecander answered before any of us had time to consider Concora's offer. "Yes!" he said.

We found Famous attached to a tree with his own handcuffs and a gag in his mouth. As one of the men began to release him, I said, "You could leave the gag if you would like." The man took his time removing the cloth. We chuckled.

"Ha ha, very funny!" Famous said.

"Come on, Famous! We are just having some fun with you," I said as we helped him back in his chair.

Concora told us that they were returning home from a trip. We briefly explained our quest.

"You will surely be sought for questioning if you are discovered among our people," Concora said. "You must be careful and make it to your destination undetected. Who knows who is hunting you?" Her words startled me. *Hunting?* Concora turned to Alecander. "Your televised image does not do you justice. You're much more handsome in person."

"What do you mean?" Alecander asked with his brows furrowed.

"We saw the news. They showed the scenes from outside the Underground Market. So much devastation." She shook her head in disapproval. "So many injured and dead!"

"Do they know who is to blame?" I asked. I thought about the remote. *The remote!* I had all but forgotten I let Alecander examine it. He had kept it in his room. It was buried beneath the wreckage of Gavaron.

"No, the report said they should be able to release more information soon. I suspect that whether or not your Gavaron was connected to the Underground Market, people will speculate that it was. It is Human nature: doubt before knowledge," Concora said.

I swallowed hard and glanced over at Alecander before shifting my eyes to Linnayah. Both of them were looking at me intently.

"Is something wrong?" Concora said.

"No . . . nothing . . . just worried about all those people," I said.

"Well, it is a shame and very disheartening that someone attacked Gavaron and murdered all your friends. Peace be with you during these sad times," Concora said sincerely.

"Thank you," I replied.

"Is there anything I can do to help you on your journey?" Concora asked.

"I think you have done enough!" Famous scoffed.

Alecander ignored Famous' reply. "No, no. Lace and the others have already done so much."

"Let me give you the name of an acquaintance of mine, Lady Verleah. If you continue in this direction you could cross paths. If you decide to visit, tell her Concora sent you. She will provide food and water, or anything else you might need. And I do mean anything."

"Okay," Alecander said reluctantly. "But first, I must ask why are you helping us? You said it yourself—doubt before knowledge."

"If Lace and the others found it necessary to aid you, I will do the same," she replied. Until I gave it some thought, "necessary" seemed a strange thing to say. However, people do not usually help others out of the kindness of their heart. Concora smiled. "If you continue going the way you were headed, you should reach some railroad tracks by nightfall. Follow them east and they will lead you to Lady Verleah."

"That's it?" Famous said. "That's all the information you are going to give us?"

"That is all the information you need. We must be on our way. Kenosis awaits our return."

We went our separate ways.

"Those people who inhabit Kenosis are so cryptic," Famous said.

"I was going to say they were weird but nice," Linnayah said. I agreed with both of them.

"What do you think? Should we find this Lady Verleah?" Kayella asked.

"It sounds like an adventure," Zira said, although her usually tough physique was beginning to look run-down.

"Are you all right?" I asked her.

"Yes, I didn't sleep very vell last night."

Alecander looked at her. "Yes, I think we should find Lady Verleah and see if she has a safe place for us to rest."

"Some food too," Bentum said, putting his fingertips to his mouth. Alecander touched Bentum on the shoulder and grinned.

We traveled several miles and only encountered two people. A small boy was playing in a field while a man we thought to be his father slaughtered a wild boar. The scraggly boy caught sight of us and waved. He enthusiastically jumped up and down, pointing in our direction and trying to catch his father's attention. But the boar's screams drowned out the little boy's excited cries.

We reached the train tracks just before sunset. Few trains still ran in the Den. Most had been taken over and converted into living quarters, medical centers, or ripped apart and looted to mend dilapidated homes. I imagine that like most occupants of the Den, Lady Verleah made do with what already existed and called it home.

"I wonder how far east we have to travel to find Lady Verleah," Linnayah said.

"We are going to find out," I said.

"I hope they have a place to recharge my wheelchair. It is starting to slow down," Famous said.

"Let's not let that be the first question we ask," Linnayah said, sounding slightly annoyed. I thought I saw her eyes roll. Famous was beginning to get under everyone's skin. I hoped that Lady Verleah had enough room to let us rest far enough away from Famous to give us all a much-needed break.

We traveled along the tracks until we needed Alecander's flashlight to ensure Famous did not ram into anyone's calves. Before Alecander had the flashlight out of the bag, we saw a train with six cars. The exterior of the cars was lit up by antique Christmas lights. We watched a woman with her back turned to us enter one of the cars.

"Should I just wheel up and announce us?" Famous asked.

"A couple of us should go," Alecander said. I grew nervous thinking about our earlier ambush by Concora.

"Cayden, come with me," Alecander said. He turned toward Bentum. "Stay here with the others. Protect them if necessary."

Bentum nodded and placed his hand on his mallet.

"On second thought, I think I will stay here and help Bentum," Famous said.

I felt a strong urge to calm Kayella when I saw tears welling in her eyes. "It will be all right," I assured her, taking her arm so she would look at my face instead of the train. "It will be all right."

She nodded and gave me a half smile. I let go of her arm as

Linnayah took Kayella's hand and drew her weapon with the other.

"You be careful," Linnayah said.

"I will. You still owe me a day in the life of Linnayah story," I teased although I really meant it.

"You come back in one piece and you might just hear it," she said.

I nodded and proceeded with Alecander toward the cars.

We covered about half the distance when we were stopped by a harsh female voice blasting through hidden speakers.

"Stop!" A dazzling light blinded us. "Do not come any closer until you declare who you are and state your business with me."

Alecander stepped forward. "I am . . . " An arrow whizzed through the air and landed at his feet. I frantically searched the area for the archer but could not find him.

"I said DO NOT come any closer!" the voice warned.

Alecander remained perfectly still. "I am . . . "

"Louder! Do you think I have super hearing?"

Alecander shouted, "I am Alecander and this is Cayden. We are traveling with our companions. Concora said that Lady Verleah might be able to help us in our quest."

After a pause, the voice said, "You should have just started with Concora's name. What if I had decided to let that arrow pierce your heart instead of landing at your feet?"

"I do appreciate your letting me remain in one piece."

"Tell your companions if they have any weapons they won't

be needed. If they want to enter my home, they must leave them outside. Don't worry. I will keep them safe until you depart."

We turned around to relay the message. The others were lit up by a spotlight and were already placing their weapons on the ground. Bentum led them toward us. I took off my gun and dropped it. Alecander did the same. We trusted Concora's word that this Lady Verleah would help us. When we were no longer a threat, she told us to enter the first train car. We did although we still had reservations.

THE LADY

THE TRAIN CAR had been gutted and all that remained of its original interior were two restored benches that ran along opposite sides. The walls were paneled with an amber colored wood. The windows were tinted. In the corner was a small table with two mugs. The smell that filled the car told us they were filled with piping hot coffee. I had not smelled that aroma since my days working for the Rawnetts. Gaming tablets sat on a table, projecting a hologram of a card game in progress.

When all of us were inside, two armed men made sure we had no weapons. They ushered us into the next car. One of the men pushed a rolling chair over to Famous. It was smaller and less cumbersome than his wheelchair. He was not very happy about it but once I started pushing him forward he stopped complaining.

"I always wanted a chauffeur!" Famous teased.

"No one said I was a very good one," I responded, pushing the chair into the edge of the doorway on purpose as we entered the next car.

"Watch it!" Famous yelled.

The next car was an empty dining area. The interior was paneled with the same amber-colored wood. Four booths on either side had burgundy leather benches and tables set with crisp white linen, fine china, tall wine glasses, and gold-plated flatware. Crystal vases with a single white rose sat atop each one. I stopped pushing Famous and squeezed my eyes shut. When I reopened them, I found the room exactly the same. Whoever this Lady Verleah was, she had exquisite taste and enough money to express it.

"I hope they offer us some wine to go in those fancy glasses!" Famous exclaimed.

"I'm hungry," Linnayah said.

"I am too," I answered.

A robust Human woman wearing a flowing black dress entered the dining car with a warm, welcoming smile. Behind her walked a woman and a man who shared my facial markings and the unmistakable violet eyes of my people. They wore matching immaculate white uniforms. They could not hide their obvious shock at seeing us. The woman in black seemed unaware that most of us were not her own kind.

"Hello, I believe I am the one you are looking for," she said pleasantly. "I am Lady Verleah. Any friend of Concora and Kenosis is a friend of mine."

"Thank you," Alecander said.

"Goodness! You all look worn out. Are you hungry?"

"Starved!" Famous practically shouted. Alecander gave him a warning glare.

"Please be seated. First you eat, then we will discuss what else you need from me. Henner and Synda will be of service to you." The three of them walked into the next car, leaving us alone. I helped Famous into a booth and made sure to sit at the booth behind him. Alecander sat down next to me and Bentum came over to join us. I watched as Linnayah attempted to nudge Kayella in my direction. Kayella shook her head when she saw I was watching and took a seat in front of Famous. She slid over to let Linnayah sit down next to her.

"Hey, come join my entourage," Famous called to Zira. She huffed and sat next to him, shoving him toward the window. "I like my women rough!" Famous laughed.

"Treat those women with respect!" Alecander demanded. He seemed upset with Famous' normal behavior. I did not blame him. We had never had to spend so much time side-by-side with Famous. We usually only had to tolerate him in small doses.

"This entire situation is strange," I whispered to Alecander.

"Why are all these people helping us? First Lace and the others, then Concora, and now Lady Verleah. Something seems off," I said. Bentum cleared his throat, letting us know he was present. I turned to him, looked around the room and mouthed, "Why are they all helping us?"

"I don't know, but I am not complaining," Bentum said.

"Bentum is right. We should count our blessings," Alecander said, not sounding convinced himself.

The servants soon brought out the food on a metal rolling

cart. Instead of family-style dining, we were served in courses: salad, soup, entrée, and dessert. I remembered serving the Rawnetts that way but had never eaten like that myself. I rather enjoyed it. I know we all did. I also had never eaten that much food in one sitting in my life. When it was time for dessert, the shelves of the cart were filled with mouth-watering sweets: crème brûlée, tarts, cakes, scones, and other desserts I had only dreamed about. I had an exceedingly hard time choosing. To be truthful, I was not even hungry by that point but could not resist the tantalizing aromas. I made sure to eat everything I was given and would not allow anything to be wasted. It took us almost two hours to complete our dining experience. I knew I would probably never eat that way again. Only the extremely wealthy had access to those types of food.

"Wine? You have wine glasses. I suppose you have wine to go in them?" Famous asked Henner, the male servant, midway through the meal.

Henner rolled his eyes and grumbled as he left the car. A few minutes later he returned with a bottle of what was probably the cheapest wine he could find.

The entire time, I kept thinking about Cresecren workers serving me, another Cresecren. We were not created to do that.

"How long have you served Lady Verleah?" I asked Synda.

"Henner came to her nearly ten years ago and I have been here about six months."

"Does she treat you well?" I asked, trying to get a better idea of what our host was like.

"No, she makes us eat rotten flesh, beats us daily and we sleep with pigs!" Henner interrupted. Synda's shocked expression told us Henner was lying. "Why do you care?" he snapped.

"I was just making sure you were okay," I replied, stunned by Henner's rudeness toward his own kind.

"Well, don't bother," Henner replied, shooting Synda a warning look.

After that, neither one spoke another word to us. They also made sure to avoid eye contact.

After dinner, one of the armed men led us through the kitchen car. It was amazingly tidy despite all the cooking that had been going on in there. Synda and Henner were busily washing dishes and did not bother to look up. My stomach slapped my insides as I thought about stuffing the last bit of vanilla mousse into my mouth. Even as full as I was, I could not help myself from sinfully admiring the leftover desserts I spied on the counter.

"I saw that," Linnayah said. "I'm still drooling too. I didn't get to taste the cherry cheesecake. Maybe later for a midnight snack." She winked at me. I returned her gesture with a crooked smile.

We found Lady Verleah alone in the next car, drinking a glass of wine and eating pieces of fine chocolate.

"Care for a piece?" she asked. Even though we all wanted to taste it, our stomachs would not allow it. "Please sit down! You are all making me nervous hovering over me." An armed man stepped inside. "You won't be needed." She waved him back outside. Reluctantly, he obeyed but remained on the platform outside the door. We took our seats. All the chairs faced Lady Verleah. Her chair was ornate, giving it the look of a throne.

"We want to thank you so very much for your kind hospitality," Alecander told her.

"It is what Concora and Lace would want for their friends. She gave you some of her finest weapons, for goodness sake! She wouldn't do that for just anyone. Besides, you are famous!"

"I certainly am!" Famous said, annoyingly arrogant.

"Before we discuss what you need, please join me for a toast." Lady Verleah held her right hand to her lips and spoke into a skeleton key. "Bring our guests some wine . . . only the best!"

Moments later, Henner emerged with immaculately polished glasses and a bottle of wine. He served the ladies first, still avoiding pleasantries. When Zira waved the wine glass away, Lady Verleah offered her sparkling grape cider instead.

"Zis looks like vine. Does it contain alcohol?" Zira asked, inspecting her glass.

"Not a drop," Lady Verleah assured her. Zira lifted the glass to her nose and inhaled. She smiled and seemed pleased with the fragrance.

I had seen the consequences of wine firsthand, so I selected the cider as well.

Lady Verleah raised her glass. "Now let us toast new friends and new beginnings!"

We all took a sip. I rather enjoyed my glass of grape cider

and eagerly accepted a refill when it was empty.

Alecander got right down to business. "We need trans-portation. We need to get to Solitare and quickly."

"I love a man who is straightforward," Lady Verleah said, brushing her upper lip with her tongue. Alecander seemed to take no notice. "I will provide you with that transportation and anything else you will need. Something about helping out those who are thought to be deceased appeals to me despite my better judgment," she said, popping another piece of chocolate into her mouth.

"Deceased?" Alecander exclaimed.

"I can see that you are not actually dead so that would then make you outlaws. Harboring outlaws sounds much more ex-citing!" Lady Verleah said.

"Outlaws?" Alecander asked, perplexed.

"Yes, your gorgeous face and that of your handsome com-panion are constantly being televised," she explained.

"What?"

"Alecander, isn't it? And Cayden? You are famous! Well, at least to those who remain connected with the world," Lady Verleah said, looking back and forth between us. Famous let out a subtle huff.

"Harboring fugitives is just the type of excitement that keeps my life thrilling!" she added.

"But we are not fugitives or outlaws or anything of the sort!" I responded.

"Oh? To me it sure looks as though you are." Lady Verleah

set her wine glass down. She crossed her legs tightly and sat up straight. "Television power on," she said and leaned back as the holographic images appeared around us.

I saw my own face looking back at me and next to me was Alecander. There was gray metal behind us; it only took me a second to realize it was an elevator. My back tightened as I recognized the images that had been taken in the elevator of the Underground Market.

"I believe you are Zira. This may be too difficult for you to view," Lady Verleah warned her.

"Nozing is too difficult for me to vatch," she replied, stone-faced.

"I can't hear. I'm deaf. What is being said?" Bentum asked Lady Verleah.

"Television closed captions on," Lady Verleah said.

As the reporter spoke, my head started spinning. Another Cresecren man flashed before me. It was the one who had handed me the satchel with the remote and called me brother. The word burned in my mind. As I began to understand what was being reported, I cringed, trying to fathom what this all meant for me, what it meant for all of us.

I was a delinquent, a terrorist, a murderer, and as far as the rest of the world was concerned, I was most likely dead! Alecander and the other mysterious Cresecren were accomplices. The man with the remote had been identified as Sutton and no one searched for him any longer because his body had been discovered in the outskirts of Solitare. I swallowed hard. I looked over at Alecander for moral support, but he was still staring straight ahead, watching the scenes unfold.

According to the news, I was the suspected ringleader, the mastermind behind all the carnage. The two reasons why I was sent to Gavaron (fighting with a Human with intent to inflict serious harm and sexual misconduct with a Human) were enough to deem me guilty.

"Sexual misconduct with a Human. That IS interesting!" Lady Verleah interjected.

I could not even muster the words to say I was not guilty of either count. I felt my brow glistening with sweat. Next, the holographic images showed dead bodies in bags against a wall of the Underground Market. I pulled my feet in as the images seemed so close I could touch them. I stole a look at Zira, who was digging her nails into the seat.

"Hell, Cayden! What did you do?" Famous could never keep his mouth shut. His voice startled me.

"Cayden and Alecander didn't do any of what they are saying! Do you really believe what they put on television? They'll project anything that will get people to watch!" Linnayah exclaimed.

"If I honestly zought Alecander and Cayden were responsible, I vould have killed zem myself," Zira said coldly. I was very thankful she thought we were innocent.

"I for one definitely do NOT believe everything I see or hear in the media," Lady Verleah said.

I barely heard her as I was astounded by the latest development in the story. Apparently, I was also responsible for the devastation in Gavaron. According to the report, I had killed myself and all of my people. *Aurora. Dahsie.* The sheer destruction of my former home flashed in front of me.

"Whoever chased us out of Gavaron didn't tell anyone of survivors," Linnayah said.

"Whoever was responsible doesn't want anyone to know you are alive. Perhaps they don't even know you survived. No doubt you are all a part of a manhunt. Whoever is responsible wouldn't want any pesky loose ends," Lady Verleah said.

I knew all anyone needed to find us was the codes on our faces. Our eyes could only be disguised by sunglasses, and those were hard to come by. Contact lenses were out of the question. They were designed so that Cresecren eyes would dissolve them within minutes if they attempted to wear them.

"Who would do this? What are we going to do?" My voice cracked. I felt defeated.

"I don't know, but you are welcome to stay here and try to figure it out. Just don't overstay your welcome. I don't want anyone poking around here. Last time that happened, I lost one of my men. And I REALLY don't like losing any man," Lady Verleah said, eying Alecander.

"We'll leave tomorrow night. I think it is best if we travel under the cover of darkness," he replied.

"Very well. I will be sure to provide you with everything I can," Lady Verleah said. She summoned Henner and Synda. "Show our guests to their sleeping quarters. I am retiring for the night." She got up and so did Alecander. He stretched out his hand and she took it with both of hers.

"Thank you," he said.

She leaned forward and whispered something into his ear, never letting go of his hand. Alecander shook his head and replied, "No, thank you."

"Such a gentleman," Lady Verleah said to him. She walked back to her chair. I could only imagine what she had asked.

"Chair descend." Lady Verleah waved goodnight as she and her chair gradually dropped down into the train car floor. This revealed that there was an underground level. "You know where I am if you need me," she told Alecander before disappearing.

I had to admit that I would sleep more soundly if we were all sleeping underground. My head was racing. I needed to talk to Alecander about our next move. I also wanted to talk to Linnayah about her apparent fighting skills before she left for home after seeing the news report. It could be the last chance I had to see her . . . ever. My mouth went dry at the thought. *What could I lose by telling her I cared for her now?*

Henner and Synda led us all to the next car. I noticed a man and a very pregnant woman sitting on a small couch holding hands.

"Lady Verleah has guests," Synda announced to them.

The man got up and extended his hand to the woman. She took it hurriedly and struggled to get up. They moved hand in hand to another couch and sat down. The woman put her hands over her belly in an instinctively protective way. The man then put his hand on her thigh, said "Couch descend" and with that, they were gone.

"So far, it looks like Lady Verleah is the only one who wants us here," Famous remarked.

"Lady Verleah is the only one who matters," Synda replied.

"Vhen is she due to have her baby?" Zira asked Synda.

"Next week with twins," Synda answered.

"That explains the humongous belly," Famous said.

"Shut up, Famous!" Zira spat. Her eyes bore through him. Bentum stepped toward Famous. Even though Bentum could not hear Famous, he had grown tired of his mouth.

"Okay, okay. . . Sheesh, everyone needs to lighten up a little!" Famous held his hands up in defense. He asked Synda, "Where am I sleeping? That wine has made me drowsy."

"Maybe if you hadn't had so many glasses," Linnayah muttered.

"We should talk about our plans," Alecander said.

"I am too exhausted," Zira said.

"Me, too. All that rich food is weighing me down," Kayella said. She had been so quiet I almost forgot she was there.

"All right, I will try to figure out a plan and we can talk about it in the morning," Alecander said.

Before Linnayah could say she was turning in too, I told her in a voice barely above a whisper, "I would like to speak to you."

"All right."

"There is only room for three of you below. The others will

sleep here," Synda said.

"I'll be staying put," Famous announced. "It would be easier for me with no legs."

"Very well. For those who are sleeping up here, Henner will show you your sleeping arrangements. Those sleeping below, please come with me."

"What did she say?" Bentum asked.

"You can sleep up here with me," I said, knowing when I had my chance to talk to Linnayah I did not want eavesdropping. I analyzed Famous' face and hoped he would surrender quickly to those glazed-over eyes and sleep heavily. The last thing I needed was his banter while I was exposing my heart to Linnayah.

"I prefer above-ground," Linnayah said. I felt giddy.

"I'll be back up to discuss some things," Alecander said.

Henner left after he showed us how our beds, disguised as artwork, folded down from the sides of the car. Famous immediately helped himself up the short ladder into bed.

"I'm just going to rest my eyes for a few minutes. And if I happen to fall asleep, you guys can fill me in at breakfast." He was asleep within a minute, snoring like a locomotive. *Phew!*

TRUTH

BENTUM, LINNAYAH, and I made small talk as we waited for Alecander.

"Maybe he fell asleep," Bentum said.

"I doubt it," I said.

"Maybe we should check. My eyes are heavy. I won't be able to keep them open much longer," Bentum said.

"All right, I will go. You two stay here," I said.

The ride down under the car was beautiful. I was inside an elevator shaft. The walls were lined with lush foliage and a waterfall trickled down between the leaves in front of me. I made it a point to make sure to show Linnayah before we left this place. The doors slid open and down a dimly lit hall stood Synda. She waved at me as I approached her. There were metal doors on each side and between the doors were large vases filled with exotic plants. Sophisticated artwork hung on the walls.

"I am looking for Alecander."

"He is in there." She pointed to a white door. The lavatory.

"Thank you."

"He isn't alone. He is with the raven-haired woman with

the interesting accent," Synda said. My eyebrows rose.

"Not what you might be thinking. The woman is quite ill. I couldn't help her; I have a weak stomach," Synda said, grimacing.

I entered the lavatory. Alecander leaned forward in a chair near a sink Zira was using to splash water over her face. He handed her a towel and she patted her face dry. I was relieved as it looked as though I had missed all the action.

"Are you all right?" I asked Zira.

"Yes. I zink it vas just all zee rich food and excitement."

"Yes, the news is enough to get anyone's stomach churning," I said as I saw color returning to her cheeks.

"Vell, if you do get sick, you have Alecander here to hold back your hair," Zira said jokingly as she smiled at him.

I smiled back. "You really should smile more often! Yours is one of those infectious smiles."

"Let's hope ve have more reasons to smile soon," Zira said as she tossed her towel into a wicker basket. "I'm turning in."

"Do you need help getting to your room?" Alecander asked.

"I'm fine. I'm pregnant, Alecander, not dying!" She winked as she walked past me. I heard the door open and close.

If I asked, I was sure Synda would have brought me a dust pan to sweep my jaw off the floor. I looked at Alecander for confirmation.

"Jinjo's baby," I said. *Wait, what? A baby? This changed everything!*

"I know," Alecander said, as if he could hear my thoughts.

I connected the dots in my head: her nervousness around Bonjú, avoiding alcohol, snapping at Famous when he remarked about the very pregnant woman, and getting sick to her stomach . . . Zira would be raising the baby alone.

"We have to protect the baby. We have to find some place safe. Some place we do not have to leave," I said. I felt even more responsible for the outcome of everything. "Maybe if I did not go that day to the Underground Market, this would not have happened. Jinjo would still be alive and would be able to help raise his child with Zira."

Alecander said matter-of-factly, "Don't kid yourself. It would have happened whether you were there or not. If you had not been there, it would have been another Cresecren in your position. Have you even thought about the fact that the day before I was chosen to be Supply Appointed? Someone must have known that I would pick you to work alongside me. You were the only person in Gavaron able enough to travel who had been sent there for fighting a Human with the intent to harm. I should have known something was up when I met little resistance choosing you as Assistant Supply Appointed."

A revelation sparked in my mind. I had been so caught up in my own new emotions that I did not make the connection.

"The man who called himself my brother. He sought ME out and gave ME his satchel with the detonator remote," I said.

"We will figure this out together like true brothers," Alecander replied.

I pressed my lips together in an unsuccessful attempt to

smile even though my heart swelled at his words. Changing the subject, I said, "Hey, so Zira actually let you hold her hair back? I would have been afraid she would have shot me!"

Alecander chuckled. "She didn't want me to at first but I told her I had a lot of experience and I promised I would NOT rub her back."

"You have experience holding hair back?" I said.

"Valarie, the woman I used to serve, spent many nights this way," Alecander said.

"She was pregnant?"

"No, she couldn't have children. That was one reason she drank. The other was that she was getting older and could not stand the thought of losing her youth. That, and the fact she was always picking the wrong men. I accompanied Valarie and made sure she did not end up in places or situations she should not be in."

I followed Alecander as he left the lavatory.

"Alec . . ." I paused to contemplate what I would say next.

"Yes?"

"I would like to tell you something."

"You are not going to tell me you are guilty, are you?" Alecander said with a smirk.

"I have feelings for Linnayah and I want to tell her before she leaves," I blurted out.

"I see."

"I know it seems futile to tell her since she will be leaving soon and I know Cresecrens are not supposed to be with Humans."

"A punishable offense. However, no one expected you to be around a Human long enough to build a bond."

"I have never felt this way before. I think it might actually be that Human emotion, love."

"*Human* emotion?" Alecander looked perplexed. "Do you believe only a Human is capable of love?"

"Well, yes. Cresecrens only take mates out of convenience."

"Are you listening to yourself, Cayden? It is true that most Cresecren people take mates for convenience, but there are rare occasions when our people do fall in love. Did you not know Bentum and Aurora?"

"Aurora was blind and Bentum is deaf. There was definite convenience there."

"You are foolish if you did not see the way they were around each another. Bentum took good care of his mate. He always made sure she was well-groomed since she could not see to do it herself. Aurora always held Bentum's arm and embraced his hand when they sat. They would sit on the sand for hours in each other's company, never tiring of each other. When they fought, they fought passionately. When she died, he wept. He feels a part of him is missing. And what about you? Do you REALLY believe you are the only Cresecren capable of love?"

I searched my memory and concluded Alecander was right. I never really knew what love was. Perhaps I still did not know. I had not had experience with love, especially having lived with the Rawnetts. Their greatest examples of love were ignoring one another and constant mental abuse.

"Have you ever loved?"

"Yes," he answered, looking down at his feet. He brought his eyes up to mine. "You know her as Valarie."

I did not expect him to say the woman he used to serve was the one he had loved.

"Valarie?"

"Yes, but that is a story for another day. All you need to know right now is that I never told her. Not a day goes by when I don't think about her. Not a day goes by that I don't wonder what would have happened if I had. You tell Linnayah how you feel or you will always be wondering."

I looked at him. For the first time, I saw the sadness in his face for what he had lost.

"Come on. We should get upstairs before they start to worry," he said.

The ride up had a volcano among the foliage. The simulated lava rumbled as we rose toward the top. Bentum and Linnayah were relieved to see us. Famous had not moved and his snoring had softened.

"What happened down there? We were beginning to think you weren't coming back. Our minds started going haywire thinking they were offing you one by one down there!" Linnayah said.

"Everything is fine. Zira isn't feeling well. We were making sure she was okay," Alecander said.

"Is it anything serious?" Linnayah asked.

"I would say it is," I said.

"Cayden meant our situation has changed. She is ill because she is pregnant," Alecander said.

"Pregnant?" Bentum asked, moving his hand to carve out a bump.

"Yes," Alecander said.

"Oh my goodness! How long has she known? Did her husband know?" Linnayah said, covering her mouth.

"She found out a week ago. She was planning on telling Jinjo but hadn't found the best time to do it before his death," Alecander said, shaking his head. I recalled Jinjo and Zira arguing, which would have made it difficult to share the news. "I had to urge her to tell me. She does not want any of us treating her differently."

"They will eventually find Jinjo's body. They'll know once they find him that Zira buried him there. They'll have questions. But, I know one thing for sure, Zira won't go back. She has nothing to go back to," Linnayah said.

Bentum let out a big sigh. "We shouldn't allow her to travel with us any more. It is not safe." He looked straight at Linnayah. "You should go home too." There was an uncomfortable silence. I knew the time was coming for Linnayah to go home.

"He's right," Alecander said.

"No!" Linnayah said, turning from Bentum's stare.

She stormed out the door. I heard the distant voice of a guard say something to her.

My feet automatically took me toward the door. I glanced back at Alecander for approval. He nodded and said, "Bentum and I will fill you in on our plan in the morning."

Outside, I met the guard's stern glare. I looked around for Linnayah. The guard pointed upward. I followed his finger to find Linnayah climbing the ladder on the side of the car.

"I would say this meets your request!" she called down to the guard.

The guard shrugged his shoulders as Linnayah took a seat on the roof facing away from us. I climbed up to join her. I glanced down and saw the guard walking away from us. He positioned himself closer to Lady Verleah's car.

"He told me I couldn't leave the train so I didn't," she muttered.

I chuckled at her cleverness. Another guard kept watch on the opposite side of Lady Verleah's car. Yet another stood on top of the farthest car from us. I was sure there were other guards out there too, even though I could not see them.

We sat there quietly. It was a nice change to relax and breathe in the warm night air.

"Your curiosity is tugging at your pant legs, isn't it? You want to know why I don't want to leave, don't you?" Linnayah asked.

"That is ONE of my questions."

"Cayden," she said as she looked at me with such seriousness my stomach knotted preparing for her words. "I . . . I can't."

"You can't?"

"I can't go home." Linnayah looked up toward the slivered moon.

"What about your mother and father? They will worry about you."

"No, they won't."

"How can you say that?"

"Because . . . " She turned to look me straight in the eyes, "dead people don't worry." Her words threw me off guard. I was unable to speak. After a long moment, Linnayah spoke, "There is nothing for me to go back to. No one for me to go back for. The truth is I should have left a long time ago, but I didn't know how. I didn't know where to go. I tried to leave before, but I was too frightened. Scared if what was out there was worse than where I already was."

Linnayah had me bewildered. Everything I knew about her, was any of it true? "You do not have a school report, do you? Do you even go to school?"

"No."

That single word burrowed into my chest. "You lied to me," I said, trying to steady my emotions.

"Lying is something I have become accustomed to. Lying is how I have survived," she said, turning away from me again.

"I . . . I . . . "

She turned back to look at me. "Cayden, you have to believe me! You are the first person in a long time I hadn't wanted to lie to. It hurt every time I did."

"How can I believe you after you just told me you are a liar!" I jumped to my feet. I wanted to know more about her. I wanted to know her story and what her life consisted of, but how would I know if she was telling me the truth?

"Please don't go. Sit back down." She patted the space I just left. I stood looking at her, thoroughly confused. "I am ready to tell you who Linnayah really is. I am tired of being deceitful. I need to tell you as only then can you decide what you want. But know one thing for certain, I am NEVER going back! NEVER! That Linnayah is dead!"

I stared into her sorrowful eyes. I sat back down. "It is not as though I have anywhere else to be. I think Alecander and Bentum can figure out our next move. Besides, I would rather not watch Famous drool as he sleeps."

Her face relaxed, showing me a small smile. "Just promise me one thing."

"I have never promised anyone anything."

"I would be honored to be the first," Linnayah said. I saw weakness and desperation in her eyes.

"What is it you want me to promise?"

"Promise me that how you felt about me when you climbed that ladder just moments ago will not change no matter what I tell you."

I took a moment to think about what that meant. I knew I cared about her, I might even love her, and if I did love her, truly loved her, then no matter what she told me, I would still feel the same way.

"I promise," I said confidently.

She took a deep breath and looked out into the night. "I was eleven when they killed my family. Pillagers came in the middle of the night to steal what little we possessed." I knew about filthy Pillagers who sought out those who had less and took what they could mercilessly. "My father was a very proud man and he worked so hard to provide for my family. My mother wasn't able to work, not after she got sick. Some of the money my father made went to my education, finding me a part-time tutor who home-schooled me. The rest of the money went to taking care of my ailing mother."

Linnayah swallowed hard. "We had a small house, a shack really. There wasn't even a bathroom inside. There were two rooms, one for sleeping and one for everything else. My mother stayed in the bedroom most of the time. Sometimes, when she was sleeping, I would pull out an old photo she had given me when I was five. I would hold it up over her face and just try to imagine her as she was when she was well. She had been so beautiful but the sickness had taken all that away. She was so fragile. I hardly hugged her any more as I was afraid I would hurt her. I wish I would have hugged her that night."

Highlighted by the moonlight, I saw a tear roll down her cheek. She wiped it away with the back of her hand. The tear stayed on her skin. I took her hand in mine to wipe the wetness away with my thumb. I did not let go. She turned to me, her eyes watery as she continued.

"I slept on the floor. I was too big to fit in the bed with my parents any more and I didn't want to accidentally cause my mother any pain while we slept. I slept across the room from the bedroom door on a layer of blankets between the bed and the wall. My mother was above me. There was no worry of her stepping on me in the night because she couldn't get up. The space was tight. I knocked my head several times on the bed frame, but I wouldn't sleep anywhere else. I wanted to be close in case my mother ever needed me."

Linnayah squeezed my hand. "That night, we had been asleep for a while. I have always been a light sleeper. I heard the front steps creaking. I froze and listened, not wanting to wake my mother. If it were just a passing critter, a raccoon or a wild dog, there was no reason to wake anyone. What I heard next terrified me. The doorknob rattled and with it so did my body. I raised my voice to yell but all that came out was a weak terrified call to my father. 'Daddy!' I said. He didn't move. I sat up with my arms clutching my blanket. I looked towards the doorway near the foot of the bed.

"I was about to call to my father again when I saw my mother's eyes were open. Her fingers were to her lips signaling me to be quiet. 'Hide!' she whispered to me. HIDE, as if there were any place to do that in our little home! I heard the sound of splitting wood and I knew the door was being kicked in. I saw my father as he leapt out of bed and grabbed the axe out of the corner of the room. That axe had become a part of our home decor the day my father traded his gun for food and medicine. It must have taken all of my mother's strength to shove me under the bed. I barely fit under it. My head turned sideways in the direction of the door. I heard another blow and the front door was open. I heard footsteps and voices, too many of them! I had heard stories about Pillagers and what they were capable of. My father had a strong heart, but he was no fighter."

Linnayah hung her head as more tears hit the top of her hand. I swept them away as I did the ones before. "I'm sorry," Linnayah said apologizing for her tears.

"No need to apologize."

She lifted her head. "I didn't think I would cry telling you this now. It has been six years since it happened."

"No one knows how long it takes a heart to heal," I said.

She paused to reflect on what I said. "I have never told anyone before."

"I am listening."

"I was so frightened thinking about my father, my mother, myself. I could feel warm wetness running down my backside and I was embarrassed. Can you imagine? It could be my last day on this earth and I was worried about peeing my pants!"

"You were eleven," I reminded her.

"My dad slammed the bedroom door closed and locked it. Like another door was going to keep them out." Linnayah shook her head. "There was so much noise. The walls were thin but I couldn't tell who was where. I heard yelling and loud thuds. Then . . . " Linnayah closed her eyes. "I heard a gunshot and it was silent for a minute. My body began trembling harder, I was sure I was shaking the bed and my mother with it. The bedroom door soon came down like the front door. I told myself not to move, not even to breathe.

"There were two voices in the bedroom and more in the other room. A light was moving around the room. 'She must be who the pills are for,' a woman said. 'She looks like death,' a man said. 'She'll surely die without these,' the woman told the man while shaking my mother's pill bottle. Then the man said that he was taking them. He was stealing the pills my mother needed to stay alive! They started to ransack the room. My mother pleaded with them to take everything but leave her pills. She tried to get them to leave the room by telling them where nonexistent valuables were in the other room. My guess is she was trying to distract them so I could escape out the window.

"The woman left the room. The man said, 'Look, Sweet Pea, I'm taking these pills! These will bring food to the table for quite a while. I won't have to pillage for a bit. So really, Darlin', you are doing a service for others. Don't worry. Since you are such a humanitarian I am not going to leave you here to suffer a long cruel death.' I heard the gun being cocked and I braced myself. My mother's voice came in a whisper, 'I love you.' I wanted to say it back but I couldn't. My mouth wouldn't form the words. I should have said it!

"A moment later, everything changed for me. I had no parents. I was alone. I can still hear that gunshot ringing out." Linnayah choked on her words before regaining her composure to finish her story. "Soon the woman returned, saying my mother had lied. Her voice didn't even waver at the sight of my mother lying there dead. 'Crazy bitch says she LOVED me before I put a bullet in her head!' the man said. They continued to rummage through my family's things. They quickly found clues to my existence.

"I knew something was wrong when everything got quiet. I stopped breathing and listened. My heart pounded in my ears. I was sure they could hear it, too. Someone grabbed my ankle with sweaty hands and I tried to grab onto the wooden slats under the bed but I couldn't get a grip. I couldn't see anything because I couldn't turn my head. They lifted the bed enough to get me out more easily. I knew I was going to die. What I saw next I couldn't have prepared myself for. They were monsters!"

"Of course they were. To do something like that to you and your family!" I cried.

"No, they were actual monsters! Well, at least, they looked as if they were," Linnayah said.

Linnayah told me about how she could not stop screaming, not even after the heinous woman struck her across her face and told her to keep her mouth shut. All the men and the woman had normal bodies but their faces were from a nightmare. They were hideous, monstrous. Their foreheads, cheeks, and chins were deformed and swollen to an abnormal size. She actually thought they might have been aliens.

Linnayah never looked back at her mother as they dragged her from the bedroom. She could not avoid seeing her father lying in a pool of his own blood. She tried to run to him but the woman had her by her hair. Her father had managed to kill one of the intruders. The man lay sprawled across the floor with blood pooling around him. The axe lay near his side. The man Linnayah gathered to be the leader picked it up and wiped it off on her father's pants and kept it for himself. They took everything they considered valuable.

"What do we do with this girl?" the woman asked.

"We just lost one of our men, so I say we keep her," the leader said.

"Isn't she a bit young?" the woman said.

"I wasn't much older than her when I joined the group. She can clean up, God knows you don't do that," the man said. The woman responded with a hiss. "She can cook, too, until she is old enough to pillage. Isn't that right, Sweet Pea, or would you rather join your mommy and daddy?" he asked Linnayah, his lips upturned into a grotesque smile as he spun his gun around his fingers once.

The Pillagers put her father's pillowcase over her head to keep her from seeing where they were going. She remembered smelling her father's scent and weeping, knowing that when it faded she would never smell it again. As they carried her to their hangout, she tried her hardest not to cry. She did not want her tears to wash away the scent. They kept her head covered until she was locked in a small storage closet. In the morning, she woke clinging to the pillowcase holding it up to her nose. Her father's scent relaxed her enough that she was able to doze off. She found food and water on the floor inside the door. She hid her father's pillowcase in her pajamas, not wanting anyone to take it from her. It was midday before someone opened the door.

It was a relief to see a youthful, fresh-faced man and Linnayah was relieved it was not one of the nightmarish monsters—until he spoke.

"Hello, Sweet Pea. It's time you get to work earning your keep around here," he said. Linnayah noticed that he was wearing similar clothing as the lead attacker.

Later, Linnayah found out that the group used saline injections in their foreheads, cheeks, and chins to disguise their appearance and become virtually unrecognizable during their pillages. After committing the crime, they would lay low until the saline had been absorbed into their bodies. If anyone in the group was killed, the others would bring the body back along with anything they thought would identify them and burn it all, including the corpse.

Linnayah spent nearly six years with the group. There were always around ten of them. A few died during the pillages but someone would come to take their place. Some arrived the way Linnayah had. She was thirteen when they began training her, giving her different scenarios and setting up mock pillages. A year later they took her out on her first pillage. I now understood where Linnayah had learned to handle a blade and what it meant to her to fight.

"I am not proud of the things I have done, though I never

killed anyone except in self-defense," Linnayah said, freeing her hand from my grip so she could fold her own hands together.

"I am not judging you. I could not imagine what you have been through," I assured her.

"I tried to run away, you know," she said defensively. "More than once."

"What happened?"

"After the first time, I was deprived of food for five days, given water only in a dirty dog bowl, and no one was allowed to interact with me. The second time, I was beaten until I couldn't open my eyes and left for dead. When I came to, Easton, the leader, said, 'Sweet Pea, you're meant to stay with me forever.' The word 'forever' burned its way into my soul and I knew I had to find a way to get out of there. I was planning on leaving the day I met you at the Supply Depot," she said, touching me above my knee like she had the night before on the couch in Kenosis. This time she pulled her hand away hastily.

"How were you planning on leaving?"

"I had convinced Easton to let me volunteer at the Supply Depot, posing as a student. Easton had his ways of getting people in places they weren't supposed to be. My plan was for Easton to believe I was staking out the place for a possible roadside raid the following month or two. I told him I thought we were capable of more than just pillaging from the poor. I stroked his ego. If we were able to take a cargo vehicle, we wouldn't have to pillage for quite some time," she explained.

"Just how were you planning on doing that? Pillagers never

attack during the day," I asked, realizing it could have been Alecander and me they would have been harming.

"No, Cayden, it was never going to go that far. I was planning on reporting back to him that I made a mistake and that there was no way to raid the vehicle. But, after everything went down at the Underground Market there was nothing to report. My only hope is that he believes I am among the dead."

"Why were you at the Underground Market? Were you really there to try to help your prostitute friend, Kiara?"

"Please don't call her that," Linnayah sighed.

"Sorry."

"I had told Easton that I learned of a man who might be able to help raid your cargo vehicle and I was going there to seek him out. He had learned to trust me and he let me go alone. Kiara and I were friends before I was taken by Easton. We used to play together in the fields by our home. She lived with her father. Her mother had died a long time ago. One night, a year ago, I had learned of a pillaging I had not taken part in. Easton and the others were carrying on about how they killed this man because he wouldn't give up a doll. The doll was raggedy and old and it only had one eye. Yet, the old man wouldn't give it up. 'He clung to it like as if it were life itself,' Easton said.

"I knew at once that the man was Kiara's father. The doll was the last thing her mother had given Kiara before she died. I asked him in disbelief, 'What did you want the doll for?' My stomach turned when I saw the doll in the mouth of his dog

Gunnar. Gunnar was flinging it around and gnawing on the helpless doll. 'What about the girl?' I asked him. He told me that there wasn't any girl and that no one else was home. I was relieved to hear that. I knew Kiara was a strong-willed person and that she would find a way to survive.

"It wasn't until a couple of months ago that I found out just how she was doing it. One of the new men in our group came home bragging about how he had gotten himself a little tail and just how little it cost him to do it. I hated the filth that came out of their mouths. He told the other men in the group to ask for a sweet little thing named Kiara if they went to the Underground Market. She had dark curly hair and was the youngest of the bunch. He said she couldn't have been a day older than sixteen." Linnayah looked up toward the sky. "I think about what it would have been like for me if I had been left behind the day my parents were killed. Sometimes, I actually think that I was better off having Easton take me with him that day."

"You were trying to save Kiara. You were not going to take her to live with your parents like you told me but you had a different escape planned that day," I said, putting the pieces together.

"Yes, I had skimmed for years from Easton and the group's haul. Never anything that would be noticed. Sometimes, I would manage to find money and I would give it immediately to Easton, stuffing a minute amount into my bra or sock. That way he never suspected anything. I had saved up enough to help me get away and survive until I could find honest work. I hadn't included Kiara in my plans until recently. When I found out about her, I couldn't stop thinking about her and how in a way I was responsible for what happened to her," she said.

"How can you think you were responsible? What happened to her was not your fault," I said.

"If I was there that day, I could have saved her father. I could have tried to convince him to give up the doll or maybe I could have protected him. Then Kiara wouldn't be doing what she is now."

"You do not know that being there would have made a difference. It may have meant you would have watched him die."

Linnayah shrugged her shoulders. "I can't go back," she said solemnly. "I stole from him."

"I would not want you to go back," I said. Linnayah smiled at me.

"Easton would always check on his loot at night, either to pump himself up before a pillaging or stroke his ego before he went to bed. As luck would have it, we had just made two good hauls in a row. We still had food from our last haul and no one was in any dire need of anything. I knew the amount of his loot was the highest it had probably ever been."

I gasped. "You did not—"

"I did!" she answered. "I took it. I took everything. I had to. There were two of us now to provide for. I never expected Kiara to say 'No!' to me. I never expected her to have given up and want to remain in hell. Easton and his crew took some-

thing from us we can never get back. They took our innocence." She looked at me and I felt the pain in her eyes. "Easton
will be pissed for sure. If he knew I was alive, I wouldn't be for
long."

"Then we have to keep moving," I said.

"Yes, but to where is the question. I still have the money.
Maybe we could pay Lady Verleah to stay here at least for a little while. There is protection here."

"I am not sure. She sounded pretty adamant about our leaving soon. And she does not really seem to be in need of money." I paused a moment before asking, "How exactly were you
planning on getting away?"

"I was going to borrow, okay, steal Yuri's car with help
from Kiara. Yuri is her boss. She could easily get his code from
him. All she would have to tell him is that she had a paying customer and he would have blurted the code out to her. I was going to take Kiara and travel as far as his car would take us,"
Linnayah explained. I raised my eyebrows at her. "Look, Yuri
could spare the car. With all the prostitution rings he owns, he
would be able to buy another one in no time. He probably
wouldn't have even blinked at the stolen vehicle. When we cir-
cled the Underground Market after the blast and I saw your
cargo vehicle destroyed, I also noticed Yuri's car. I know he was
in the building. Don't hate me for saying this, but I hope he
died that day in the Market."

"I could never hate you." I was certain of those words.

"It is nice to have a friend. I haven't had one of those in

years." Linnayah sighed, rubbing her temples.

"You have a headache?"

"Yes, I have been thinking too much." Her laugh lightened the atmosphere.

"Let me help," I said, scooting closer to her. "You are not going to throw me from the train if I rub your shoulders, are you?"

"You can take your chances," she teased. As she sat up straight, I could tell I would not end up with dirt between my teeth.

I rubbed her shoulders while reflecting on our conversation. Her skin and hair were soft despite her harsh lifestyle. I used to have to rub Mr. Rawnett's shoulders after his weekends to help him with his headaches. Rubbing Linnayah's shoulders was much more pleasant.

My intention to tell her how I felt was delayed after hearing her story. She would not be leaving anytime soon. I was ecstatic at the idea of spending more time with her. Instead, I asked her, "Where is the money?"

"I have a small amount on me. The other part of it, well, I have to get to know you a LITTLE better before I share that information with you."

"Do you think Easton had anything to do with the explosions at the Underground Market?" I soon regretted my question.

"What? No, they don't have access to that kind of material. Wait! Do you think I had something to do with it?" she said defensively, craning her neck around to see my face.

"No. No," I said, not willing to lift my hands away from her silky skin. "I would be lying, though, if I said it never crossed my mind for a brief moment."

She raised her voice. "No!" She stood up.

"No! Look, Linnayah, I am sorry I thought that you might have had something to do with the—"

We were suddenly surrounded by darkness. All the Christmas lights and the lights inside the train went out.

I glanced at Linnayah. She was looking forward. I followed her intense gaze. I realized her last statement was not meant for me. Two sets of lights were coming toward us. My stomach tried to lunge upward into my throat as I feared a replay of the events at Gavaron. The lights moved the same way as they had the day Linnayah and I had gone fishing. I saw a third set of lights in the distance. There might have been even more, but I was not planning on sticking around to count.

EQUALITY

"GIDEONS! Like the ones on the beach," Linnayah whispered.

"We have to go!" I gasped as I saw the guards rapidly retreating into the train cars.

My heart raced and my adrenaline was on full power. We had little time until the vehicles were upon us. There was a slight chance they might breeze right past if they had not seen the lights of the train. From inside the cars, an alarm sounded.

We flew down the ladder and raced inside. The floors were illuminated by faint lights.

"What the hell is going on here?" Famous grumbled. "Can't I get a good night's rest anywhere?"

A guard pulled open the side door. "Come with me. Lady Verleah summons you all."

"What about Kayella and Zira?" I said.

"They are already with her."

Bentum stomped his foot in frustration. He could not see anyone's mouth in the darkness. "What is happening?" he demanded.

Linnayah moved close to his face and said, "Time to go!" She took Bentum's hand and pulled him behind the guard. Famous was already working his way down the bed ladder. Alecander ran over to hold the chair steady for him while Famous jumped from the ladder to the chair. We were in the next car when the lights of the gideons beamed through the windows. As we descended into Lady Verleah's quarters, the guard headed toward the door and readied his weapon for battle. *Have we led the gideons here?*

"How on earth did they find us?" Linnayah asked.

No one answered.

We found Lady Verleah in her glitzy nightgown. Synda was helping her put a fancy robe over her shoulders. Henner stood silently in the corner with his face still displaying his dislike for us. Kayella sat on the edge of Lady Verleah's enormous bed. Zira steadied herself against a side table. Famous' wheelchair was in the corner. Famous hurriedly transferred himself into it. Panels with screens wrapped around the entire room. Some showed scenes from outside. I saw the lights of the gideons turn off, set by set.

"It seems you have attracted some unwanted visitors," Lady Verleah said. She crossed the room toward the far wall. The panel showing the live feed seemed to move along the wall with her. When she stopped, the live feed was on a panel in front of her.

"We are truly sorry." Alecander said.

"Tsk! Tsk! No need to apologize! How could you have

known you were being tracked?" She raised her arm and pulled down a wall vase. A floor-length mirror on the wall slid to the side, revealing a doorway.

"Hurry now! You must be going. We can't have them find you here, can we? I am in no mood for bloodshed tonight," she said, waving us toward the newly open exit.

"Bloodshed," Kayella repeated feebly.

Linnayah looked at Kayella and said, "No one is going to hurt you or any of us, understand?" Kayella nodded.

Lady Verleah reached inside her robe pocket, pulled out something, and pursed her full lips to kiss the object before handing it over to me. "Take this," she said. It was a thick stiff cream-colored cloth, rolled up and tied with a red string. "When you approach the gate, make sure you hold it up for the Keeper to see. The Keeper will bring you to Amaury. Give it to him. Now go. I have to attend to our newest guests."

"Thank you for helping us," Alecander said before leading the way through the doorway.

Lady Verleah smiled and said, "I haven't had action around here lately so maybe I should be thanking you for letting me know I am still alive." She smacked her own meaty backside while turning to walk away. I could hear her laughing as I exited the room. Behind us, the door slid shut.

I was happy to be away from Henner's disdain. We were in a narrow hall, lined up single file. I placed the cloth Lady Verleah had given me into my satchel. Our feet clanked against the metal floor as we walked. I heard a commotion up ahead. We halted.

"What is going on?" I said impatiently. I wanted to get as far away from whoever occupied those gideons.

"It's a dead end!" I heard.

"Our weapons are here!" Alexander exclaimed.

I was perplexed. I began searching the hall for clues as to what to do next. I saw the same panels around the hall and metal horizontal bars above our heads and along the walls. I heard everyone beginning to panic. I turned around and headed back toward the way we came. There must have been something Lady Verleah forgot to tell us.

I only took a few steps before an abrupt movement of the hall caused me to lose my balance. It was moving forward. I bumped into a screen panel. It lit up, displaying scenes from inside the cars and the surrounding area, including the top of the car where Linnayah and I had been sitting. These screens were equipped with sound. I knew then that Lady Verleah had been listening as well as watching us.

I grabbed a bar above my head. So did the others. Famous locked the wheels of his chair. Soon we felt our direction shift. My companions touched the screens to have a clear view of what Lady Verleah was up against.

One of her guards fell from the train and landed headfirst on the ground. Whoever the attackers were, they were in no mood for negotiations or discussions.

"Please don't let anyone else die!" Kayella whimpered, turning away from the screens and covering her ears.

Kayella's plea went unheeded. A ball of fire erupted out of the top of one of the cars. It hit one of the gideons, causing it to catch fire and crash. The men inside the gideon scampered out, took cover, and opened fire. The other gideons began firing at the train. The sounds made me cringe and I wished I could turn the volume down. I took a step back and gripped the metal bar behind me, squeezing it as I continued to watch the screen. *Smoke, gunfire, fire!* My eyes shot around the horrific scene. Lady Verleah's men were managing to keep the intruders off the trains. I searched the screen for Lady Verleah, but I could not find her.

"Make it stop!" Kayella begged. I could see her body shaking. "We brought this upon them." No one replied. We all knew she was right.

Linnayah looked at me in desperation. I leapt forward, pounding the screen in front of me. It went blank. The others followed my lead and soon the only sound in the hall was our labored breathing.

It must have been another ten minutes before we felt the underground train slow down. I fought the urge to turn on a screen. The train came to a full stop. A door to the side of us opened vertically. Bentum and Zira exited first with Famous right behind them. Alecander coaxed Kayella out of the car and Linnayah followed her. I tapped the screen and nothing happened. I pounded it with my fist but still nothing. Alecander came back to see what I was doing. He had his crossbow slung over his shoulder.

We heard a commotion outside. Alecander turned quickly, grabbed his crossbow from his shoulder, and sprinted back out. I gave up on the screens, swung Mercy up off the floor, and followed Alecander. My heart nearly jumped from my chest at what I saw: Kayella was on her knees facing us while a man I believed was the Keeper held a knife against her neck. Kayella's eyes filled with tears and her bottom lip quivered. Zira, Famous, and Linnayah had drawn their weapons.

"Are there any more in the train?" the Keeper demanded.

"No," I replied. I started to open my satchel to retrieve the cloth Lady Verleah had given me.

"You move again and your friend NEVER moves again!" the Keeper threatened.

"Damn it, Cayden! Don't go getting us killed!" Famous said.

"I have something in my bag to show you. It is from Lady Verleah. I am supposed to give it to Amaury. Can you take us to him?" I asked as I steadied my legs and tried not to move.

"What is it the Lady has given you?"

"A cloth."

"Show me!" he said. "Slowly! The rest of you, lower your weapons."

I pulled out the cloth and held it forward to give the Keeper a clear view. Instantaneously, the cloth darkened until it was nearly black, revealing the reason Lady Verleah had kissed it before handing it to me. Her kiss was all that was left of the original cream color.

Satisfied with what he saw, the Keeper pulled his weapon away from Kayella's neck. She crawled forward until Bentum could help her to her feet. She was shaking visibly as Bentum tried to calm her.

The underground area was almost blinding, being made entirely of polished metal. It was built with ramps and stairs leading upwards from two train docks. We followed the Keeper up some stairs while Famous took the adjacent ramp. The Keeper carried a crossbow larger than Alecander's. At the top of the staircase, he led us down a long corridor to a locked door. He placed his hand on a touchpad near the door and it opened. A heavily armed man met us. He said nothing but questioned us with his dark brown eyes as he stood up from his chair. He had been watching the screen that showed the docking area.

The Keeper led us down a ramp and across an empty room towards three doors. He stopped at the door on the left. He again put his hand up to the door pad on the wall. The door opened, revealing an underground garden in a spherical room. It was warm and bright. Herbs, vegetable, fruit plants, and flowers encircled us.

The Keeper led us through the garden toward a new set of doors.

"It is late, so most everyone is asleep. Keep your voices down and try not to cause a commotion. You will find Amaury in the Grand Hotel lounge," the Keeper said. The doors before us slid open.

We entered a quiet underground town. A wide path separated two sets of buildings with signs such as A&A's Salon and Barber Shop, The Watering Hole, Pop's Restaurant, and General Store. I looked upwards and for a moment I was not sure if we were underground. There were stars shining above us. Linnayah gasped. Our hands touched as I turned to look at her and she grasped mine, letting it go when she heard Kayella say, "It's lovely here."

My mind went back to Linnayah's wish for Kayella and me to be together. I frowned, reflecting that I had not told Linnayah how I felt about her. A Human and a Cresecren were forbidden to be together—that much was true. Linnayah would be publicly ridiculed and likely spend time in jail. I would have been sent back to Gavaron. However, that was no longer possible. The world was different now. The old rules did not seem to apply anymore.

"I think I'm going to like it here," Famous said as we passed The Watering Hole. Its windows were lined with bottles of spirits. I rolled my eyes.

It occurred to me that I should concentrate to see if this place was as real and as charming as it seemed. I took a few deep breaths and closed my eyes. When I opened them, the same charming town still stood before me.

We walked along the path looking for the hotel. Dim lights made it easy for us to make our way. We entered the hotel to find a gray-haired man sitting with his back to us in front of a fireplace. My eyes wandered around the room. It was very quiet with only the sounds of the fireplace filling the air. The man got up and turned to face us. I made sure this time to have the cloth ready. I held it outward for him to see.

"Hello! I am Amaury," he said as his friendly Cresecren eyes met mine. Amaury appeared to be about forty. His dark skin did not have many wrinkles and his gray hair had deceived me. He wore a silver ear cuff that fit snugly on his outer ear and came down onto his upper cheekbone, providing a clear view of his barcodes. The ear cuff covering part of his face looked like the letter *N*. "Ah, Lady Verleah has sent you," he said, taking the cloth. "Please come and sit. You all look weary."

We all took seats as Amaury walked over to the fireplace and opened the cloth. We were silent as he read. He tossed the cloth into the fireplace where it instantly disintegrated. Amaury turned to face us again saying, "Do not worry about Lady Verleah. She and her warriors can handle the attack. As a precautionary measure, help has already been sent."

"Relieved to hear that," Alecander said. "I am Alecander. This is Cayden, Linnayah, Bentum, Kayella, Zira, and Famous."

"Are you putting us up in this hotel for the night?" Famous asked.

"Yes, my friend," Amaury said. "You will find plenty of room here. It is quite hospitable but first let us discuss why you are here. It will not take long as I know you are weary."

"We are here because some dumbasses annihilated our home and before that I think the same dumbasses blew up the Underground Market. Those same dumbasses are shooting at

Lady Verleah and her people right now!" Famous exclaimed. *Well said!* For once Famous was right.

"Perhaps I can shed some light on those . . . dumbasses," Amaury said with a crooked smile.

"Please do!" Famous replied.

"First, I would like to welcome you to my dream, our dream! Welcome to Novus!" Amaury said with his arms outstretched toward the town.

"What is this place?" Famous inquired.

"A place to start over, a place to begin, a clean slate . . . " Amaury said.

"New?" Alecander said.

"Precisely! Novus is the Latin word for new," Amaury explained. "This is a place for Cresecrens and Humans who have proven their loyalty to the movement to start fresh."

"Movement?" Alecander asked.

"With the funding and help from The Truce and those who support the mission, we have been able to build this humble underground town. It is a safe haven for those who believe in freedom and equality," Amaury said.

"Lady Verleah is protecting this secret," I said.

"Yes!" Amaury said enthusiastically.

"And the Keeper is there for good measure," I said, realizing its level of security and the amount of manpower and weaponry that would be needed to penetrate this underground oasis.

"And there are others, too, who stand to protect it," Amaury added. "You cannot begin to understand the level of dedication that goes into protecting Novus."

I thought about Lace and the others and wondered if they were all aware of this Novus.

"I thought The Truce was supposed to be a peaceful group," Famous blurted out.

"They are, but they also understand that in this day and age, there is the need to defend and protect what is right," Amaury said.

"You have a lot of guts bringing us here. You don't know anything about us, yet you let us in as if we are your best friends," Famous said. It seemed like a good point.

"I know enough about you. I know that most of you are Cresecren and that at least one of you is affiliated with The Truce." He paused to give us time to confess. When no one answered he said, "Zira, I am sorry about your loss. Jinjo was such an inspiration to the movement and a unique soul."

"Zank you," she answered.

I was shocked to find they were part of The Truce. Zira and Jinjo had advocated for the release of my people and that we not be created only to serve Humans. The Truce's motto "WHO Are We to Play GOD?"

"We will take good care of you for the duration of your stay. We will get you all the medical care you need to make sure your baby is well taken care of," Amaury told Zira.

"Did I hear him right? You're pregnant?" Famous asked, but Zira ignored him.

"Speaking of medical care," Amaury said, focusing the

conversation on Bentum. Amaury began moving his hands using sign language as he spoke. "I can get you help with your hearing if you would like." Bentum looked at him suspiciously. "You don't have to give me an answer right now. Just think it over. And Famous, you must grow tired of that wheelchair. What if you had no need of it ever again?"

Famous scoffed. "Sir, with all due respect, don't promise me something you can't deliver!"

"I never make promises I cannot keep." He turned to Linnayah. "You, though, you are the one I am most curious about. Lady Verleah gave me no information about you, young lady."

"There isn't much to tell," Linnayah answered, casually glancing in my direction. I saw her plea for me to keep her true past secret.

"Time will tell. Time always tells," Amaury said. Linnayah shifted uncomfortably.

Lady Verleah had said nothing about Linnayah because she knew nothing. In this situation, the fact that Linnayah had been a Pillager would seem to be pertinent information. But I knew Linnayah was really a good person in a bad situation who was also looking for a new start.

"Now onto the dumbasses!" Amaury seemed enthused. "We have not been able to determine who they are exactly, but we are definitely working to find out."

"Well that's a relief," Famous said sarcastically. "I'll tell you who they are. They obviously are people who got a problem with us Cresecrens. They showed up at the Market when

Alecander and Cayden were there and tried to pin the disaster on them. Then they show up in Gavaron trying to kill us. Then they show up at the train we just so happen to be occupying. I gotta tell you I'm not even sure I trust anyone in this room!"

"What do you mean?" I blurted out defensively.

"Look, Cayden, you and Alecander were at all three places, all three times, and nothing happened to either of you. You weren't blown up at the Underground Market. You brought these two lady friends to Gavaron and subsequently it is attacked and again you were not injured. We all know how close you and your buddy Bentum are. So obviously he would make it out. Poor Aurora had to be a sacrifice for the plan or perhaps you were going to make it back for her, but you were too late."

Bentum sprang forward and took a swing at Famous. Amaury blocked Bentum's fist by grabbing his wrist and holding it steady.

"I'm sorry but it has to be said," Famous continued. "Okay, so maybe you weren't involved but what about these two?" He pointed at Linnayah and Zira.

"What about them?" I said, growing agitated.

"What do you really know about these two? This one fights with a blade like some sort of ninja warrior." He wiggled his finger in Linnayah's direction. "And that one—"

"How dare you accuse me of being affiliated with zose murders!" Zira slapped him across his face. Famous sat stunned, holding his cheek. It was the second time Famous had been slapped by a woman in the past two days.

"Enough speculations for one night! You are all tired and I am sure it adds agitation to the mix. Please, let me show you to your rooms," Amaury said, gesturing down the hallway.

Famous scowled. "Good idea!"

"Are there others staying here?" Kayella asked shyly as we entered the hall.

"Yes. Most everyone who occupies Novus is away on . . . business. By tomorrow night, things will be livelier around here. Most of the town sits empty waiting for the right time for it to be full of those it was meant for. Those like you and me."

Each of us was given our own room. Linnayah's was across the hall from mine. I hoped she would not hesitate to ask me if she needed anything. The rooms were quite spacious with all the amenities of a home. Famous had inquired about the house across the street, finding out it was where Amaury lived. He told us there were similar houses for other town officials.

Instead of exploring, I headed straight for what I hoped was a bedroom. As soon as I laid eyes on the king-sized bed, I placed Mercy gently on the side table, tossed my satchel to the floor, climbed onto the bed, and kicked off my boots. It was more comfortable than my sleep pod. I thought about meeting Amaury. Novus had possibilities. I thought about becoming someone of high importance someday. Lying flat on my stomach, I quickly feel asleep.

SURPRISES

I WAS still groggy the next morning from a night of dreaming of running, constantly running. As my vision cleared, an outline of someone's face startled me. I scrambled away from it, tangling my arms in the covers. When I was free, I reached for Mercy. I was thankful my gun was still on my bedside table.

"Cayden, it's me. I'm so sorry! I didn't mean to scare you!" Kayella's soft voice said.

I blinked, trying to focus. "What are you doing in here?"

She sat on the bed as I lowered Mercy and put it back on the side table. "I came in last night . . . " she began.

"How did you get in?" I asked, upset that I had not even been aware of an intruder in my own room.

"The door was unlocked. I knocked but you didn't answer so I let myself in," she said as she smoothed back her auburn hair.

"Why did you come in here? What are you doing on my bed?" I asked defensively, annoyed that she could get onto my bed undetected as I slept.

"I couldn't sleep. I was scared. I went to Linnayah's room,

but she didn't answer. I tried her door and it was locked. I was going to knock on Zira's door, but she needs rest for her health and the baby's. Cayden, you are the closest companion I have had since Dahsie died. I feel safe around you. Even though I was so very tired, I couldn't sleep because every time I closed my eyes I would see everything all again, all that DEATH!" *There it was, that word again.* Kayella had come to find me in the middle of the night and warned me not to go to the Supply Depot. She had been so frightened that day too. "In here, if I opened my eyes I would see you and I wouldn't be afraid. You were sleeping peacefully and I didn't want to disturb you. The bed is rather large, so I hoped you wouldn't mind. I didn't have time to rethink my decision because as soon as I laid down and closed my eyes, I fell asleep." Kayella lowered her eyes.

"I am thankful I make you feel safe and that we are friends. Most of all, I am just glad we both had a good night's sleep," I said truthfully.

"Thank you. I will make arrangements to room with Linnayah if our stay is extended past today," Kayella said. She stood and fidgeted with her clothes. "I'd better get back to my room so we can shower." She became flustered. "I mean so you can shower in here and I can shower there at the same time. Well, it doesn't have to be at the same time. Um, never mind! See you later!"

Kayella had forgotten that she had locked the door to my room. When it did not open, she became flustered to see me standing behind her. I saw a notification flashing on a screen next to the door and moved closer. Kayella got the door open and looked over her shoulder. I startled her by being closer than she had expected. I reached over from behind her and touched the screen. As the message appeared, it said in Amaury's voice, "Breakfast 9:00AM at Amaury's residence."

"Good morning!" Linnayah said. I began to panic. *How will this look to her?*

"Morning," Kayella said, hurrying to her room.

Before I could say anything, Linnayah winked. "I knew you two would make a cute couple." She headed down the stairs. I swung around and kicked the floor, stubbing my toe. I cursed, then I noticed the time. I did not want to miss breakfast. I had eaten more food in the last few days than I ever had before and was thoroughly enjoying it. And I wanted to talk to Linnayah about how things are not always as they seem.

The town ceiling was beautiful. The clouds floated slowly across the warm sunny sky. I knocked on Amaury's door. A spunky little Human girl about seven years old answered.

"Hi, come in. My parents and everyone else are in the dining room," she said, skipping in front of me as she showed me the way. "I like your bag," she said to me over her shoulder.

"Thanks," I replied.

The little girl's lopsided pigtails bounced up and down as she hopped into her seat next to Amaury. He wore the same ear cuff as the night before. I had a feeling it symbolized some sort of leadership ranking and he was never without it. She patted the seat next to her and said, "Sit next to me. I'll share my eggs with you if you'd like."

I was not the last one to arrive. Kayella still had not made it. Everyone was already seated drinking coffee, tea, or as in the little girl's case, orange juice.

"Welcome, Cayden. I see you have already met my daughter, Terra," Amaury said, patting the little girl on her head. "And, Terra, you will be eating all your eggs this morning by yourself." It was obvious that my face gave away my thoughts. "Terra isn't my biological daughter. You know that isn't possible. I courted her mother from the time Terra was three. We were married last year." *Married?* I must have heard him incorrectly. I felt he was reading my mind when he added, "Married. Yes, you heard me right. Here, in Novus, it is allowed. Who has the right to tell us whom we love and whom we do not?"

While I was trying to comprehend what I had just heard, Lady Verleah appeared in the doorway from the kitchen. She called back over her shoulder, "Another guest has joined us."

"Cayden, I believe you have met my wife, Lady Verleah," Amaury said.

"Ye . . . Yes, good morning," I stuttered in disbelief. "Happy to see you are well!"

"I told you she could take care of herself, didn't I? I am so glad to have my sweetheart home a little early from her outing."

Lady Verleah joined us at the table, kissing her husband on the lips, and winking at Alecander.

"I always make it back to my family," Lady Verleah said.

"Did you find anything out about those . . . " I remembered the girl sitting next to me and chose my words carefully, "people?"

"Yes, they came looking specifically for your group. We will discuss that after breakfast." Someone I was not looking forward to ever having to see again emerged from the kitchen. Henner and Synda made their way around the room. Synda was taking orders on how everyone wanted their eggs while Henner asked me what I preferred to drink. There was a knock at the door. Instantly, the energetic little girl hopped up to open it. Kayella entered and sat at the table, not making any eye contact with me. Breakfast was uncomfortable with Henner's unwanted presence and constant reminder of his distaste for us.

"Can I wear my pink, sparkly dress to the party tonight?" Terra asked her parents.

"I think you look lovely in your pink dress! That is a fine choice. Now, go and get yourself to school before you are late," Amaury said. She gave her parents a loving embrace and bounded toward the door.

"School?" I asked. I was surprised they had the resources to provide it.

"Yes, and we also have a doctor, engineers, and many other patrons willing to work and live here. The outside world is struggling. Here, we have plenty of resources. Our safe haven has become a place for Humans and non-Humans to start new lives, to feel whole and at peace. A child can run off to school without her parents worrying about her. It is how the world should be."

"Sounds too good to be true," Famous interjected.

"Ah, but it is true," Amaury said. "You are welcome to find out for yourself."

"I don't plan on leaving anytime soon unless you plan on kicking us out," Famous said.

"You are welcome to stay as long as you like. You are the reason Novus was built," Amaury said.

"I may never leave! Now what is this about a party? Are we invited?" Famous asked.

"Of course, you are our guests of honor," Amaury said. "It is a welcome party and celebration of Novus' remaining safe and our location secret. We are also honoring those who have fallen for the cause and we will include those you have lost."

Alecander directed the conversation back to the attack last night. Lady Verleah told us that she was a step closer to finding out who they were. We were relieved to hear that despite all the destruction and chaos we saw, she only lost the man who had fallen off the car after being shot. Lady Verleah's reinforcements had arrived swiftly and the gideons retreated. The damage to the trains was repaired immediately. They were inspecting the abandoned gideon for clues. Those who had occupied it had escaped.

"They will be back and we will be ready!" Lady Verleah said.

When we left Amaury's to see more of the town, Lady Verleah stayed at home with Henner and Synda. As Amaury put it, she deserved a day of relaxation before the festivities tonight.

"What is on the agenda for the day?" Linnayah asked Amaury.

"I thought we would pay the good doctor a visit and have Zira see him for a checkup. Is that all right with you, Zira?"

"Yes, I should go. I haven't been to a doctor in years," Zira said.

"Then, how do you know you are actually pregnant?" Famous asked without hesitation. I knew he had not thought about his question before he asked it. Of course, with Famous that was always the case.

"A voman knows!" Zira snapped.

"I want to see the doctor, too. I want to hear!" Bentum said.

"Then so be it! You will go with Zira to visit Doc Ace," Amaury said. I saw hope in Bentum's eyes.

"I'll go with you both," Kayella said. "Maybe he can prescribe something that can help me sleep." She looked at me. I gave a slight nod, showing her I thought it was a good idea. That did not help my situation with Linnayah since she saw the little exchange and smiled slyly. I shook my head in defeat.

"What about me?" Famous said.

"What about you?" Amaury answered.

"About my legs," Famous said, looking down at his wheelchair.

"You will experience a new life. The specialist will be arriving today. You will pay Doc Ace a visit too. We want to make sure you are in good health to begin the process," Amaury said.

"Process?" Famous asked, sounding a little concerned.

"No worries, my good man. You will be well taken care of. We will not make you do anything you do not approve of." Amaury's words soothed Famous' creased brow. "Come, let's get you all over to see Doc Ace. The rest of us will take a town tour."

We left those who needed the doctor's care with the knowledgeable Human, Doc Ace, and his humorous Cresecren trainee, Hemmingway. *A Cresecren allowed to become a doctor!* If I did not see it, I would have never believed it! Hemmingway said that he could have either become a doctor or the town comedian. What shocked me most was not that he was training to become a doctor. It was that he was given a choice. Doc Ace was a highly intelligent, older gentleman. Half the time, I did not know what on earth he was talking about. He seemed to be very confident in his ability to help each of my companions. His office was inviting with soothing instrumental music playing softly in the background. The rest of us followed Amaury as he said, "Let's see . . . you have already seen the garden. You may enter it and take a closer look at any time. It is lovely. I suggest you visit it during the evening hours. It is quite a spectacular sight!"

"I'd like to see it," Linnayah said.

"I'll take you tonight," I said. "I mean, you would like to go see it and I would not mind seeing it myself. We could go together."

"Sure," Linnayah said.

"We'll start at the tailor shop. I informed Havarty we would be there as soon as possible. I'll have to remember to send the others over after their appointments," Amaury said.

"Really, it is not necessary. We're fine," Alecander said.

"Oh, but you can't go to the party in these clothes, can you? They're fine clothes, don't get me wrong, but they just aren't celebration clothes. For goodness sake, Cayden, you are missing a piece of your shirt. Don't worry, we are not wasters here. You will wear the same outfit to all special occasions with minor alterations. Some of our people even trade evening wear if they find someone close to them in size. Please, it is our pleasure. Now come, Havarty is waiting."

Havarty had a small chin, light brown eyes, and a matted tuft of orange-red hair on top of his head. He had a nervous laugh but was very cordial.

"My goodness, Havarty, you have such lovely things!" Linnayah exclaimed. She acted like a giddy child, running around and admiring one shiny thing after another.

Havarty blushed. "Thank you!"

"We can start with you, my dear," Amaury said to Linnayah. "Come. Come let Havarty work his magic." She climbed eagerly onto a pedestal in the center of the room.

Havarty studied her for a moment and then walked over to a corner where material of all different colors lined the wall. He pulled out a lilac one and brought the material back to the pedestal, draping it around Linnayah. It was not just a bolt of material but rather a partially made gown.

"This one will be perfect with your blonde hair and it will set those blue eyes blazing!" Havarty said.

"It is just lovely! I love it!" Linnayah exclaimed. I smiled as her eyes lit up. Havarty went on about how he would make Linnayah's gown, what he would add, and what he would take away.

"I have never worn a party dress," she said gleefully. "In fact, the one I am wearing is the first dress I have ever owned. And I don't think it is fit for a fancy party."

Havarty scrunched his nose and nodded.

"You look fabulous in anything," I said. As soon as the words left my lips, I wished I could take them back. They sounded better in my head. I was embarrassed to have said them out loud.

"She certainly does," Alecander added. I hoped he said it to make me look better.

She giggled and said, "Oh, thank you, Alecander!" as if I had not said it first.

Alecander glanced over at me with a look that said he sympathized with me. I gave him a look that could have set his eyes on fire. He raised his shoulders in question. Instead of explaining myself, I turned my attention back to Linnayah.

"You have to get undressed down to your undergarments," Havarty said. Linnayah looked stunned. Havarty's cheeks became rosy again. "So I can get your measurements! A curtain will come down around you and after you are undressed I will take a 360° 4D photo. I need it to finish making the gown. If you are uncomfortable with that we can do it the old-fashioned way. I could take measurements but it will take much longer to see your finished product. With the 4D picture, we can have more fun. We can build your whole look together privately— hair, makeup, shoes, jewelry, everything! So you can see the look before anyone else does."

"Let's do it your way," Linnayah said.

"Why don't you gentlemen take a look around and let me know if you see anything you like," Havarty said.

I moved away and acted as though I cared about a color chart on the wall. I could hear Havarty pulling the curtain around Linnayah. I kept my head turned away from it as I fought the images trying to creep into my mind. I saw a shimmering fabric out of the corner of my eye and a mirror above it. I saw the reflection of skin. I was not sure if it was Linnayah's arm or leg, I was only certain that it was hers. I felt I was intruding on her privacy and looked away.

"You may get dressed now," Havarty said to Linnayah. "Now, who is next?"

Alecander and I did not spend much time picking out what we would wear. I just let Havarty do whatever he thought was best. Alecander did not give him much help either. Our suits were similar in color but not in style. Havarty explained that he was going more for a youthful look for me and a debonair look for Alecander. Linnayah approved of both. We left her oohing and aahing about her new look with Havarty. She was so lost in conversation that she did not even seem to realize that we left. I had to admit, though, that, I could hardly wait to see her in the dress.

Amaury showed Alecander and me around the rest of the town. He started with Novus Town Hall. We opened the doors to an empty room filled with bleacher-style seats. The arched rows of seats faced each other. I excused myself to use the restroom after all the orange juice I consumed.

When I emerged, I did not see Amaury or Alecander. There was an open door where a solid wall had stood. I stepped through the door intrigued and amazed by what I saw: a shooting range, training dummies, weapons that hung on the far wall, and a much larger training arena than Kenosis. I walked to where Alecander and Amaury were looking through plate glass into a small empty room.

"I was just telling Alecander that this is our combat training room. You two should give it a go," Amaury said.

"What do you say, Cayden?" Alecander asked.

"Sure. Why not?"

Amaury chuckled. "I'll set an easy scenario since neither of you have experience." Amaury approached a black box. He punched in a set of numbers that opened it and pulled up a small computer.

Inside the room, I looked over at Amaury for some sign of what would happen next but as soon as the door shut behind us, the room went pitch black. Alecander put his back up against mine. Soon the lights came back and there was a man who towered over us standing a couple yards away. His eyes were half-crazed. Behind me, Alecander shifted to the right. I briefly thought about closing my eyes and focusing on reality. However, that would defeat the purpose of training. This was a mock scenario of something that could happen. Besides, I was not even sure my ability applied in this situation.

"You call him easy?" I assumed Amaury was grinning on the other side of the glass.

The giant lunged at me and I leapt to the side. I felt the warmth of his body heat above my chest as the giant's fist caught the neckline of my shirt and tore it open. Out of the corner of my eye, I could see an image of another behemoth.

"What? No weapons to defend ourselves?" I said.

The giant reached behind him and grabbed a blade.

"Why not give him a gun?" I whispered to myself, a little worried Amaury might have heard me.

I heard Alecander struggling, but I could not see past the giant. He lunged at me with the knife and I dodged him again. I backed up into a stool that had not been there a moment before. I picked it up and slammed it over the giant's back, breaking off a leg of the stool. He growled as he climbed to his feet, lunging at me and this time piercing the skin of my left hand. Blood began gushing although it was not painful. I could not feel my hand at all nor use it. I saw the broken wood and grabbed a fat leg of the broken stool, holding it up against the giant. Alecander slammed into my side, and the collision caused me to lose my balance. He saw my injured hand and his eyebrows furrowed.

"I wonder which of us has it worse?" Alecander asked as he moved his face to give me a full view of it. His eye was swollen shut. Seeing the makeshift weapon I held in my other hand, Alecander hurriedly picked up another leg off the broken stool. I noticed that my giant lagged in his response between attacks, which allowed me to assess the situation.

The enormous man was breathing heavily and swaying back and forth. I took a deep breath and yelled at the top of my lungs, swinging the stool as hard as I could against the giant's side. My weapon broke in half and the only effect it had on the giant was to make him angrier. He grabbed me by my neck, lifting me up and then slamming me down. I temporarily lost the use of all of my limbs. The giant snarled and slowly approached me, holding the knife over his head. I frantically searched around for something to fend him off. On the floor was a splintered half of a stool leg. I reached for it but it was just beyond my fingertips. The giant lunged at me. I used the forearm of my injured hand to keep his knife-wielding hand at bay. I attempted once again to grab the splintered wood. This time I was successful and swung my palm up as hard as I could straight into the side of the giant's neck. I watched as his eyes rolled back as he lost consciousness. I braced myself for the weight of his body to fall upon me. Instead, the giant disappeared. I looked at my hand only to discover I was no longer holding anything. My injuries, however, remained.

Alecander's grunts caused me to turn in his direction. Alecander was hanging from the shoulders of his giant as the behemoth slammed him over and over against the wall. Alecander had a grip on the giant that was enough to make his face turn crimson. I sprang to my feet. I saw Alecander's stool leg lying next to his foot. I swiped it off the floor and smashed the giant over the head. He fell to his knees. I watched as Alecander mustered the energy to kick the giant hard from behind. Moments later, the giant disappeared along with all the stool pieces. I helped Alecander up off the floor. His eye looked much worse than it had earlier. We patted each other on the back as we caught our breath. We could see our reflections in the glass. My shirt was intact and my hand was not bleeding. Alecander did not have a swollen eye.

Amaury opened the door and gave us enthusiastic applause. "Shall we go again? Perhaps on a more difficult level?"

Alecander and I looked at each other and answered in unison, "No!"

"Perhaps another day then," Amaury said, amused.

I enjoyed the company of Alecander all day and was glad the subject of my glare at Havarty's shop did not come up. It was like old times, just the two of us. We spent some time playing chess in Amaury's backyard. It would have been a perfect afternoon since I won a match. But Henner kept scowling at us.

CHANGE

Havarty had my suit delivered at 6pm. A woman and a man with emerald eyes, probably in their mid-twenties, who wore tight-fitting sleek black body suits with high white collars, stormed into my room as soon as I opened the door. Their hair was short, spiked, and dyed a silvery-white. They moved like they were extensions of each other and finished each other's sentences. The woman walked behind a chair carrying my suit that moved along by itself. The man trailed an oversized hand-bag atop a small black trunk which also moved by itself.

"We don't have much time. We still have your friend Alecander to attend to," the woman said.

"Yes, you are to meet everyone in the lobby . . . " the man added.

". . . at 7pm sharp," the woman said.

"This is . . . " the man began.

"Addison." She finished his introduction. "And this is . . . "

" . . . Adam." He finished hers.

"What exactly are you here to do?" I questioned.

"Doll you up, sweetheart!" Adam said.

"Um, no! That is quite all right," I said, putting my hands up in defense.

"Nonsense!" Addison replied.

"No, really I can manage on my own," I said to them.

Addison tossed my suit from the chair onto the couch. "Sit!" I complied. "Thank you," she said, patting my shoulders. Her chair carried me into the bathroom.

"Please let us do our jobs without any more fuss. I promise you will look . . . " Adam said.

" . . . simply fabulous!"

As they unloaded their gear, they moved swiftly and grace-fully like two swans swimming across a lake.

"Shame on you!" Adam said. "And to think you would have gone to the ball looking like . . . "

" . . . the ugly stepsister." Addison finished his sentence with a crooked smile.

"You do have a rich dark hair color." Adam reached toward my hair to inspect it. Before he could touch it Addison said, "Wait!"

Adam stopped. "Ah yes, the suit!" Addison rushed out to retrieve it.

"Do us a favor," Adam said, looking at my satchel and gri-macing. "Leave that here tonight. It simply won't do."

A half hour later, I found myself standing in the doorway of the bathroom being admired by Addison and Adam as they ap-proved of their work. I thanked them for their incredible job. They planted a kiss on opposite sides of my face and like a whirlwind were out the door.

"Have fun, Cinderella!" Addison said.

Adam added, "This look will last WAY past midnight!"

I turned around to face a full-length mirror. I was impressed. I almost did not recognize myself. The shorter haircut really did set off my eyes as Adam had said it would. I laughed as I realized I was admiring myself. I had refused to allow Addison to apply any makeup. After some convincing, I did allow her to moisturize my face. My periwinkle, collarless shirt was form-fitting and very comfortable. The ebony military-inspired jacket was a bit stiff. I was instructed never to button up the jacket so my belt made of a black bendable metal with a darker periwinkle buckle could be seen. I approved of my black dress boots, also military-inspired. I admired Addison's addition of the pewter pocket watch on a long beaded chain. I picked the watch up to examine it closely. It was engraved with a filigree N which I assumed was for Novus. I turned the watch over. There was an inscription on the back that read, "Let your life begin."

I heard a ruckus in the hall. Alecander was pushing Adam out of his room. Addison's hands were on her hips, showing her disapproval of Alecander's actions.

"It was only a simple injection!" Adam pouted.

"Your face would have been flawless for the evening!" Addison added.

"I rather like my crow's feet!" Alecander said, tossing their bags into the hall and slamming the door behind him. I chuckled.

"Your friend is . . . " Adam said.

" . . . irrational!" Addison finished.

"He has no sense of style!" Adam said.

"It is simply a shame. He is so handsome. With our help he could be stunning!" Addison added.

"Ugly stepsister!" they said in unison. I quietly closed my door, leaving them in the hall to collect their things. Thinking about what it must have been like in Alecander's room caused me to laugh out loud.

I checked the time again. It was still twenty-four minutes before I was supposed to be downstairs. I looked out the window to see people busily getting ready for the big event. Tables, chairs, ribbons, fresh-cut flowers—Cresecrens and non-Cresecrens alike helped to prepare for the festivities. I had never been to anything like this before. The Rawnetts never threw any parties, keeping mostly to themselves and not wanting anyone to see what their home life was like. The closest thing to a celebration at the Rawnetts was the twins' birthday party.

I decided to go down even though I would be early, but I could not wait to see Linnayah and the others. I checked on Mercy to make sure she was still where I had left her. I placed my satchel on the shelf beside her, feeling naked as I left it behind. Amaury and his family were already in the lounge. Little Terra spotted me and skipped up to me as I approached. She did not wear pigtails this evening but instead her hair twinkled with tiny white lights woven into a loose bun on top of her head.

"Where's your bag?" she asked.

"I left it in my room."

"Too bad, I like that bag."

I winked. "So do I."

"I brought my pink one that matches my dress," Terra said, showing me her purse and spinning in a circle.

"That is a very pretty bag and you look lovely." She beamed.

"Can I sit next to you at dinner like I did at breakfast?" Terra asked.

"I think you have an admirer," Lady Verleah said from the couch near the fireplace.

"If it is all right with your mother, then it is all right with me," I said.

Lady Verleah nodded. Terra jumped up and down, clapping her purse against her hand. Just then, I noticed a woman standing near the fireplace and staring into the flames. Her auburn hair reflected the firelight. She wore an olive gown that hung low in the back. She turned around as I stepped further into the lounge. I was surprised to see that it was Kayella. Her gown reached just above her knees and her silver high heels showed her copper-painted toes. Her hair was swept off her face in a complimentary side-do, with ivory and copper vines intertwining through her curls. I had never before seen her with makeup and it suited her well.

"Hello, Kayella."

She looked down at her freshly painted fingernails. "Hi."

"You look lovely," I said, trying to catch her eyes.

"Thank you," she said, adjusting a strap on her gown.

"Do I look that ridiculous?" I asked, trying to lighten the mood.

"What? No! You look great!" Kayella let her eyes meet mine.

"Well, since you would not look at me I thought maybe it was because you were trying not to laugh." I fought off a smile.

"I would never . . . " she began, obviously mortified.

"I am joking, Kayella. I was just trying to get you to look at me."

She laughed nervously as she looked past me. Her eyes grew wide. It was Alecander.

"My, you Cresecren boys do clean up nicely!" Lady Verleah said.

Alecander did not require Addison and Adam's help to complete the "debonair" look Havarty envisioned. He did not have to try to look handsome, he just was. His suit was dark charcoal. Unlike mine, his had lapels, an ascot, and a rich plum vest. Black lace boots completed his ensemble. Havarty had referred to it as a Phantom of the Opera piece.

Behind Alecander came Zira, her arm interlaced into Bentum's. They were both dressed elegantly all in black. It was fitting given their recent losses. Zira had on a black sequined beret. A yellow tulip was attached and served as a remembrance of the one Linnayah had given to Jinjo after he died. Bentum's suit was also a Phantom of the Opera piece. He wore pewter hair chains that ran along his closely shaven head.

We greeted them and I asked Zira about her doctor's appointment.

"It vent vell. Zee babies and I are all healzy," she said.

"Babies?" I said.

"Yes. I made Doc Ace check zree times to be sure zere vere, in fact, two of zem. I zink Bentum has some pretty big news to share also."

"I do!" Zira stepped out of his way as everyone realized he had understood what Zira had said without having to read her lips.

"You can hear!" Kayella exclaimed.

"It's funny. You all don't sound anything like I imagined," he chuckled.

"What did Doc Ace do?" I asked.

Bentum put a finger to his right ear and flipped over what he called the tragus, the small pointed cartilage of the outer ear, to show us where Doc Ace implanted a hearing device.

"I don't even notice they are there," he said.

"What about Famous? Were they able to do anything for him?" I asked.

"I don't know. We were excused to go to Havarty's. We haven't seen him since then," Bentum said.

Other guests began to emerge from their rooms. Amaury had stated that more occupants would be arriving and joining Novus this evening. They greeted us warmly in passing. A feeling I was not familiar with kept sneaking up inside of me and disappearing only to return every time I thought about seeing Linnayah. It was a sudden warm feeling in the pit of my stomach. As quickly as it came, it would disappear when I became involved with what was going on around me.

A Human woman on a Cresecren man's arm approached us. This seemed to be a common practice. I hoped it improved my chances with Linnayah. I saw the woman's silvery spiked hair and emerald green eyes and recognized Addison. She had added a metallic fuchsia jacket to her ensemble, refreshed her makeup, and highlighted the tips of her spikes fuchsia to match her new look. The man walked with a slight limp and occasionally leaned on her. He wore chrome glasses with light gray tint even though we were indoors. Those glasses must have cost a fortune.

I looked closely at the man behind the glasses. My jaw dropped as I read his jaw. We shared the same birth month and I recognized the birthdate.

"What's the matter? Haven't you ever seen a pretty lady before?" Famous said, twirling Addison around with one hand. Addison giggled.

"Your legs!" I said amazed.

"What? No mention of my Adonis new look?"

"You look fabulous!" Kayella chimed in.

"Thanks to my date here, Addison. She said that lightening my hair would match my personality." Famous spun Addison around again. Again she giggled. Light hair to match his personality? Really? Was she talking about the same Famous we all knew and barely tolerated?

"Are you wearing makeup?" I could not resist the jab.

"A little. Addison said it was essential to accentuate my features." He lifted the glasses for everyone to have a clearer view of those features. "As for my legs, I can't express how it feels to walk again. I owe Doc Ace and the specialist, Doc McGriffin, my eternal gratitude. Especially since without my new legs, I couldn't slow dance with my new lady friend." He squeezed Addison. If I had eaten, I would have lost my dinner. Addison seemed like a level-headed young woman. *What did she see in Famous?*

Famous began a long-winded story about how Doc Ace and Doc McGriffin made him a bionic man. I tried to listen, but I lost interest as I anticipated seeing Linnayah at any moment. It was almost 7PM. I heard that Doc Ace and Doc McGriffin had taken Famous to a lab with some top-secret "stuff."

"It just so happened that they had these beauties," Famous said, lifting his pant legs to reveal flesh-colored parts "from a man who lost his life last year in a tragic accident. I knew I was supposed to walk again! I just knew it! It wasn't right when my legs got blown to hell but they have risen! And they came back improved. Well, they will be improved once my brain can learn to keep up with them so I won't be stumbling around or stepping on pretty ladies' feet." He winked at Addison, who blushed. "I'll be faster than you, Cayden."

"What?" I said as I was forced back into the conversation.

"I said, I will be faster than you. So fast, if we raced, I'd be sipping a glass of wine at the finish line while you were still crouching down to begin."

"I highly doubt that!"

"Give me a little time to get used to these limbs and we will see."

"Sure, take all the time you need and then we will see who will be sipping what at the finish line." *The man gets a new pair of legs and suddenly he thinks he can do anything.*

"You're on!" Famous said, shifting his weight which caused him to lean into Addison. She did not seem to mind. *He should lay off the booze tonight, although that could be fun to watch.*

I was so caught up in Famous' challenge that I had not noticed the room had grown quiet. Someone let out a low gasp. A woman had just entered the room.

Little Terra broke the silence, rushing to the woman's side. "You look so beautiful, Linnayah!"

My heart skipped a beat when I saw her and adrenaline sped through my veins. I had never felt like this before and it made me uneasy. Linnayah bent down toward Terra and said something that made the little girl laugh. Terra skipped off to share the joke with her mother. Linnayah's face lit up as she looked our way and began to walk toward us. My hands began to sweat. I suddenly wanted to take my jacket off. She looked phenomenal. Even that word did not seem to do her justice.

Famous, Bentum, and Zira stopped her to share their big news. I admired her while she caught up with them. She wore a stunning golden gown that reached the floor. Every once in a while her copper sandals would peek out as if to say hello. Her hair was pulled up high in the front and draped down her back. A copper-leafed tiara sat upon her head and a matching bracelet wrapped around her right bicep. Hair chains ran along the sides of her head and intertwined to hang down her back. Tiny crystal stars on the chains twinkled as her hair moved. Her torso was hugged snuggly by a sparkling V-neck top. Her makeup enhanced her features as I am sure Adam told her while applying it to her fresh face. I could not stop looking at her perfect lips. She looked like a princess or maybe a goddess.

Amaury and his family got up to join the festivities outside. Terra ran over to take my hand, leading me to my place next to her at our table. *My first party and my date is a seven-year-old girl. Well, at least I have a date!* Linnayah met my eyes long enough to exchange a smile before we left the hotel. Terra kept swinging my hand up and down all the way to our seats.

There were many more people than I had expected. As soon as most of the guests were seated, the lights of the town began shifting to an evening setting. The sky dimmed and classical music started to play. We feasted on delicacies and had nonstop conversation. We filled each other in on our day's activities. I looked around the table, truly enjoying my company, and surprisingly that included Famous. The seven of us had become a family unit in such a short time. Perhaps we could start over here in Novus. It felt promising.

Havarty made his entrance, being sure to be fashionably late. He smiled and waved while he rushed to take his seat, tipping his fedora as he greeted people. I spotted Adam looking at his sister from time to time. Famous probably made him uneasy so he felt the need to keep an eye on them.

Amaury took the podium in front of the Grand Hotel. He threw a purple neck flag for those lost in Gavaron into a large burning pot. We watched as the flames grew higher. Lady Verleah tossed in a piece of wood from her train for her fallen warrior. When Amaury spoke of those lost in the Underground Market, Zira stood and Bentum escorted her to the flaming pot. She took the yellow tulip from her beret, gave it a gentle kiss, and dropped it into the flames. We had a moment of silence.

"Tonight we honor those we lost, not in mourning but in celebration of the lives they led. We also celebrate those who survived and were brought to us here in Novus!" Amaury concluded.

After the solemn ceremony, the transition back to the party atmosphere was well done. Trays of exquisite desserts were placed on each table. The music switched from classical to faster dance tunes. A band appeared above us with four fantastic musicians suspended above the dance floor, one in each corner. Their formal jackets changed colors with the rhythm of the songs, casting colored lights onto the dance floor. Two were Cresecren. I was fascinated by the fact that they could play drums. Normally, Cresecrens were not given the luxury of learning anything for recreation. The other two musicians switched between singing and playing a variety of musical instruments such as guitars and keyboard. When the songs had lyrics, the drummers joined in with the chorus.

I looked over at Linnayah as she began to feel the beat and watched as her shoulders and head found their rhythm. I had never danced a day in my life. In fact, I had rarely listened to any music. Once, I saw Mr. Rawnett force his wife to dance with him while he was in a drunken stupor. It was not a very good example of people moving together with music.

Terra must have been reading my mind. "You wanna dance with me?" she asked, her face sticky with chocolate ganache. A fast song with a heavy bass beat was playing.

"No, thank you," I said politely. Terra's bottom lip quivered.

"You don't want to dance with me?" Her voice was an octave higher than usual.

"No, no, it is not that. I am sure you are a great dancer. It is just that I . . . " I did not even have the courage to tell a child.

Terra leaned in and whispered, "You can't dance, can you?"

"No. I cannot."

"I'll tell you a secret." She leaned in closer, her eyes widening. "Daddy couldn't dance either until Mommy and I taught him how."

"Really?" I said. Amaury had just taken Lady Verleah to the dance floor. He looked as though he knew what he was doing.

"Don't be afraid. I'll teach you like I taught Daddy. It's a fast song. This is easier and more fun than a slow song. Later, you can ask Linnayah to dance," Terra said.

"Linnayah, huh?"

"Are you kidding me? Your eyes popped out of your head when you saw her in her dress and you got that look my daddy sometimes gives my mommy. I'm not six any more. I know what I am talking about," she said, licking chocolate ganache off her chin.

I took my napkin, dabbed it in my water, and reached over to clean her face. "All right, since you seem to know what you are talking about, young lady, you can teach me, but only on one condition. Let us keep the Linnayah information just between us."

"Ok, but I think everybody already knows that information," she said, taking my hand and leading me to the dance area.

I tried not to look around to see what Linnayah was doing. I had a hard enough time learning to dance without that distraction, trying not to step on anyone's feet. Finally, a slow song played. I took the opportunity to ask Terra if she would like to take a break and get a drink.

"You don't know how to slow dance either, do you?" Terra asked.

"No. I do not."

"It is very easy. You just put your right hand on the lady's upper back or hip. The other goes in her hand and you spin around slowly, moving to the music," she said, demonstrating for me with a phantom partner.

"You really are a great dancer!" I said as I walked toward the bartender to order drinks. She swelled up with pride.

I heard a voice behind me. "Care to dance?"

Linnayah stood there, waiting for my answer with a small smirk on her face.

"He would!" Terra answered. "He knows how because I just taught him!" Terra gave me a shove on the back of my legs, pushing me toward the dance floor.

Linnayah took my hand. "Great, because Hemmingway just asked me to dance and Kayella needs a partner and I thought of you. You know she's shy, so I decided to ask you for her." *Linnayah, the matchmaker, was back.* Hemmingway, the would-be doctor, stood there with a big smile that showed his perfect teeth. His violet eyes sparkled. I looked back at Terra, hoping she could save me from this situation. Unfortunately, she had already gone to get a drink. She waved back at me with her free hand like a joyful mother seeing her child off on his first date. Linnayah let go of my hand and took Hemmingway's outstretched one. My throat tightened as she said, "You two, don't let me down! I'll see you on the dance floor." To add insult to injury, Hemmingway winked at me as they slid toward the middle of the dance floor. He wrapped one arm snugly around Linnayah's waist. I wanted to wrap my arms around his neck.

"We don't have to dance if you don't want to," Kayella said.

I turned to face her. "No, I want to dance with you. I am just not sure how."

"I don't know how to dance either," she said. "Linnayah tried to show me but it wasn't long enough for me to know what I am doing."

"Then let us go look like we do not know what we are doing together," I said, holding out my arm to escort her to the dance floor. I took a position toward the back so we would have some privacy and a clear view of Hemmingway and Linnayah.

Hemmingway looked as though he had danced with many partners. I naively and awkwardly tried to follow his lead. I stepped on Kayella's foot attempting a maneuver Hemmingway performed flawlessly with Linnayah. I think I saw him roll his eyes at me. I took a deep breath and closed my eyes, recalling what little Terra had said: "You just put one hand on the lady's back or hip. The other goes in her hand and you spin around slowly, moving to the music." I breathed in deeply, repositioned my arms and listened to the rhythm of the music. I was relieved when I was sure Kayella's toes were fairly safe. I actually started to enjoy myself. The music changed and threw us off the beat but we managed to pick up the new rhythm.

"We aren't so bad together," Kayella said. "I mean at dancing." Her cheeks flushed.

"You know, this is kind of fun."

"Cayden, can I talk to you about something?" I did not know much about women, but I did know that those words meant it was about to get serious.

I straightened my shoulders and said cautiously, "Yes."

"You know Linnayah has been trying to get us together."

"Yes."

"Well, I want you to know I had no part in it. I don't understand her determination to get us together when she obviously has feelings for you herself."

"She does?" I said in shock. My heart fluttered with the news.

"I don't think she realizes it or maybe she just won't let herself realize it," Kayella said.

"I have not exactly noticed any signs."

"Well, it is mostly the way she looks when she talks about you or the way she stares at you when you aren't looking," Kayella said. It was hard for me to comprehend.

"She told me you wanted to be my mate and she has been trying to get us together ever since," I said.

"Linnayah has a good heart. I did tell her I had thoughts about becoming mates. Once she heard that, she vowed to help me, ignoring her own feelings toward you. She is a true friend. But I want to be a true friend to both of you." I looked at her questioningly. "Cayden, come on, you haven't looked at me once during the whole time we danced until I addressed you."

I did not know what to say. She was right. I *had* been watching Linnayah. It was hard to take my eyes off her.

"I don't want to be matched up with someone who will always wonder WHAT-IF. You care for her, not me," Kayella added.

"I care about you."

"But you don't LOVE me. And that is more powerful than

anything else in this godforsaken world. When you find it, you should never let it go." She reached up gently and grabbed my chin to make sure she had my undivided attention. She had never looked so serious in all the time I had known her.

"I do not know what to say," I said truthfully, feeling apologetic.

"Whatever you do, don't say you are sorry because you can't help who you fall in love with. Besides, I want to be with someone who loves me back," Kayella said. I felt even worse with the realization that Kayella had just told me she loved me and I could not return the sentiment. She read the sadness in my eyes.

"What did I just tell you? No apologies." Her eyes glistened. I leaned down and kissed her gently on her forehead.

"Now, go ask Linnayah to dance before Hemmingway sweeps her off her feet. He is quite the catch, you know," Kayella said, lightening the mood.

"Are you sure?" I said, not wanting to leave her alone on the dance floor.

"Go on! Go!" she said playfully shoving me towards Hemmingway and Linnayah. I looked back and Kayella gave me an encouraging smile.

I passed Famous and Addison, who looked more like they were hugging rather than dancing. I was not certain whether it was because Famous was still not comfortable on his legs or if he was just using it as an excuse to get closer to Addison. Probably a little of both.

I was not paying attention to where I was headed and ran into someone from behind. All I could see was a mane of wild pink hair tossing around. I apologized as he turned around.

"No worries, friend," he said, smiling.

"I was not watching where I was going," I said.

"Good thing I was done. I wouldn't want to waste a good drink," he said, tipping his glass over to show me that it was empty. I relaxed at his casual attitude and friendly hazel eyes.

"Nice to see a new face around here. The name is Crowley," he said, extending his free hand.

"Cayden," I replied as I shook it.

"Well, Cayden, you seem to be on an important mission, so I will let you get back to the girl." He winked. *Was I THAT obvious?*

Before I reached Linnayah, the music changed. I was thrown off by the upbeat music and paused where I stood. Defeated, I looked back for Kayella for some sign of what I should do. But Kayella was making her way toward Alecander and the others.

I felt a sudden firm grasp on my shoulder and turned to see Adam. "Follow me!" he said mysteriously.

I gave up on my mission of dancing with Linnayah and followed Adam to the refreshment bar. He handed me a drink and led me toward a more private area in front of the movie theater.

SECRETS

We STOOD for a moment as we sipped our drinks. Adam seemed to be scanning the area for any potential eavesdroppers. I thought how perfectly he matched his sister in his black jacket with fuchsia accents. I wondered if they ever shared clothing since they were about the same size.

"What is it, Adam?" I asked.

"Things here in Novus are not as they seem," Adam said cryptically, facing away from me.

"What do you mean?"

"Laugh," Adam said.

"What?" I was beginning to think Adam might not be all there.

"What I mean is pretend we are talking about something less serious. Relax your posture and laugh as if I am telling you a joke," Adam said seriously before he let out a laugh of his own.

"Okay." I chuckled despite not understanding why.

"That's better." Adam forced another chuckle.

"This is getting a bit strange," I told him.

"Tell me something, Cayden. Don't you think it is a little weird to be having a party after the deaths of so many? Don't you find it strange that no one here seems like they are in mourning?"

"We are celebrating their lives. You heard Amaury," I reminded him.

"That is all fine and dandy, but what about your friends Bentum and Zira?"

"What about them?" I said defensively.

"Cayden! Relax and smile! Please!" He sounded so convincing I did as he asked. "They just lost their loved ones, yet they are partying and having a great time, not feeling any sorrow."

"There has been no time for that. We have constantly been moving," I said.

"Yes, I know, and no one is expecting you to leave anytime soon. Look at them. Look at all of them," he said.

I took a good look at my friends. They all seemed to be enjoying themselves. Kayella, whose side I had just left, had no sign of sorrow on her face. She smiled and laughed along with Zira, Bentum, Alecander, and the others at the table. Famous seemed to be in his own personal heaven, wrapped in Addison's arms. Linnayah moved around the dance floor with Hemmingway as if she had not a care in the world. I searched my own feelings for any sorrow for the death of those lost. I felt nothing.

"What is going on?" I demanded.

"It's Amaury's way of keeping the peace," Adam said solemnly.

"What do you mean?" I asked.

"Amaury is exercising his ability to control the environment or, should I say, controlling those in it."

"You mean he is controlling our minds?"

"More like masking them," Adam said, laughing in an attempt to cover the seriousness of the conversation. "By keeping emotions under control, Amaury can ensure a happier, safer life. A life that no one would want to leave and one that anyone would want to fight to remain in."

"Why are you telling me this? Why not Alecander or Zira or anyone else?"

"Alecander was not exactly the warmest in welcoming Addison and me into his room earlier. Bentum and Famous, as a result of Amaury's generosity, received body parts they desperately wanted. I do not know that they would be willing to listen. Kayella, well, she seems so fragile, and Linnayah has been at Hemmingway's side most of the night." My stomach tightened with his last words. "And Zira, well, since I have never been around a pregnant woman before, I just don't know how to deal with one."

"Zira does not have the plague. She is carrying children!"

"Sorry. It is just that she is also a bit rough around the edges. Honestly, I am afraid of her." I understood what Adam was saying. At first impression Zira did give off that feeling.

"Is anyone besides us aware of this information?" I asked as I patted Adam on the back, trying to look chummy.

"No, I don't believe anyone besides Amaury and Doc McGriffin, who I believe created the mind-masking serum, is aware of its existence. It is distributed in our drinking water," Adam said, throwing in a laugh for show when he noticed Amaury crossing over to the refreshment bar.

"How do you know all this?" I asked in an accusing tone.

"Lady Verleah had booked my sister and me for an early beauty appointment today. She instructed us to enter quietly without knocking so we wouldn't disturb her husband's meeting. We did as we were told, but Lady Verleah was not in her bedroom where she had told us she would be. We waited patiently for ten minutes before time became our enemy. We needed to stay on schedule or we would not get to everyone else who requested our services for the event. And, we always get to everyone.

"I told Addison to stay in the bedroom in case the Lady came in while I went out to see if I could locate her. I made sure to be very quiet as I did not want to disturb Amaury and his private meeting. The door to the backyard was open and I saw Lady Verleah in her garden. I tried to get her attention by waving but then I heard voices. Amaury and Doc McGriffin were sitting nearby. I backed up into the doorway when I overheard them talking about the serum. As soon as I heard enough, I ran up to the bedroom. Lady Verleah showed up two minutes later. It took everything I had to control myself!"

"The specialist?" I said, referring to Doc McGriffin.

"Yes. Apparently, he also specializes in toying with people's emotions."

"I have not met him."

"He is at the table furthest from us. The one by himself who is smoking," Adam said. Elderly and frail-looking, the doctor looked harmless. But if I had learned anything from my travels, looks can be deceiving.

"To feel no sorrow? Is that so bad?" I asked, questioning myself as I said it.

"This isn't a temporary thing! This is something Amaury plans on doing permanently. He plans on taking away all negative emotions: anger, disappointment, jealousy. It's not right! It just isn't right! Shouldn't a person be able to express how they feel? You may be Cresecren, and I may be Human, but here you will be nothing if you can't express yourself!" Adam's hand shook and liquid from his glass spilled on the floor in front of him. His smile was crooked as he held his glass up as if to toast me.

I followed his charade, tapping my glass to his and saying, "Yes! They should!" I held the glass to my lips but could not bring myself to drink. *This is madness!* "Have you told Addison?"

"I haven't and I don't plan on telling her," Adam said.

"Why would you not tell your own sister?"

"Addison hasn't always been the cheerful girl you see now."

I saw that she was still on the dance floor with Famous. They were drawing a lot of attention. Famous was getting used to his new legs quite nicely. He seemed to have no difficulty finding the rhythm of the music. They looked as though they had been dancing partners for years.

"Addison was severely depressed before we came here," Adam continued. "Every night was horrible. I'd fall asleep wondering if she was going to be there in the morning. It pains me to say this, but I got to the point of wishing she would be gone. I was beyond exhausted, always checking in on her, always making sure she didn't drink herself to death, overdose, or slash her wrists. The day Amaury found us he asked if we had any special skills. I told him that we were extremely good with beauty and fashion. Ever since we were little, we would get into our mother's things while she was away during the evening, making what we finally figured out was not an honest living. She was a lady of the night. I saw Novus as a new life, a new chance. A place where perhaps Addison could become whole again."

"What about your mother?"

"She died a few years before Amaury found us. Our father had left us long before that. But our mother did leave us what she thought was valuable."

"What was that?"

"She left all her gentlemen clients to Addison and to me she left Addison's distraught heart. That is why I cannot tell Addison. She has a purpose now. If we left, it would kill her. I can't kill my sister!" Adam could barely conceal his distress.

"But why are you telling me this?" I asked again.

"I think we better separate. I don't want any suspicions. Plus, I don't want to underestimate a man who has the ability to dull a person's emotions. I am telling you because I want you to remove something else from Addison's life that I do not think is good for her." He no longer forced a smile as he turned to watch his sister.

"Famous," I said. With that, Adam walked over to a small group of people. He laughed and smiled, as if our conversation had not just happened.

My head was spinning. What should I do with this new information? We had just arrived. I had just begun to see Novus as a place I could really start over with Linnayah, Alecander, and everyone I cared about. Where would we go next? I decided to let it go for the night. Let everyone enjoy themselves and relax. They deserved it. They needed it. In the morning, I would invite everyone to my room to tell them what they all needed to know.

I tugged on my pocket watch chain to remove the watch from my pocket. I had no intention of checking the time. I flipped over the watch to stare at the inscription once more. "Let your life begin." I squeezed the watch as if to crush it before placing it back into my pocket.

I searched for Linnayah. She and Hemmingway had stopped dancing. He whispered in Linnayah's ear before leaving her side. I wished I could have heard what he said. I was steaming under my jacket knowing that he was so close to her. I remembered that Amaury had said the garden looked spectacular at night. I saw my chance to ask Linnayah if she would like to go and see it. I made my way over to her, passing Adam. He did not look in my direction nor acknowledge my presence.

"No Hemmingway?"

"He went to the restroom."

"Amaury said the garden was spectacular at this time of night. He suggested we check it out. I thought you might like to come with me sometime tonight," I said.

"Sure. How about now?"

"What about Hemmingway? You seem to be enjoying yourself."

"I was until he wouldn't stop telling jokes and trying to make me laugh."

"What is wrong with that?"

"It is hard to hold a conversation with someone who doesn't take you seriously and turns everything you say into a joke."

"Perhaps he is nervous."

"A little tipsy maybe, but definitely not nervous! I have never met someone so full of himself. He actually told me that I was worthy of being on his arm! Come on, we can discuss Hemmingway's antics on the way to the garden," she said, taking my hand and pulling me toward the garden.

"But he will be looking for you!"

"Maybe, but if I am in the garden with you, he won't find me. And the joke will be on him for once."

"That bad, huh?" I could not suppress a grin.

"That bad!" Linnayah scooped up the bottom of her dress in one hand and took off toward the garden. I chased off after her. I slowed so I could take off my jacket and admire her from behind as she ran along in front of me.

"You let me win!" she said breathlessly, opening the doors to the garden.

"No, I did not!" I lied.

"Yes you did!" She was laughing as she turned around to face me. "You were on my heels plus you still had time to take off your jacket!"

"Okay, maybe I did let you win," I admitted.

"Humph!" she said turning back around to enter the garden. "Oh, Cayden! Amaury was right. It is spectacular!"

The doors closed behind us. Faux stars shone down upon us. Lights built into the pavement led the way through passageways in the garden. Twinkling tiny lights illuminated some of the flowers and plants, while their sweet scents were intoxicating. We absorbed the peacefulness with each deep revitalizing breath. Our hushed voices were the only sounds.

"Can I see your jacket for a moment?" Linnayah asked.

"Sure," I said, handing it to her. I thought maybe she had caught a chill. Instead, she tossed it right over my head.

"Hey!" I exclaimed, reaching up to yank it off.

"No! You can't remove it until you count to thirty!" She giggled. I remembered playing hide-and-go-seek with Bonjú, back in Kenosis. I smiled, anticipating the same game with Linnayah. Her shoes indicated the direction she was heading. *This will be easy.* She stopped and I thought she had found her hiding space. I finished counting and pulled the jacket from my head and headed off in the direction I had heard her take.

I followed the path for a short distance until I found Linnayah's sandals resting on a bench. *Clever! This will be harder than I originally thought.* I always did love a challenge, especially when there was a beautiful prize to be found. I searched around for her, looking behind bushes and trees.

"Where are you?" I called out, hoping for a giggle or some movement to give away her position. But there was only silence. I thought I saw someone holding a weapon. As I approached cautiously, it turned out to be a bronze statue of a gardener holding a shovel. I chuckled at my misjudgment. I walked closer to get a better look. I studied the gardener's face. He looked young and full of life. Linnayah leaped out from behind it, startling me. She grabbed my waist and we tumbled backwards as I lost my balance. She landed on top of me and rolled over onto the thick grass. We laughed. I adored the way her face lit up in the darkness. We stared up at the stars.

"I could lie here forever," Linnayah said.

"So could I."

Linnayah rolled over onto her side and propped her head up with her hand. I had a clear view of her face. There was a blade of grass on her left cheek. I reached up to wipe it away.

"Grass," I said as I swept it from her soft skin.

"Maybe I wanted it there."

"You could tell Havarty it is the latest fashion."

"You know, it would tie in well with his new line. We could call it 'Mixed Elements' and I am privileged to be the first one wearing it. See?" Linnayah pointed to her tiara and hair. "The leaves are of the Earth and the stars are of the Air."

"That explains why the women hovered around you when you first showed up to the party," I said.

"Yup! They were all interested in seeing what Havarty had created and if they could get their dresses altered for the next event."

I rolled over on one elbow to bring my eyes to Linnayah's level. "A woman can wear anything she wants but a man will still notice."

"Who says she's wearing it for a man?" Linnayah huffed. "Maybe she wants to look nice for herself. Not every woman needs a man."

"Sorry!" I said, rising off my elbow and holding my hands up in defense. I noticed my pocket watch had come loose from my pocket. I hurriedly shoved it back in as if to hide the inscription from Linnayah. I did not want those words to taint what was happening.

"Really though, Cayden, I could have come to this party wearing a garbage bag and you would have taken notice."

"Yes," I admitted and added, "I noticed you were a gorgeous lady with a slightly odd taste in fashion."

"You think I'm gorgeous?" She blushed as she rose off her elbow to a sitting position.

"Definitely," I said sheepishly.

"You are too cute! If Addison saw what you have done to your hair, she would probably whip out her comb and get right to work on the dance floor," she teased.

"It is your fault," I said, attempting to fix my hair. "You threw my jacket over my head and knocked me to the grass."

"So sorry for trying to have a little fun. Here, let me help you. You're making it worse." She leaned over and tousled my hair, pulling out a twig. She showed it to me and tossed it aside.

"Hey! Give that back! I was starting the transition to 'Mixed Elements,'" I said. She laughed. She traced my sideburn with her finger. She followed what she was doing with her eyes. I held my breath as she turned so that our eyes met. She leaned forward slowly and stopped short when we heard music. I wanted to find the speakers and squash them with my bare hands. I exhaled in defeat and watched as she turned her head to listen.

Linnayah said, "Slow music. They must play it for the plants. Did you know it has been proven that talking to plants and playing music to them helps them grow?"

"Wow . . . that is so interesting," I said sarcastically. She turned back to face me and smiled.

"Aren't you going to ask me to dance?" Linnayah said.

"Well, I thought about it earlier but I have never danced. And, well, there was the whole Hemmingway thing."

"There is NO Hemmingway thing," Linnayah said, annoyed.

"All right, I will dance with you, but not right here. Not in front of him," I said in a serious tone, pointing at the statue of the gardener.

Linnayah laughed. "Come on," she said, grabbing my hand. "I saw the perfect place." She led me past the statue and behind a tree to a more private grassy area. "Is this better?"

I pretended to be looking around to see if anyone was watching. "It will do."

"Good!" she said, letting go of my hand and sliding hers up to wrap it around my neck.

"Wait!" I said, removing her arm from my neck gently. "I should probably remove my boots or you may not be able to walk back to the party."

"I do want to keep my toes," she teased. "Hurry! Get those things off before the song is over. They may not play another."

I tore off the boots and tossed them by a small bush of white daisies. I smiled as I hurriedly picked one. I was sure Linnayah had not seen my action. I stood up with one arm behind my back and the other stretched toward Linnayah. She took my hand and placed it on her hip, then gestured for me to give her my other hand. I slowly brought it around, revealing the white flower. Her eyes grew larger in delight and she covered her lips with her fingertips. I placed it in her hair behind her ear. She took my hand in hers and we started to dance. Just as I began to catch up to the rhythm of the music, the song changed. I clumsily adjusted to the new beat.

"Relax, Cayden, you're not letting yourself enjoy the moment," Linnayah said. She was right. Instead of living this moment to its fullest, I was worried about stepping on her feet or throwing her off the beat. My shoulders were so tense and hunched that I looked like a soldier in battle rather than a man dancing with a lovely woman.

"Sorry, I am new at this," I said apologetically.

"Just close your eyes, let the music inside your soul, and relax," she said soothingly. Linnayah's beauty was distracting. The way the corners of her lips turned up in a soft smile as she spoke made me feel lightheaded. I closed my eyes and breathed in slowly, trying to match the rhythm. It worked. Within a short time, I felt more confident. *What's this?* I could feel Linnayah's hand loosening in mine. I almost opened my eyes, but I decided against it. She led my hand gradually to her waist. I was a bit confused by this move but I did like where it was going. She then removed her hand from mine and gradually moved it up my arm, causing the hair on it to rise at the sensation. She pulled her body closer as she slid her hand up onto my shoulder. I still did not want to open my eyes. I was afraid it would ruin the mood or, worse yet, discourage her. We danced this way until she slid her hands up behind my neck, pulling me in even closer. I could feel her warm breath on my neck.

"Hey, Linnayah! You in here?" My eyes flew open as a male voice rang through the foliage.

"Hemmingway!" she whispered, annoyed.

"He must really want a dancing partner," I said, trying not to sound disappointed.

"I have your shoes," he continued. "I know you're around here somewhere! You're not hiding from me, are you?"

I bent down reluctantly to put my boots back on as Linnayah went to reveal herself to Hemmingway and retrieve her shoes.

"There you are!" Hemmingway said. "What are you doing out here alone? Waiting for me?" I tied my first boot as if it had done something wrong to me. I began tightening the laces of the other in the same manner.

"Thank you for my sandals," Linnayah said.

"I went to the bathroom, came back, and you were gone!"

"Did you stop by the bar too? Goodness, Hemmingway, you reek of whiskey!"

"Liquid courage!"

"For what?"

"To do this!" Hemmingway said to Linnayah as I finished tying my shoe. My heart raced as I heard her struggle and squeal under his alcohol-laden lips.

I tore past the tree like a tiger on the hunt and spotted Hemmingway pushing Linnayah against the statue. One filthy hand grasped her buttocks. She struggled to free herself from his embrace. I knew that Linnayah could fend for herself, but I could not stand to see her like that for one more second. I tore Hemmingway off Linnayah and hurled him to the ground.

"What'd you do that for?" Hemmingway whined.

"I would have just as soon have punched you but I am hoping you are one of those people who will wake up tomorrow from your drunken state and regret what you did here!" I shouted.

"Are you okay?" I asked Linnayah and noticed her rubbing

her back.

"Yes, I'll be fine," she assured me as her eyes grew wider. She shoved me aside and kicked an oncoming Hemmingway between the legs. He dropped to his knees with his mouth hanging open and his face scrunched up in agony. His hands cupped the injured area.

"Damn, Linnayah!" Hemmingway gasped.

"You think just because a girl dances with you, it gives you the right to grope her? You're lucky that kick was not full force. Remember that next time you think about doing something stupid like this again!" Linnayah grabbed my hand and pulled me away from the wounded man. Once we were back on the path, she let go of my hand. I worried that was the end of the fairy tale moments we had just shared. I found a little comfort in knowing she was using both hands to rub her back. We stopped by the entrance to the garden, where I asked her to wait while I retrieved my jacket.

"Did you want to go back to the party?" I asked her.

"No, I'm going back to the hotel. I need to get off my feet. Would you like to come with me or would you rather ask Kayella to dance some more?" Linnayah asked, looking away from me.

"There is only one person I want to dance with and she cannot do that right now in her injured state," I said. She smiled at me and took my arm as I led her back towards her room.

FEELINGS

WHEN WE REACHED Linnayah's door, I was not sure what I should do next. Linnayah relieved the awkwardness. "It's still early, would you like to come in?" I nodded, trying not to look too eager.

"I never did thank you," she said as she kicked off her shoes.

"Not necessary."

"Thank you," Linnayah said, placing one palm on my chest. She stood on her toes to kiss me softly on the cheek. She paused for a moment before dropping back down to the floor. I stood frozen, wondering what it meant. *A thank you and a simple gesture from an appreciative woman. That is what it meant.*

"Make yourself comfortable, take off your boots if you'd like, and stay awhile." I took off my jacket and hung it over the back of a chair, then removed my shoes. My socks were dirty from our garden entertainment. I rubbed my feet together to try to dust them off.

"It was fun while it lasted," she sighed. "I just wanted to pretend a little longer. Pretend one evening that I was someone else. Havarty said he had never seen anyone so excited about the whole process of getting ready for the event. He said I was the perfect person to wear a particular piece he was working on. I told him I didn't want him to go through all the trouble since he already started working with me with the lilac gown. Havarty said that it wasn't any trouble and that it would please him if I was the first to wear it. It sounded so glamorous! I couldn't resist. I can't remember the last time I felt that kind of anticipation and excitement," she said dreamily.

"I know what you mean."

"I think I will get out of this dress but I am leaving the tiara on a little longer. I feel like a princess." She giggled.

While I waited for Linnayah to change, Hemmingway consumed my thoughts. I wondered if he was simply an unpleasant drunk or a pompous jackass. I heard Linnayah howl from the bedroom and I rushed to the door.

"Are you all right?"

"Yes, sorry. I tried to get this thing off over my head and I twisted my back while doing it. Geez, it really hurts!" she said.

"Can I do anything to help?" I asked. I cursed Hemmingway under my breath.

"Um, just a second. Step inside the door but keep your eyes closed."

"Okay," I said, doing as she asked.

"If you peek, Cayden, I swear I'll do what I did to Hemmingway to you!" she warned.

"I know you will."

"I'm going to stand in front of you and you are going to lift this dress up over my head, okay?"

I gulped. "Just let me know when." I heard her dress swishing as she walked toward me. Linnayah took my hands and placed them on either side of her dress.

"In a second, just pull straight up and I will get one arm out and then the other." I nodded, gulping again.

The procedure went smoothly until a small grunt escaped her lips. "Sorry!" I said.

"It's okay. It's not your fault," she said. "You can turn around and open your eyes. I'll be out in a minute. Thank you for helping."

I opened my eyes after I was facing the opposite direction and fought the urge to look back. When I remembered what Linnayah did to Hemmingway, it made the decision much easier. "Do you need help getting your clothes back on?" I could not help asking.

She laughed. "I think I'll be fine."

"I was not trying to be funny," I said, feeling offended.

"It's just that men usually ask if they can help take your clothes off, not put them back on."

"I suppose you are right," I said as I left the room, feeling uncomfortable. She giggled again.

Wearing a silk lilac camisole with matching silk pants, Linnayah emerged a few minutes later. "Havarty sent these over. You probably have a pair in your room, too."

I grinned. "I hope mine isn't EXACTLY like yours." She

laughed.

"The color just is not right for my complexion," I said in my best Havarty impression.

"You're silly!" she said. She crossed the room to sit on the couch next to me. As she sat down, she grimaced.

"May I take a look?"

"It's fine really but you can take a look at it if you want." She turned so I could see her back. I lifted her camisole up over a raised pink area that was beginning to bruise.

"He must have pushed you pretty hard," I said, lowering her camisole.

"I felt a jagged part of the statue pressed against my back," Linnayah said.

"Let me see if I can find anything that will help," I said, leaving her on the couch to search the medicine cabinet in the bathroom. "Found something!" I called back. It was a soothing pack. "I am going to hold this on your back. It will be very cold," I warned. She nodded before I gently lifted her camisole.

"Thank you."

"You are welcome. Tomorrow we can have Doc Ace look at it if you like, just to be sure you are really all right."

"No, thank you! I'll be fine. I do not want to be anywhere near where Hemmingway might be." I did not blame her. I did not want her to be anywhere near him either.

"All right," I agreed.

"I have to apologize to you about something," she said, still facing the other way.

"You do?" Linnayah turned to face me. "Hey, I cannot ice your back while you are facing me," I said.

"Here," she said, taking the pack from my hand and leaning back against the couch to trap the cool pack in place.

"Good idea," I said, not really meaning it. I tried hard to contain my disappointment. I wanted to keep icing her soft-skinned back.

"Although I still think you and Kayella make a cute couple, it was none of my business to try to get involved. You two seem to be getting along nicely. She was a little braver than I had imagined. Going to your room last night—"

I interrupted her. "You are right about it being none of your business but you are wrong about Kayella and me. We are nothing more than friends. What you may think happened last night certainly did not!"

"That is what Kayella told me this evening, too," Linnayah said. "Actually she told me much more than that."

"Did she?" I was extremely interested.

"Besides the usual mind-your-own-business stuff, Kayella told me to be true to my own feelings. She also told me I couldn't control whom I fell for and I couldn't make anyone love anyone else."

"Sound like pretty sound advice."

"Yes, but the truth is that I am not ready to be true to my feelings."

"Why not?" I tried desperately not to sound disappointed while remembering Kayella's thoughts about Linnayah's feelings toward me.

"I don't know. I'm afraid, I guess. Afraid things will get complicated if I unleashed those feelings."

"I can understand those fears," I said sympathetically.

"I can handle myself, you know, I mean like fighting or fending for myself. I don't want to lose the security of not having to worry about someone else. Love can make you vulnerable."

"You were going to take your friend Kiara on your journeys if she agreed to leave the Market with you that day. You were willing to look after her," I said.

"I know, but she didn't leave with me and I don't have to worry about her. I started to think it was best for me that she stayed because survival would be easier. I am only responsible for myself. Then I met all of you . . . Zira, Kayella, Bentum, Alecander, and even Famous." She paused. "And you. You are all finding places in my heart. Part of me wants to flee but a bigger part of me wants to stay. You all are the closest thing I have had to a family in many years. You remind me of what it used to be like before all the chaos, before my parents died. Tonight was the first time I really felt like Novus could be a place for us to have a chance at a normal life."

I felt like a lowlife for holding in what I had just learned about Novus from Adam. *How could I tell her after what she just confided in me? But how could I not?* I struggled with what to do. Linnayah adjusted her tiara and I decided to let her be the princess she deserved to be for one more night. I would tell everyone before breakfast, and then they could make their own informed decision about Novus.

"I am not sure what to say," I told her honestly.

"Don't say anything. I like how everything is right now. I like just being here with my friends."

Although I wanted more, I did as she asked. "I will always be here for you."

"Thank you," she said.

I stayed with her for a while, talking about things like our favorite colors or favorite time of the day. We kept our conversation light. When Linnayah grew weary, she took the daisy from her hair and placed it on the table next to her. She then took off her tiara and put it next to the flower. I stood up and let myself out so she would not have to get up. As I left the room, I reminded her I was just across the hall if she needed anything. Linnayah smiled and thanked me before I closed the door. I leaned against her closed door for a moment, taking a deep breath. As soon as I had the chance, I detached the pocket watch. I thought about throwing it down the hall and watching it shatter into pieces as it hit the wall. Instead, I dropped it into a dark-colored vase before entering my room.

INFORMANT

I DID NOT sleep well. In my effort to let everyone get the rest they needed and enjoy one more night here in Novus, I neglected to grasp the toll it would take upon me. I woke early and called everyone to my room before breakfast.

"What do you want?" Famous said.

"I have some news. Well, some information on this place called Novus," I said. I clenched my fists as I anticipated how the conversation might go.

"What kind of information?" Alecander asked.

"The kind that could change your opinion about Novus . . . about Amaury," I said.

"Oh, get on with it!" Famous scowled.

I avoided eye contact with Linnayah as I told them everything Adam had said to me. To spare Famous' pride, I withheld the reason why Adam chose me.

"That's ridiculous!" Famous retorted.

"Maybe it isn't," Zira said. "I haven't felt much sorrow for Jinjo since shortly after arriving here. Even now, as I speak, zere seems to be a mask."

"I haven't thought of Aurora much either since our arrival. I haven't felt the ache of her being gone. I haven't even thought about why I haven't felt anything. Why can't I feel any sadness?" Bentum said.

"It is the first step in suppressing what Amaury considers negative emotions," I said.

"Sounds like he is trying to create a type of utopia," Alecander said.

"When did you find this out? Last night at the party?" Linnayah said.

I was forced to meet her eyes. "Yes." I confirmed what she already knew.

"Why did you wait until now to tell us?" Linnayah said, sounding agitated.

"Let me ask you all a question first," I said, pausing for any other comments but everyone was silent. "How did you all sleep last night?"

"Fine," Kayella said.

"Like a rock," Bentum answered.

"Best sleep I have had in days," Zira said.

"When I was done entertaining Addison, I was out cold," Famous said. The ladies grimaced.

"I fell asleep where you left me and didn't wake until this morning," Linnayah said with a stinging tone. I knew I deserved it. I had had plenty of opportunities to tell her last night, but I just could not bring myself to ruin the evening.

"I slept well too," Alecander agreed.

"You all needed that rest desperately. You did not need a reason to get riled up. What harm did it really bring any of you? If it makes you feel any better, the burden of carrying the information was almost intolerable. I barely slept," I said.

"Well, I am not staying here. That's for sure. No one is going to play God with me," Famous said.

"I agree," said Bentum. "People have taken enough rights away from our kind. I will not let them take my feelings too."

"I'm leaving too. I don't know vhat effects his potions vill have on zee babies," Zira said.

"I sure as hell am not staying here!" Linnayah's words shot fire. I hoped that she would learn to forgive me.

"Then we leave today," Alecander said. "I would rather take my chances out there than become a puppet for someone else's amusement in here."

"I'm not leaving," Kayella said in a small voice. We all turned to look at her in bewilderment. "Nothing you will say will change my mind. Don't try to convince me otherwise."

"Why on earth would you want to do that?" Famous as usual said exactly how he felt.

"I do not see the harm in it, that's all. I want to stay. There is food, shelter, and a comfortable atmosphere. I feel safe here. So what if Amaury is trying to create the perfect environment? It's more than most people outside of Novus are trying to do. Most people in the Den create a negative, hostile environment. I like not feeling sorrow. I like closing my eyes and actually going to sleep. I like feeling like a part of a functioning society.

This is the most fun I have ever had in my life. Amaury was telling me they could find a job for me. Maybe I could work alongside Havarty. He said he could use an assistant. I am great at being someone's assistant. You all know that. Besides, if I leave, I know I am as good as dead. I don't ever want to feel that kind of terror again. I AM NOT LEAVING!" We could not ignore the seriousness of her plea.

"Well, stay! I'm not telling anyone how to live their life and neither should any of you. Otherwise you are no better than the Humans who created us," Famous said.

"He's right," Alecander stated.

I did not know how to feel about Kayella's decision. How could we leave her behind? But then again, how could we ask her to come with us? I was not sure if Kayella referred to her being unwilling to fight or if she was talking about falling victim to emotions and the effects they would have on her. Either way, the outlook for her if she left Novus was grim.

"For my sake, I would prefer if you didn't say why you were leaving. I don't know if Amaury plans on revealing what he is doing but I don't want to cause a disturbance," Kayella said.

"Give the girl a pit and she'll ask for the whole peach," Famous grumbled.

"That is fine with me. We will leave Novus without causing a stir," Alecander answered for everyone.

"Whatever you say, boss," Famous mocked.

"What about my hearing?" Bentum said. "I do not want to lose it again. I just got it back!"

"Holy crap, how could I not even think about my legs! The hell I'm giving my legs back! I'm not giving back these runners without a fight!" Famous slapped his thighs with both hands.

"We will talk to Amaury calmly and rationally, telling him of our plan to leave and Kayella's plan to stay. We will see what Amaury has to say about his very generous gifts," Alecander said.

They were gifts. Would Amaury ask for them back if we were leaving Novus? The devices must be very expensive. There would be questions if anyone found out about the aid Bentum and Famous received. Amaury would not want the secret of Novus to get out.

"I vant to clear somezing up," Zira began. "I know some of you might be vondering how much affiliation I have vith Zee Truce. I am not affiliated vith zem at all. It vas Jinjo vho gave money to zee cause against my better judgment. I heard stories of a place vhere Humans and Cresecrens alike could call home. Alzough I vas not against zee idea, I vas also not for it. I had only met Amaury once before vhen he came to collect vhat Jinjo had pledged. It vas vhat Jinjo and I argued about last. I do not expect you to believe me, but I trust zat you do, or else I vould not be here now standing amongst you all." I recalled how angry Zira was with Jinjo the day I met them.

"You have not given us any reason to mistrust you, Zira," I said.

DEPARTING

WE TRIED NOT to be obvious about not drinking any tainted liquid. We did not want Amaury to know why we were leaving Novus. Alecander, Bentum, and I met with Amaury and Lady Verleah after everyone had eaten. We thought it best to leave Famous out of the—hopefully—civilized discussion. Alecander took on the role of the group leader.

"We would like to thank you sincerely for all that you have done for us: providing us a place to safely recuperate, showing us your hospitality with the lovely party, bestowing gifts greater than we could imagine," Alecander began.

"You sound as if you are leading up to a negative. Are you planning on leaving us?" Amaury sat up in his chair. Lady Verleah turned from us to look at her husband. Her face held a glint of concern.

"Yes, with one exception," Alecander said.

"Oh. Who has decided to join our Novus?" Amaury looked toward his wife as if to let her know everything was under control. She faced us and attempted to relax.

"Kayella. She wants very much to remain here. The rest of

us would like to press on. We have business to tend to in the outside world," Alecander said.

"I see," Amaury said, contemplating. "Well, you are free to leave. Naturally, Novus will be sorry to see you go but will be eagerly awaiting your return." Alecander glanced at me and Bentum shifted his feet. Amaury understood the uncomfortable silence. "You do not plan on coming back, do you?" His last word carried a higher pitch.

"No," Alecander answered.

"Well, I am glad one of you decided to join us here in Novus," Amaury said. "It was a pleasure having you with us. Please take what you need before you go as I am sure your travels will be challenging. Know that you are ALWAYS welcome back."

"We appreciate that," Alecander said. "We know you want Novus to remain a secret. I give you my word that we will not share its whereabouts."

"I am sure you will not," Amaury said confidently. "When do you plan on leaving?"

"Today," Alecander said.

Amaury sat back in obvious disappointment. "I had hoped you would stay a little longer."

Lady Verleah called for Henner using her skeleton key ring. He appeared with a look of disapproval when he saw us. "Henner, our guests will be leaving us," she said. "Go and fetch Synda and prepare food packs and water rations immediately. Leave the packs in the hotel lobby within the half-hour."

Henner replied, "Yes, Lady Verleah." A small smirk appeared on his face before he disappeared. *What did this man have against us?*

"I will personally escort you to the Keeper and he will show you on your way. I will be in the hotel lobby in a half hour," Amaury said, looking at his watch.

"Thank you," Alecander said.

"What about my listening devices and Famous' new legs? I suppose you will want those back," Bentum asked, sounding worried.

"They are gifts. Think nothing more of it," Amaury answered.

Bentum let out a deep breath. "I wish I could repay you!" he exclaimed, obviously relieved.

"In a way, you already have. You brought Kayella here. Now our family has grown. There is no greater gift you could have given me," Amaury said, sounding pleased.

We retreated to our rooms to collect our weapons. We left Kayella in the lobby talking to a young woman with a long scar across her face. I wondered how she acquired it. There was a knock on my door. I opened it to find Kayella and Synda. They each grabbed one of my arms.

"There is no time. We must get the others!" Synda said. I looked into her deep violet eyes and saw that she was terrified.

"Wait!" I said, prying myself from her grasp. I snatched Mercy off the side table and grabbed my satchel. Kayella banged on Linnayah's door. "What is this about?" I demanded.

When Linnayah opened the door, she frowned at Kayella. "I was trying to relax for a few minutes before we had to leave. Who knows how long it will be until I can do that again?"

Kayella grabbed her by the arm and pulled her into the hall. "We have to go . . . NOW!" Kayella pleaded.

"I thought you were staying," Linnayah said, confused.

"Get your weapon! You are going to need it," Synda said convincingly enough for Linnayah to disappear momentarily before returning with her staff.

Kayella and Synda had already gone down the hall knocking on the other doors. I was surprised to see that Alecander was in Zira's room. Synda rushed us all there.

"Now tell us what is going on!" I demanded.

Synda said, "Please, you must all go—"

Famous interrupted her. "That *is* the plan. Didn't you hear?"

"I don't mean with Amaury! You will surely die if you do that. I'm foreseeing my own death in speaking to you now. I locked Henner in the refrigerator. It is only a matter of time before Amaury discovers him. Amaury isn't planning on you leaving alive."

Growing clammy and lightheaded upon hearing those words, I forced myself to focus on the conversation.

"Why would Amaury want us dead? He said we were free to go," Alecander asked.

"You really think Amaury would let you leave Novus with all your knowledge and the costly devices he gave you?" she said.

"Surely, there have been others who have left freely," Alecander said.

"That is just it. There has only been one who wanted to leave Novus and never return. As soon as he stepped out of Kenosis, he was murdered. A few have the privilege to exit to the outside world and they are sworn to secrecy to protect Novus and they always return to it. Those select people stand to lose a lot if they ever break that promise," Synda said.

"What is Amaury's plan for us?" Alecander asked.

"Please, if we stand here we will all die, which would defeat my purpose for being here now," she said, moving toward the door. "No more talk. Follow me."

"Why should we trust you?" Famous said.

"Because I wasn't the one who poisoned your food packs in case you survive the ambush Amaury is planning. Henner is guilty of that," Synda said, opening the door and stepping into the hall. "We must move quickly!"

"What is Henner's problem with us anyway?" I angrily blurted out.

"He can't help it. It isn't his fault. Doc McGriffin recently diagnosed Henner with Paranoid Personality Disorder. Basically he believes you all came here to harm or exploit us. Instead of getting help for Henner, Amaury uses him to his advantage."

"That is just not right!" I said, with sympathy toward Henner replacing the anger.

We followed her down the stairs into the lobby. There was

only a young couple who sat in the corner lip-locked and paying us no mind. We walked across the lobby, calmly pretending nothing was amiss. We almost made it to the door when we saw Addison through the front window. We paused but Synda hissed, "We must keep moving!" Addison walked in past her. She raised her eyebrows when she saw Famous.

"I ran into Terra and she told me you were leaving. I had to learn the news from a child. You were just going to leave without telling me?" Addison's voice cracked.

"Look, Doll, I kinda don't have a choice here," Famous said.

"We have to go now!" Synda said, sternly looking down the street. The kissing couple stopped and looked at us. One was the young woman with the scar Kayella had been talking to earlier.

"I'm real sorry, Addison, but I have to go," Famous said, moving past her.

"Then I'm going with you," she said.

"What?"

"You heard me!" she said, following us out of the building.

Famous looked defeated. "You're not going to make this easy, are you?"

"That's just it, Famous. I'm not going to be anyone's easy anything! I'm coming with you!" Addison stomped her feet like a two-year-old about to throw a tantrum.

"Okay, okay!" Famous said as Synda picked up her pace.

"This is madness. We are about to walk right past Amaury's

residence. What if he sees us?" I said.

"Oh, so you don't want Amaury to know you are leaving? How would you like it if I began to scream?" Addison said, puffing up her shoulders.

"No! Addison. Shhhhh!" Famous said, cupping his hand over her mouth and drawing the attention of a passerby. Famous let her go right away. He gave her a hard kiss on the lips to appease the passerby, who had stopped dead in his tracks. Addison became molasses in his arms. I rolled my eyes. The passerby continued on his way. "She's coming with us!" Famous' tone was so final that no one replied. Addison silently gloated at her victory.

"We aren't passing Amaury's house, but we must hurry inside the Delivery Post," Synda commanded.

"This is a fine time to be mailing something!" Famous said.

Synda ignored him as she paused at the Delivery Post door and lowered her voice, "Once inside we must detain the worker." She swung open the door and we followed her in.

"Hi, Synda!" the woman behind the counter said.

"Hello, Blynn," Synda replied.

She was our old Supply Appointed, whom Alecander had replaced. We thought she and her assistant, Phillip, whom I had replaced, had been transferred down south to the new Cresecren ground. She recognized us and looked as though she had seen a ghost. "You are not dead?" Blynn cried.

"No, and you are not working down south in the new Cresecren grounds with Phillip," Alecander said.

"I did go with Phillip. Then Amaury helped me fake my own death so I could join him here. Phillip was here, too, for a while but he has since returned, choosing the old way of life. He was so set in his ways. That old man," she said, smiling.

"We didn't see you last night. I thought everyone went to those shindigs," Famous said.

"I wasn't feeling well. I am much better today. So what are you all in here for?" Blynn asked.

Synda glanced behind us and said, "Now! There isn't a moment to lose."

Famous let go of Addison's hand, jumped over the counter, and wrapped his arms around Blynn. Alecander ran around the other side and grabbed some wire hanging on a hook. Blynn shrieked, confused by what was happening, and tried to escape from Famous' arms.

"We don't want to hurt you, Blynn. Please be still," Alecander said. Blynn stopped struggling as Alecander pried Famous from her and sat her gently on a nearby chair. He glared at Famous.

"What is this all about?" she demanded as Alecander tied her hands with the wire.

"We want to leave but Amaury will kill us if we try. I have news for you. Phillip never made it to where he was headed," Famous said coldly.

"Don't be ridiculous!" Blynn said. Her graying hair flew back and forth as she shook her head. She looked to Synda for an explanation.

"It is true," Synda said. Blynn swallowed hard as she looked back at us. The disappointment in her eyes was grueling to watch.

A high-pitched voice startled me. "Hi, Cayden!"

I swung around, lifting Mercy. I saw little Terra standing near the door. I lowered my weapon.

"Hi, Terra," I said calmly.

"What you doing?" she asked.

"We were just about to mail something." It was the first thing that popped into my head.

"Oh, really? What are you mailing?"

"Um . . . " I looked around for someone to help me out.

"Aren't you supposed to be in school or something?" Famous asked.

"There's no school today, silly. It's Saturday!"

"Well, you should be running along," Famous said. "We grownups are very busy. We don't have time for children right now."

Terra pulled in her lower lip and bit it. "Okay." She turned to leave.

"Terra," I called gently after her. She turned slightly. "Can you please not tell anyone you saw us here? What we are mailing is a secret," I said, smiling tenderly. Terra nodded and left quietly.

Seconds later, we heard a commotion from outside. A group of men and women ran toward the Grand Hotel. They did not appear to be armed but as the last of them ran by I saw the edge of a sharp object poking out of his sleeve.

Synda pushed Blynn aside. Behind Blynn were numbered parcel boxes. Synda pulled a key out of her pocket and opened number 11. The box appeared to be empty.

"You have a key to that box? I always wondered why we didn't," Blynn said.

"Hurry, Synda!" I cried.

Synda put her hand in the box and pushed against the back. It slid inward. Part of the wall to the left side of the boxes opened, revealing an exit.

"We go now!" Synda commanded.

Synda led the way. Alecander made sure Zira, Kayella, and Linnayah entered before he followed. Bentum was right behind. Addison ran past Famous before he had a chance to stop her. Famous ran in after her, saying, "Woman, you are impossible!"

The front door swung open and a young man clutching a blade rushed in. As I pulled Mercy's trigger, he threw it. I ducked. A second later my arm seared in pain as my attacker fell convulsing to the ground. Amaury trained his men well. The young man's dagger had found its way into my left shoulder. An instant later, Amaury came into my view. He paused upon seeing me, his vengeful violet eyes glaring at me. I am sure what he saw was anger masked by sheer fear. I only got a glimpse of his massive gun. It looked like it could drop a horse. I bolted to follow the others. The passageway door closed behind me and I could hear Amaury thrashing against it on the other side. I had a vision of the silver *N* resting on Amaury's

cheekbone. It stood as a bold reminder of what he would protect at any cost. I knew it was only a matter of time before we
would meet again.

LOSS AND LOVE

As I contemplated pulling out the blade, I was thankful it had not hit any vital organs. Regardless of the pain, I did not think I could actually bring myself to kill anyone. I still could not bring myself to switch Mercy to kill mode. I tried to rotate my arm and found I could barely move it. My shoulder seared with pain. Blood soaked through my shirt. I wiggled my fingers to ensure there was no serious nerve damage.

I hurried on behind the others, constantly looking back. It was still a shock to see Famous running and moving so quickly down the hall. He looked back and saw my injury. He sprinted to me and pushed me in front of him without saying a word so he could help me if I collapsed.

We followed Synda up a flight of stairs. Famous said, "If I was still in that wheelchair this would have been a bit of a challenge."

I swung Mercy over my other shoulder as I climbed the stairs, using my right arm to grab the railing. I lost my balance. I tried to grab on to the railing with my injured arm, yelping in pain as I stretched to reach it. This caught the others' attention.

They stopped and turned to look at me. I heard them gasp.

"I am fine. Really. Keep moving!" I ordered, trying to look as though there was not a three-inch blade stuck into my shoulder.

As I stepped off the stairs, a ground-shaking blast erupted behind us. I knew it was Amaury's way in. *So much for peace inside the Novus walls.*

I looked back and saw Famous trying to regain his footing on the stairs. I grabbed him instinctively with my right hand and grasped the railing with my left. I screamed in agonizing pain. He clutched my arm as I pulled him up.

Synda yelled to us, "It isn't much further now!"

We came to another door. Synda hurriedly punched in a code. It opened within seconds and we emerged into sunlight. We could hear our pursuers below us. We had to keep moving. I heard weeping. I knew at once that it was Kayella. Things could not have been more crushing for her. I recalled her response in Kenosis when Lace attempted to hand her a weapon. Kayella had refused it and crouched against the wall, holding her knees up to her chest and slowly rocking back and forth. I felt the need to protect Kayella and keep a watchful eye out for Linnayah. I knew Linnayah could take care of herself but I wanted to make sure that when she was ready, I would have the chance to tell her how I felt about her. The sun blazed and I regretted not drinking some of the water Henner served at breakfast. My mouth was dry and beads of sweat were already rimming my brow. Of course, the hot pursuit was adding to my sweltering. The pain in my arm started to fade as it was almost numb.

"You don't look so good," Famous said to me.

"I can honestly say I have never felt worse," I said feebly as my stomach churned.

"Here, let me help you," he said, words I do not think I have ever heard Famous say to another living soul. He took Mercy from my shoulder and slung her over his own. I would have fought him for her if I had the strength. Famous pulled me toward him and wrapped my good arm across his shoulders, which helped me press on.

"Thanks," I said.

"We must move toward the hills and take cover. It is our only chance at survival!" Synda shouted.

I had to keep moving but there was something wrong, something terribly wrong. I could not feel my left arm and shoulder any more. I contemplated saying something to Famous but ultimately what could he do to help? He was doing enough already.

We began climbing a hill and I slipped. I almost took Famous down with me but he pulled me back up. Kayella was no longer crying but I still heard her sniffling. *How could I tell her looking like this that the outcome of this day would be positive?* I tried to stand up straighter but my efforts were thwarted. I could no longer feel my hands and fingers. I attempted to wiggle them once again only to discover they would not budge. I felt a tightening in my upper chest. Fear took over and I began to panic. My breathing grew labored.

"Cayden, you all right?" Famous asked, sounding far away. I turned my head to confirm that he was still supporting me. His face faded in and out with every step we took.

"We must take cover and protect ourselves!" Alecander shouted.

Addison ran to Famous' side. She was saying something but I could not understand it. All I knew was that she was pointing to my shoulder. I looked at it and saw the blood was now taking on a hint of blackness. *Poison!* I had heard of the poison, Widow's Shadow, but had never seen it in action. I knew there were only two cures: cutting off the poisoned limb before it contaminated other body parts (most importantly the heart), and death. The knife must have been laced with the deadly poison. Everything around me went black.

I gurgled as I came to. I was alone. I heard gunfire and shouting. Our pursuers were upon us. *Wait! I was alive and my breathing was no longer labored.* A metallic taste filled my mouth. Suddenly, I wanted anything to drink. I would have drunk stagnant water if it were at my feet. I attempted to sit up and felt something in my right hand. *A flask!* I sniffed the contents of the bottle and finding no foul smell, took a swig. *Water!* Cool, refreshing water caressed my tongue and lips. I drank until the flask was empty. As I set it down, my chin dripping wet, I closed my eyes for a second and concentrated on feeling my arm. I was overwhelmed with excitement when I could. I had heard of phantom limbs and wondered if that was what I felt. Had someone taken my arm?

I prepared myself for the worst as I turned my head, and was shocked to see my arm still intact. The sleeve of my shirt had been torn off and the blade removed. Something iridescent masked my injury. It was the same substance Lace had used the day we met her to seal the door of the tunnel to Gavaron. Someone had used it now to seal my injury. I bent my arm gently and wiggled my fingers to test my motor skills. My arm was a little stiff but otherwise functional. I noticed Mercy perched at the end of my fingertips. I stared at her for a long moment as I refocused on reality and the sounds of battle. Beneath those sounds, I heard uncontrollable soft crying. *Kayella!*

She was hiding behind a large boulder. A series of bullets took off a small portion of the boulder in front of her, shattering into hefty shards on the ground. Kayella screamed. I swung over and grabbed Mercy with my right arm. Her attacker was moving steadily toward her, firing his triple-barreled gun in her direction. He was toying with her. I propped Mercy up and lined him in my sights, but my vision was still hazy. The indigo ray whizzed by the man's face, drawing his attention to me. I swallowed hard as he swung his weapon in my direction. He had figured out that Kayella was no real threat and I was the one he needed to destroy first.

I prepared to fire Mercy again, hoping this time she would find her target. It would be a shame for someone to have saved me only to die now. I blinked, trying to focus. In that brief second, Lace mounted the man's shoulders and drove a blade into his chest. It was the same blade that had pierced my shoulder. The man fell lifelessly to the ground and Lace scouted her surroundings like a lioness surveying her kingdom. Her aunt Concora appeared in my peripheral vision. Lace met my eyes and gave me a quick encouraging nod before stalking her next victim with Concora by her side.

I felt groggy as I stood. It dawned on me that Concora and Lace were supposed to be acquaintances or maybe even friends of Lady Verleah. Why would they be helping us? I had no idea. But my immediate goal was to reach Kayella and make sure she was all right. I would also be on the lookout for Linnayah, Alecander, and the others. *They have to be okay!*

I shook my head vigorously, trying to get a better grasp on reality. It seemed to help. I could see Kayella's feet and ankles. They had not moved since I focused on them. My heart sped up as fear engulfed me. *She has to be all right!* I still had not had the chance to tell her things were going to be fine. I took longer strides toward her all the while scanning my surroundings. I could see weapons firing, hear gunfire, and was comforted to see Alecander was still alive. I saw Concora and Lace but no one else. Alecander had recently fired his bow and it was returning from its target. My stomach turned and I choked down bile as I white-knuckled Mercy's handle. Somewhere in the chaos Famous shouted profanities. *Shut up, Famous! You are making yourself an easy target.*

"Kayella!" I called as I rounded the boulder. There did not appear to be any sign of trauma but she did not acknowledge me. I stared at her chest and watched as it rapidly rose and fell. *She was alive!* "Kayella!" I said again, this time in a softer voice as I squatted to her eye level. She did not flinch. She was dreadfully pale and her eyes held a hollow stare. Kayella was in shock.

"Kayella, it's me. Cayden," I said as calmly as possible while I tried to line my unfocused eyes up with hers. I quickly scanned the area to make sure we were safe before meeting her eyes again. I thought about the words I wanted to say even though I did not know if they were true. I said them anyway. "Kayella, listen to me, everything is going to be all right." My vision returned fully but Kayella did not. I took her face in my hands. Despite the hot weather she felt cold. I repeated myself. If she heard me, she gave no indication. I could not leave her yet I could not let the others fight alone. They needed my help. A woman's bloodcurdling scream jolted me. *Please, not one of ours!*

I did not know the first thing about battle. I had had a day of training back in Kenosis with Lace when she gave Mercy to me. I also had the hour in Amaury's training area with Alecander, but neither was enough. I had speed but that was useless if I tried to pull Kayella to safety. I also had to find out if my companions were okay. I heard rustling in the bushes behind me. I swung Mercy in the direction of the sound, ready to fire. I contemplated shooting blindly but disregarded that thought immediately.

A voice from the bushes hissed, "It is Amil, Lace's brother. Do not shoot!" His hand emerged from the bushes followed by the rest of him. I was relieved to see him. He whispered, "I will take Kayella to safety and then rejoin you in battle. This is a war we cannot lose." He bent down to pick up Kayella. Before the bushes concealed him, he looked back at me. "You have a gift of sight. Use that to your advantage."

I peered around the boulder. I saw the two men who had been with Concora on the day that she ambushed us. I watched them take down one of the enemies with their bare hands. But then the smaller one, who had hit me over the head that day, fell face-first into the dirt, a blade sticking out of his back. A few yards away, a man I assumed to be his killer ran from the scene without looking back. He was out of sight before I had a chance to react.

I almost felt fully recovered. I took a step out and saw Bentum struggling with a man who was ripping at his ears. Alecander hit the man from behind with his shoulder, knocking him to the ground. Bentum grimaced in pain, grabbing at his ears. The man dropped tiny silver disks and stomped on them. Bentum's face filled with rage as he pounced on the man, mercilessly punching him in the face. Alecander pleaded with him to stop but Bentum was unstoppable. Alecander and I finally pried Bentum off the man, who lay cowering on the ground.

Lace and Concora approached us. Suddenly, the man Bentum had been pummeling pulled out his knife, but instead of attacking us took off running toward Novus. His foot caught on uneven ground. He tripped and fell onto his blade. I cringed and vomited at the sight of blood gushing from his body.

I wanted nothing more than to be in the safety of Kenosis with Linnayah and my companions. We could play hide-and-go seek with little Bonjú and push the images far from our minds. As I envisioned Kenosis, I worried again that I had not seen Linnayah, Zira, Famous, Synda, or Addison in quite some time.

"I last saw your friends headed this way. The mouthy one who now has legs and the woman who clings to his arms," Lace said as if she heard my thoughts. "We must find them and head to the safety of Kenosis."

"What about Linnayah, Zira, and Synda?"

"I have not seen Linnayah or Zira."

"I am sure they are fine," Alecander said, trying to reassure me. "They can handle themselves."

That knowledge did not ease my mind. We moved toward where Famous and Addison were last seen. We passed dead bodies, apparently the victims of Bentum's mallet. My stomach heaved as I choked down what little I had left in it. The noises of battle and struggle seemed to have subsided.

"What about Synda? The Cresecren woman," I asked Lace. "Tell me she was not harmed! She helped us leave Novus. She risked her life to save us."

"Synda is dead," Lace answered, looking away from me.

"Who killed her?" I said. When Lace did not respond or look me in the eyes, I grabbed her upper arm to force her to look at me. It was a stupid reflex. I knew she could kill me with little effort but I had to know how Synda died.

She looked at me solemnly. "I have lost dear friends, too. I do not wish to lose more, so we better keep moving," she said quietly. She was right. We needed to get out of there or risk being overwhelmed by the size of the force Amaury would gather.

"It won't be long until the next strike," Concora said. "We must move now!"

We found Famous bent over someone whom he seemed to be strangling. We rushed to his aid, ready to assist him. But instead, he was administering CPR to Addison. I was stunned to see that he was crying. I did not know he was capable of such emotion.

"I told her not to come with me. You all heard me, didn't you?" he said. "Why didn't you listen to me, Addison? You should have stayed with your brother! Adam could have protected you!"

He bent down to listen to her heart. We all stood perfectly still so he could hear the faintest of sounds. "Addison, please get up!" Famous turned and said to Lace, "Give her some of that voodoo medicine you gave Cayden."

The mystery of why I was still alive had just been solved. "It cannot bring people back from the dead," Lace said gently.

"Give it to her!" Famous commanded, his eyes burning into hers.

Lace bent over Addison, feeling for a pulse on her neck. She put her cheek to Addison's lips, to see if she could feel any breath.

"She is no longer with us."

"Give her the damn purple potion!" Famous thundered.

"It won't do any good and it is all I have left. It must be saved."

"Please!" Famous pleaded.

"I cannot help you. I am sorry."

"She does not lie to you. The girl cannot be helped," Concora said. "The elixir must be saved."

"Those bastards killed her! They were her friends but they had no problem killing her," Famous raged, holding Addison's hand.

"They did what they believed they had to do to protect Novus," Concora said.

I thought about her brother Adam and his attempt to save her life, only to have it end tragically. *How would he take such news? Would he remain in Novus without her?* No doubt he would hear a different tale of her death than the truth. They might even say she was killed by Famous himself. I hoped for Adam's sake he chose to stay in Novus, as only death awaited him outside those walls.

"We must go!" Lace said, looking over her shoulder.

Amaury and a number of his followers approached. I recognized Crowley, whose wild pink mane stuck out even from a distance. I had had a pleasant, albeit brief conversation with him the night before. Now he would kill me if he got the chance. Suddenly Crowley, then a second later the man beside him flew sharply backwards and fell to the ground. Someone had taken them out from long range. Amaury and the others fired blindly in our direction.

Even amid our extreme danger, though, I could not bring myself to move Mercy off taze mode. I aimed for Amaury but missed. I was much better at hitting a stable target. Our hidden sharpshooter took out two more of Amaury's men. Amaury was infuriated by the shot I had fired at him. He took aim at me. I backed up into Bentum, who was readying his own weapon. As I did, I shot again and hit the gun of a woman who had run up beside Amaury.

The impact knocked her into Amaury, who staggered and pushed her off. Then he grabbed the side of his neck as blood gushed from it. I am certain Amaury would have been dead if I had not interfered. It threw the sniper's aim off, wounding Amaury but not killing him. The woman stepped in front of Amaury to get a better view of his injury. A moment later, she collapsed onto Amaury and fell to her death.

Amaury bent down to rip off a piece of her vest and applied it to his injury. It was instantly drenched with blood. He gestured to his followers to continue on and they obeyed. But many were cut down and the rest retreated to safety. He glared for a moment in my direction, then turned and fled with the others. I had a feeling it was not the last I would see of Amaury.

Famous bent down and lifted Addison. He stumbled and refused anyone's attempt to help him.

"I have my horse. If you carry her beyond the hills, he will take her the rest of the way to Kenosis," Lace told Famous.

Famous reluctantly let Alecander carry Addison part of the way to a chocolate-brown gelding tethered to a tree. As we approached the horse, a large blade whizzed by Lace and embedded itself in the tree. The gelding bucked. Lace pulled the blade out of the tree, causing bark to fall at her feet. She scanned the area. Alecander set Addison down to free his hands.

From the woods came a figure I recognized instantly. Fear consumed my limbs. The Keeper of Novus stood before us.

"I'll take care of this," Lace said. Before anyone could react, she ran toward him to match wits in combat. Bentum raised his mallet but Concora pulled his arm down quickly. She shook her head, telling him that this was Lace's fight.

Lace raised the knife and charged toward the Keeper. He remained motionless. I worried that if he did kill Lace, he surely would kill us as well. I grasped Mercy, hoping to give us a fighting chance at survival. If I sensed that Lace was losing, I would not hesitate to fire.

Lace flung the dagger. The Keeper stood his ground. *Was this man looking to die?* He caught the knife by its handle as it missed him. *How could she have missed?* Lace continued to charge and pounced at his neck. He grabbed Lace around her waist and interlocked his hands. I watched in horror. He had the strength to squeeze her to death.

I was stunned by what I saw next. He slid his hand up to the nape of her neck. Instead of crushing it, he lovingly stroked her long curly dark locks.

"Is that . . . laughter?" I whispered to Concora.

"Let Lace have a moment. She has not seen her husband in months." She took the gelding's rope from the tree.

"Her *husband?*" Famous repeated. "I thought he died? That is not the same man in the picture."

"The man in the portrait was Lace's first husband, Bonjú. This is Lace's new husband, Kai," Concora explained. It made sense. Little Bonjú was named after his birth father. "Help me put the woman on the horse."

"The woman's name is Addison!" Famous spat.

"Addison will have a proper burial in Kenosis," Concora said to Famous soothingly.

I had never seen Lace's face so radiant. She was beaming. I imagined little Bonjú would also be excited to see him. Thinking about seeing Bonjú again made me smile.

When Lace and Kai approached us, their demeanor seemed to soften. My companions and I still had our reservations. Why was Lace's husband working for Amaury? I knew if they wanted us dead, they would not have fought to save us.

Famous whispered to me, "What the hell is going on here?"

"I wish I could answer that. But, for now, I think we should go with them. We really do not have a choice. Besides, if they wanted to kill us, we would be dead already. They helped us against Amaury's men."

I grabbed Bentum's shoulder and let him know we were continuing with Lace. His head was wrapped with a piece of cloth. I smiled encouragingly. When I was certain Bentum was no longer looking, I said, "I wish you could still hear me, my friend."

I had to ask Kai about Linnayah and Zira.

"The two women you speak of are in grave danger. I fear they will not make it through the night," Kai said.

"What do you mean? Has Amaury taken them back to Novus?" I balled my fists and felt the blood rush to my head.

"I fear it is much worse than even that."

I glared at Kai, angry at his vagueness. I could not stop the growl that broke from my throat. "Where are they?"

"She who fills your heart with desire is in the soiled hands of the Pillagers. Lady Verleah saw to it that they came for her."

"Easton!" I hissed. Suddenly, it all became clear. Somehow Lady Verleah knew about Linnayah's jaded past but she never said anything to Amaury or anyone else.

"The outside of the train cars are equipped with surveillance devices," Kai continued. "She learned all she needed to know about Linnayah the night you arrived." I felt violated, knowing that the way I remember those special private moments atop the train car would forever be changed. "Lady Verleah could not risk Linnayah's kind tainting Novus. Your friend's past was too sordid for even the Lady to feel she could reform her," he added.

"But Linnayah was trying to make a better life for herself! She was looking for her own Novus," I cried. I turned to Alecander and said, "I have to find her. I have to help her get that second chance."

PILLAGING PILLAGERS

Alecander always seemed to understand me. Though he did not know the whole story about Linnayah, he still trusted me. He also knew how I felt about her. I could not let her die and I could not let Zira die along with her. Linnayah had said she needed a friend and I was that friend. From what I knew about friends, you did not forsake them.

"Then we go together," Alecander said firmly.

"This Easton, he won't kill them right away," Kai said. "The girl has something he wants. He will make her pay for what she has taken. The other woman is merely a pawn in his game and will be tortured. She will wish for death before it inevitably comes."

Death! There was that word again, haunting me to the depths of my being. I was determined for it not to prevail.

"If it wasn't for Lady Verleah watching from afar, I would have attempted to rescue them. The Lady would have had us surrounded in seconds. There are eight of them: six men and two women. I hesitated in sending them toward Kenosis but I wanted to slow them down. I told them there was a shortcut through the east side of Kenosis to their destination," Kai said slyly.

Lace smiled. Kai's misdirection could give me time to catch up with them. Especially if they ran into any challenges that Kenosis could deliver. I turned to Bentum and explained everything. I told him he should go to Kenosis with the others. He shook his head and said, "Linnayah is one of us now. I am going with you."

"You are not leaving me out of the action!" Famous added.

"I'll take Addison home," Concora said. "My duty is to protect Kenosis. As for the rest of you, I will see you at the dinner table. Your plates will be set, so do not disappoint me."

"We will not," Kai said.

I was glad one of us was that confident. When the adrenaline slowed down, my knees began to knock together. Beads of sweat covered my brow. It took everything I had to ignore what my body was doing.

"I believe we can catch them before too long. We know a *true* shortcut," Kai said.

"If you can keep up," Lace teased. I got the feeling she was directing her comment at me. I recalled I almost got my head lopped off trying to race her before. "Remember, as we approach Kenosis, stay in my path." She would not have to tell me that again.

We all took off in Lace's footsteps. I was not sure what we would meet. But I had never felt so much a part of anything in my life.

My life ran like a movie through my head as we searched for Easton and his small army: the time with the Rawnetts, playing chess with Alecander, the night on the top of the train with Linnayah, our dance in the garden. I chose to hang on to that blissful moment when I held her and felt the warmth of her breath on my neck. I could almost feel the heat of her body next to mine. Knowing Easton would not let Linnayah or Zira go without a fight, I struggled to hold on to the feeling of her warmth. Famous' new legs made it easy to keep up. With a few more weeks of practice, he would be a worthy adversary in a race. He might even win.

We could hear yelling in the distance, a quarrel between a man and a woman.

"It is surprising they made it this far," Kai said to us.

I could see them. They were stopped. We kept ourselves hidden and made as little noise as possible.

"They are on riders," I whispered to Kai.

I admired the polished bronze vehicles. Riders could carry one or two people and were capable of extreme speeds. They moved effortlessly through the terrain, either on the ground or slightly above it.

"How could we have possibly caught up to them so quickly?" I asked.

"Because we know the land and they do not. They have met obstacles to get here. I see they are down a man and a woman and one rider," Kai said.

Kai was right: there were six people left. A couple of them

looked as if they were mending wounds. One of the riders' rear wheels sparked neon red, which indicated it was damaged. Another rider had a metal storage carrier just big enough to hold Linnayah and Zira. I knew Linnayah's tongue was as sharp as a serpent's as she spat words to the man who approached her. I assumed it was Easton. He slapped the top of the carrier as if he were quieting dogs. He held a ragged cloth.

"I have never heard you speak so many words!" he said. "Frankly, I liked it when you just shut up and did what you were told! But, I have the feeling THAT Linnayah is gone now! Torturing you will be much more pleasurable than I had anticipated!"

I thought Easton was going to open the carrier to gag Linnayah. When he did, we would have a chance to rescue them because Zira and Linnayah would help us outnumber them. We split into pairs. Bentum was to shadow Lace. Famous was with Kai and Alecander would follow me. Kai would lead us and confront Easton, demanding the return of Linnayah and Zira. Kai advised us to avoid more bloodshed.

I wondered if Easton had led some of his people into the craft the very same way as Linnayah. They could share similar heart-wrenching stories and were not killers but merely survivors.

I kept those thoughts with me as we approached them from different angles. Lace partnered with Bentum. Kai advised Famous to grasp his right shoulder and not let go no matter what. Kai told Alecander to do the same to my shoulder.

"Well, then, lead the way," Alecander said, placing one hand firmly on my shoulder and drawing his crossbow with his other.

Easton was my main focus. My eyes darted about instinctively, watching the Pillagers for any indication they were aware of our presence. Silence surrounded us. I could hear nothing, not even my own footsteps, nor my own heartbeat pulsing in my eardrums. I felt Alecander's grip tighten on my shoulder. I fought the urge to look back at him and continued to focus on the enemy. I looked toward Kai and Famous. They continued to press on, their weapons at the ready. Soon we would all be out in the open.

In the distance, I saw two enormous mountain lions approaching fast. Their teeth jutted out of their black lips as I heard their vicious growls deep within me. I knew Alecander saw them, too, as his grip tightened on my shoulder.

I no longer saw anything but the glorious creatures. I closed my eyes hard, clenching them tightly before reopening them. I hoped I would once again be able to discern the difference between reality and the unwanted fantasy realm.

When I reopened my eyes, I could see everything else as it was seconds ago, relieved that the lions were no longer present to increase the danger. My hearing returned to normal. I heard my pulse beat heavily in my ears. My shoulder burned with the clenching of Alecander's fingers. I turned my head to examine him. His hand was steady on the trigger. I gasped as I saw him aiming his weapon in Bentum's and Lace's direction where I had seen the lions approaching. I swung around with my right side and came down hard on Alecander's bow as he pulled the trigger. My shoulder seared from being ripped from his grasp. The arrow whipped through the back of Lace's hair. She swung her head in our direction.

"Retract!" Alecander summoned his arrow.

I did the first thing I thought of to make Alecander follow me. It was insane and stupid but I had no other choice. I grabbed his crossbow. I knew if I could get the crossbow away from Alecander he would desperately want it back to protect himself. Hopefully I could get him to follow me toward Easton. The arrow startled me as it reentered Alecander's crossbow.

Alecander did as I hoped and continued to stay close behind me as if seeking cover while reaching for the crossbow. It must have been a sight to see from afar. Under any other circumstances, it certainly would warrant a chuckle. I had to get him into the safe realm, the reality realm, and then I knew I had to do something drastic to bring him back. I only hoped our friends would get to Easton before we did.

Lace ran forward off to my side and Bentum broke off a few yards to the side of her. Bentum's mallet hovered near his waist. It was difficult to steady Mercy and keep Alecander's crossbow away from him. Thankfully, I had speed.

Easton undid the lock of the carrier. Linnayah seized the opportunity to use her feet to kick the door against Easton's chest, knocking him back. By now, Easton's crew had seen us and drew their weapons, waiting for their leader to tell them their next move.

"You have got to be joking," Easton said laughing as he regained his footing. Linnayah was out of the cage. Zira had her legs dangling over the edge, ready to drop to the ground. Easton had drawn his gun and aimed it at the women. His eyes kept darting between Kai and Famous and Alecander and me, unaware of Bentum and Lace. I hoped it was a good time to bring Alecander to reality. I did not have much time nor did I care whether or not the lions still appeared to him. I came to a dead stop and swung my arm back as Alecander crashed into me. He was still crouching as he moved forward and I hit him hard in the side of the face.

"Sorry, my friend," I said, still looking forward and hoping that his face did not hurt as much as my arm throbbed.

"Thank you, I think," Alecander said, snatching his cross-bow.

Lace had already taken down one of Easton's men. He lay motionless next to his rider. A young woman cradled her injured arm as Bentum guarded her. She obviously had no fight left in her.

Feeling more secure with Alecander standing next to me, I looked in Kai's direction. He said something to Famous, who held his weapon ready. Linnayah and Zira were free of their temporary holding cell but they were still held captive by Easton and his gun. One of the three men near the front spotted Lace and Bentum, warning Easton who quickly repositioned himself. He kept the gun pointed at his captives.

"Let me tell you how this is going to work. I'm gonna be generous and give you back this dark-haired beauty but I'll take Sweet Pea off your hands," Easton said.

I watched Linnayah scowl at hearing her unwanted nickname. The way he said it made my skin crawl.

Kai spoke. "We will be taking both women with us."

"Look, I have no fight with you. What do you want with her anyway? She'll rob you blind when you look the other way and leave you after you take her in and give her everything she needs to survive. That's how she repays kindness."

"Kindness!" I could not stop myself from interrupting. "You think killing a child's parents and kidnapping her is *kindness?*"

"I see it more as I took a fragile girl out of a destitute situation and gave her strength to really live," Easton barked.

My finger played with the trigger of my gun. I even contemplated switching to kill mode.

"You are sick!" I said.

"You must be lover boy, Cayden, right? Lady Verleah told me about how Linnayah got all sentimental and opened up to you. It must have been such a romantic sight: the two of you under the moonlight on a train sharing your innermost secrets!"

My face flushed with anger. The moments Linnayah and I shared would now forever be tainted.

"Sweet Pea, why don't you tell Cayden now how I taught you to survive, put food in your hand, a roof over your head, and a safe place to sleep. Also, tell him how you repaid such kindness by stealing from the very person who gave you life. The way I see it, I gave you your life and I have every right to take it away," Easton said, moving toward Linnayah.

Linnayah spat in his face. The man deserved much more, but the gesture confirmed how we all felt about him. Then she did something that shocked us all. She apologized. Her harsh look grew softer as she said, "I'm sorry! I shouldn't have done that. Easton, please forgive me!" Easton looked just as shocked as everyone else.

"You're damn right you shouldn't have! I have a mind to pistol-whip you!"

"Please, don't do that. I'll give you what you want, but please promise me one thing," Linnayah begged, her eyes glistening with moisture.

"I don't promise anything! Sweet Pea, you of all people should know that."

"I didn't quite tell you the truth when I told you I didn't have the money any more."

"How so?"

"Yeah, how so?" Famous, as usual, had trouble keeping his thoughts to himself. I too wondered where the money was.

"Once you have what you want, you leave us be," Linnayah said.

"Where is it?" Easton demanded.

"Cayden, give Easton the money before someone gets killed."

I had no idea what she was talking about. *Was she trying to get* me *killed?* I searched her eyes for an explanation. She lowered her hand and pointed toward the side of her waist. *When did she have time to put anything in my satchel?* It did not feel any heavier than usual.

I unhooked my satchel from my shoulder. I looked once more at Linnayah. She motioned to me with her lowered hand to toss it to Easton.

"Hand it over gently," Easton said.

I took a few cautious steps forward.

"Don't give him the money, Brainless! Once he has that he's going to kill her," Famous shouted.

Easton grinned. "Your friend's right, you know."

Bentum smashed his mallet down on the back of a rider. The injured woman at his feet let out a startled shriek. I swung my satchel over my shoulder with all my might, propelling it toward Easton.

Linnayah shot forward with a kick to Easton's back, pushing him in Lace's direction. The satchel hit Easton's chest and the strap slapped him across the face before it fell open onto the ground. Lace ran toward him. In all the confusion, Easton managed to hold on to his gun and fired a single shot at her. She lay motionless on the ground.

Kai cried out her name and all became utter chaos. Bentum ran to Lace's aid. I fired Mercy toward Easton when I thought I had a clean shot. Zira had a mission of her own: to disarm him. As she dashed toward Easton, my shot found her instead. She fell, her body shaking violently. *Zira! The babies! What have I done?* Easton chuckled. Linnayah rushed to comfort her. The only thing I was thankful for was that I had had the sense not to turn Mercy on to kill mode. If anything happened to the babies, I would never forgive myself.

I heard yelling and commotion up ahead and knew without looking that Kai and Famous were engaging in battle with the other Pillagers. Alecander fired his crossbow. I felt its arrow whiz by my right ear and hit the injured woman, who had drawn a blade and aimed it toward Bentum as he knelt beside Lace. The woman slumped over and fell onto Bentum's back. When Bentum saw the arrow in her chest, he looked up to thank Alecander. Alecander said "retract" to his bow. The arrow ripped from her chest, splattering the ground with droplets of blood as it cleaned itself before reentering the crossbow. I felt my blood drain from my face. *Alecander had killed someone!* The Den was a far more dangerous place than I had ever anticipated.

Easton grabbed Linnayah's hair, pulled her up against him, and jammed the gun to her head. They struggled. Her defiance only caused Easton to press the gun deeper into her temple. Easton squeezed Linnayah tighter around her neck. Her face reddened as she fought to escape his hold.

"Stop! She cannot breathe!" I shouted.

"That's the idea, Violet," Easton called back to me. Singling me out as Cresecren made me loathe him even more. "I'm getting on this rider and you are going to let me leave or you will be responsible for Linnayah's dying here today."

Linnayah attempted to shake her head, but the movement was so slight I barely noticed what she was doing.

"Don't worry, Sweet Pea. If you pass out, I'll take GOOD care of you," he said, brushing his lips against her cheek. It made my skin crawl. I gripped Mercy tighter and did not take my eyes off Linnayah. I wanted to remove this evil from Linnayah's life once and for all. She could not start her life over as long as he was alive. He would always be looking for her. I did not have a clear shot. I was not about to risk repeating what I had already done to poor Zira and her unborn children.

Easton stepped back and pulled Linnayah against him. "Look! This is the way this is going down. I am going to get on one of these riders and ride on out of here and you are going to let me do it or it's simple—she dies."

I took a step forward. "You will not get your money back that way."

"It's beyond money now, it's the principle. Besides, my luck brought me another big score on our last moonlit outing. Fools were acting and living like they had squat when all along they had enough money to hire protection. Bet they wished they had paid for that protection before they died! It still blows my mind as to why they chose to live the way they did. Living in squalor, pretending they didn't have much. I'm still kicking myself for not asking one of them before I made damn sure no one would ever know the answer."

"You are insane!" I yelled. I watched as he inched closer to the nearest rider. I knew just how capable he was of cold-blooded murder.

"Drop your weapons!" he shouted. "I said drop them or she dies right here! Right now! My getaway would be much easier if I killed her now." His backside bumped up against a rider.

Alecander growled to let me know he did not like Easton's demand. I agreed but could not take the risk of losing Linnayah. I tossed my weapon as far as I could to the side. Alecander sighed and followed my lead. His crossbow landed right next to Mercy.

Easton's eyes followed each of my friends' movements, making sure they disposed of their weapons. Zira was still shivering on the ground. Easton knew she was no danger to him. Bentum, upon seeing what Alecander and I had just done, tossed his mallet aside and it landed hard into the dirt. His face was stern and angry as he held Lace's head steady. I was not positive, but I believed I could see her chest rising and falling. My heart skipped a beat at the possibility of her surviving and seeing her with little Bonjú again.

Famous' eyes met mine. I was sure he could read the determination and pleading in my eyes as he reluctantly tossed aside his handcuffs. They had proved to be a worthy weapon. Kai was not so easy to convince. He held his knife tightly.

"A stubborn one, aren't we?" Easton chuckled. "Cayden, it's time to say goodbye to your girlfriend." Easton turned to look me dead in my eyes as he pressed the end of the gun into Linnayah's temple. She grimaced from the pain and reopened her eyes to look into mine. She was telling me goodbye. It was worse than any torture I could ever physically endure. My body began to shake as I thought about her dying, right then, while I watched. She looked so terrified. A lump filled my throat. I did not want to be without her. My eyes welled up and for the first time in my life, I felt as though I would cry.

I barely breathed as I pleaded, "Please, if it is revenge you seek, kill me. I will die in her place." I meant it. Linnayah jerked at my words. I wanted Linnayah to have her chance at her Novus even if it meant I would not be there to see it. *What had I ever done with my life to try to better it? At least Linnayah had made the effort to become a noble person.*

"You would die for a Pillager? The world really is full of fools," Easton said. "Tell you what, first I shoot her then I'll kill you. You'll die together, Romeo and Juliet, forbidden lovers."

I stopped breathing and locked on Linnayah's crystal blue eyes, knowing full well it would be the last time I looked into them. I could not believe this very man killed her parents years ago, sparing Linnayah's life then only to take it now. No one should have so much power.

"You are no god!" The words fell from my lips.

"Your choice of words is odd for your last ones. Shouldn't you be professing your love or saying your goodbyes instead of wasting your breath insulting me?" Easton asked.

I did not even have time to think about what I would say to her. I opened my mouth, wanting her to know how I felt. It sickened me that it would be the only time I would have to tell her. I could not believe it would be how she found out how I felt about her.

"I—" I began.

An object flew through the air, catching a glint of the sun before it punctured Easton's arm. He howled in pain and released Linnayah. She pushed back against him, knocking him hard onto the rider. I sprinted towards her as she ran towards me. My heart leapt as I recognized the blade as belonging to Lace. She was sitting up. My attention quickly turned back to Easton, who had already mounted the rider. I knew I had to pursue him. I could not let him get away. He would forever be looking for revenge.

I grabbed Linnayah's hand and gave it a squeeze. Alecander had already reached our weapons and tossed Mercy to me. He shot his arrow at Easton and it skimmed the bottom of the rider as it passed beneath.

I pulled Linnayah closer and kissed her on her forehead. Her grip tightened on my hand as I reluctantly pulled it away to pursue Easton. He already had a good head start. My only hope was that the land would play its mind tricks on him.

"I'm going with you!" Linnayah said, grabbing my hand again.

"But you are safe now!"

"You won't be if you go after him alone!" she cried.

I started to tell her no. She ran to the broken rider, retrieving her staff. I knew I did not have time to argue with her and she would not let me go alone. I caught a glimpse of Lace and she showed me where the bullet had impacted one of her iridescent spheres. The shield spread across her torso, capturing the bullet before it could do any serious damage.

I mounted the first rider I believed to be working even though I had never driven one. Linnayah wrapped her arm around my waist as she swung her leg over the rider. Starting it was simple, getting it to go anywhere was another story. I recalled a story Famous had told about a midnight ride with Quinso Vardo. He had never ridden one before either but Quinso had just received his new toys and wanted to take them for a ride. Famous said it was so simple even a four-year-old could drive it.

"You have never driven one of these before, have you?" Linnayah asked.

"No," I replied as I figured out how to get it moving.

"Don't look back at me. Keep your eyes where you are going!"

I yelled back to Linnayah, telling her to keep her eyes closed and sing a song to help distract her. I also wanted her to close her eyes to keep her from worrying about my driving. I would worry enough for the both of us.

"You'll be sorry you asked me to do that," she said in all seriousness.

FACE TO FACE

IT WAS NOT long before I saw Easton. Just as I did, Linnayah took her arm off my waist so I automatically slowed the rider.

"Don't slow down, keep going!" Linnayah sang off-key. I could not keep a smile from forming on my lips.

Easton was an experienced driver and weaved in and out of trees and around bushes with ease. I, on the other hand, often scraped against them. Each time I did, Linnayah sang even louder and more off-key and squeezed my waist tighter.

"Sorry!" I said.

"If you want me to stop singing just say so!" she sang.

I worried about what I was going to do when I caught up to Easton. Then he began swaying back and forth, ducking and swatting frantically at the air in front of him as if fighting some invisible foe. *Here was my chance*! I could handle what he might be seeing; however, Linnayah would be of no use. I slowed the rider enough for her to jump off. She had her staff in one hand, the reason she had been holding onto me with just one arm. When I was sure she was fine, I sped forward.

"You better come back!" she shouted.

"I will!" *I hope!*

Easton continued to battle his invisible foes. Agonizing groans escaped his lips as he raised his injured arm to defend himself. He grabbed the blade stuck in his upper arm, howled as he ripped it from his flesh, and began slicing the air. I tried to clear my mind by closing my eyes and then reopening them. I hoped to erase the images and noises that were attacking Easton before they started to attack me. As I approached the back of Easton's rider, it came to a sudden stop. Whatever Easton was battling had his full attention. The anticipation of seeing what Easton was fighting terrified me. I slowed my rider as I lifted Mercy and took aim. I knew I needed to fire before Easton's attackers began to strike me. Nothing mattered more at that moment than survival. I switched Mercy to kill mode but I could not make my finger pull the trigger. No matter how evil Easton was, he was still a man.

As I approached Easton's rider, I saw myself in the side mirror. The intense and weathered look on my face startled me. Easton's image took over the mirror and I watched him smile. He spun around and fired in my direction. As I saw the corners of his mouth turn up, I impulsively jerked the rider to my right. The bullet grazed my armpit and I winced. Easton had no qualms about killing me. He was not fighting any invisible foe but was just plotting against his real enemy: me. The man was not only devious but was cunning as well: he had ripped the blade from his own flesh and put on a believable show of fighting an invisible evil while plotting to kill me.

I fired Mercy at Easton's rider, blasting a hole in its tail. The rider wobbled uncontrollably, sparks flew, and I heard a high-pitched hissing noise as it short-circuited. The rider flung Easton up and over the front end where he plowed head-first onto the rocky ground. Lace would have been proud of me. I dismounted my rider cautiously, approaching Easton's motionless body like a hunter anticipating retaliation from an injured but still dangerous prey. I kept Mercy aimed at him.

I nudged him with my foot, half-expecting him to swing his gun around and fire. At such close range, Easton would not miss. I raised my free hand and wiped away a drop of sweat from my brow. Easton shifted his body and raised himself slowly, holding his injured arm. His gun lay near his feet. I kicked it away. It smacked against a large rock. I breathed easier, knowing it was out of his reach.

"Aren't you going to help me up, Violet?" Easton said sarcastically. He faced away from me, which made me suspicious.

"The day will never exist when I would do that," I said as I gritted my teeth. "I prefer that you stay where you are."

"You're not thinking of shooting me, are you?"

"You leave me no choice. Even with the promise of letting you go, you would never stop looking for Linnayah."

"You are right," he said. I shifted uncomfortably. "Before you decide to take my life, may I at least stand? You will want to look me in the eye when you kill me. Shooting me in the back is the mark of a coward. Are you a coward, Violet? Let me leave this world with my dignity intact."

Easton's chatter made me nervous. I did not trust him. Before I could answer, I heard rustling behind me.

"Cayden, you are not a murderer!" Linnayah's said. I felt her gently touch my shoulder.

"I have no choice," I said, looking at the back of Easton's head. Once again, I shifted uncomfortably. Mercy shook in my hands.

"You always have a choice, Cayden. Lower your weapon, Cayden. This is my fight, not yours."

"You are not a murderer either," I said, reminding Linnayah that she never intentionally killed anyone during those dark nights spent pillaging. She had killed in self-defense only. She fell silent and seemed to be thinking about what I said.

"While you two forbidden lovers try to figure out who is going to send me over to the other side, I'm going to stand up so I can die like a man," Easton grunted.

"You are not a man!" Linnayah said. I imagined Easton in his monstrous pillaging form with his saline-injected face and wished that he appeared that way now. Maybe then I could pull the trigger. I imagined all the people whose lives he had taken or destroyed, all the devastation he had created, and how killing him would rid the world of such an evil being. Linnayah was right; I was not a murderer. I lowered Mercy as Easton got up from his knees, still holding onto his injured arm. I looked at Linnayah. She paused briefly before lowering her staff.

Just before Easton jumped to his feet, he turned his shoulder slightly toward us. I caught sight of his bloody arm. *Lace's knife*! I had all but forgotten about it. It was no longer stuck into his shoulder.

It all happened so fast: Easton let go of his injured arm, spun around, and raised the blade. It caught the sun and the reflection was blinding. I fired Mercy instinctively and watched, horrified, as Easton grabbed at his heart and fell backward. Strands of his hair were flung across a rock. I gasped as I backed up and swallowed hard. My mouth was as dry as the barest of deserts. I dropped my arms and Mercy fell to the ground.

I do not know how long I stood there. Seconds turned into minutes as I stared at Easton's body, searching for some sign that I had not killed him. When I came out of my trancelike state, I realized Linnayah had cupped my face in her hands and turned my face towards her. I saw her lips move but her words did not register.

I squeezed my eyes shut, then reopened them and tried to focus on Linnayah's soft lips. I began to hear her words as if someone was turning up the volume in my head. Her voice grew louder and louder.

"You are not a murderer," Linnayah said adamantly. "Do you hear me? You are *not* a murderer!"

I still could not speak. Instead, I nodded my head slowly. Linnayah's lips curved into a small smile and she kissed me gently on the cheek, then pulled her head back so she could look into my eyes. Her touch seemed to be my lifeline, pulling me back to reality.

"What was that for?" I asked.

"Saving my life."

Alecander had been standing behind us. He gave me a look of encouragement and squeezed my left shoulder.

"It has been a very long morning. Go back the way you came and meet up with the others. Kai and I have this under control," he said.

I nodded.

Kai bent down toward Easton's body. I watched as he checked for a pulse, knowing full well he would not find one.

"What happened to the rest of his crew?" I asked.

"We sent them on their way. I don't think we will have to worry about them any more. They will not know what to do without their leader," Kai answered.

"Why do you suppose Easton did not just try to outrun us on his rider?" I asked Linnayah.

"Because his pride was more important than his survival and he underestimated us."

EPILOGUE: FAMILY

Kenosis was just as we had left it. Bonjú greeted us with warm hugs and sticky hands. Elza purred at Famous and rubbed against his legs. Famous sat down gingerly on the couch holding his side. Elza leaped into his lap and began licking his wounds. It shocked us when Famous did not push the cat away. By evening, Kayella had pulled herself together and warmed up to Amil, who had been caring for her since he carried her back from the battlefield. I was truly grateful for that.

"What are you doing?" I asked Linnayah, who was pushing a chair up against a wall and reaching for the portrait of the late Bonjú. Everyone turned their attention to her.

She turned and gave me a wink as she flipped over the portrait to show that it was lined with money, lots and lots of money.

"Well, hot damn!" Famous exclaimed.

"When did you have the time to put that there?" I asked.

"When you were sleeping. You are a very hard sleeper," she giggled.

"Why would you leave it here? You did not know you would ever be back," I said.

"No, I didn't. But I wanted to give back, I wanted to be sure Bonjú had a good life, much better than I did."

Lace walked over to Linnayah and embraced her.

"You haven't gone soft on me, have you?" Famous said, bending down to rub behind Elza's ears. She purred louder. "I bet Addison would have really loved you."

Just before sunset that evening, we buried Addison, Synda, and Roberto who had died protecting me. I did not even know his name until after his death. Namid had been with Roberto. He was also the sniper who had shot Amaury in the neck. Namid had stayed behind to insure our safety back to Kenosis. When he felt it was clear, he returned to Kenosis. With the help of Amil, who had returned as promised, he was able to bring back Synda's and Roberto's bodies.

The cloth that covered Synda's lifeless body slipped off of her face. Before Kai could hurriedly cover it back up, I discovered how Synda had died. Her death was the most disgraceful way a Cresecren could die. Whoever killed her brutally removed the markings from her face, and left her to die a painful, excruciating death. He was trying to prove a sick point. Something metal near Synda's hand caught my eye. It was wrapped up in her garment. I rushed over to aid in recovering her and I inconspicuously grabbed it out of the entwined cloth. I held it tightly in my hand. An image crossed my mind of Linnayah under a similar sheet if I had not pulled the trigger against Easton. I fought to push the image out of my head. As if Linnayah could see the image too, she took my hand in hers and gave it a gentle squeeze. An unspoken thank you. When no one was near I unclenched my hand to discover what I already knew was inside. Amaury's ear cuff. It must have broken off in the struggle. *Amaury murdered Synda!* I do not know exactly why but I made the decision to keep the information to myself and keep the broken ear cuff.

After the burial, I learned that Kenosis had been Synda's home. Years ago, she worked for a man who played a cruel game. The tyrant would release her into the wild, then hunt her like she was an animal. If Synda could evade him until dawn, he would never play the game with her again. He would track her and taunt her by purposefully missing shots, which made her try even harder to escape. Sometimes the game would last for minutes, sometimes for many agonizing hours, and it always ended the same way. He used tranquilizer darts to bring her down.

Synda would wake up hanging by a thick rope wrapped around her ankles and strung up like an ornament. She was always naked, gagged, and filthy. He would torture her by teasing her with an extremely sharp blade. He barely had to touch her before an open wound appeared. When the tyrant decided he was done, he would cut her down, throw her clothes at her, and take her home. Cuts and scrapes on her body, coupled with bruising around her ankles, would stay as reminders until the next hunt.

The tyrant's mistake, this one time, was releasing her into Kenosis. As the game progressed that day, Bonjú Senior could no longer accept the behavior of the tyrant, fearing the man would kill Synda. Bonjú made sure that the man would never find Synda or Kenosis again. After a while, Synda became family.

I recalled what Lace said earlier about not being the only one who had suffered loss. Lace had lost her first husband, Bonjú, along with many other inhabitants of Kenosis to a rampant disease before the cure was developed. I learned that Lace had almost died herself but received the medication necessary to save her life and that of her unborn child, little Bonjú. With death fresh in my mind, I thought of all the inhabitants of Gavaron buried beneath the debris. Someday, maybe, we will make it back to give them a proper burial, one that they truly deserved.

I breathed in the warm air, saddened by the day's events and relieved to be in the company of friends. Friends I had only just met but to whom I felt loyalty and comfort in just knowing they were near. It did not even bother me when Desmin let out his occasional unwarranted belly laugh.

Once we were back inside, the questions about Amaury, Lady Verleah, and Novus began. Concora said she became acquainted with Lady Verleah some time ago, though she never revealed the true location of Kenosis. Lady Verleah was trying to recruit those who lived in Kenosis to become a part of Novus. When Concora began to suspect that something was not right about Novus, Synda volunteered to help. Kenosis' occupants as a whole agreed that Lady Verleah and Amaury would see sending Synda into Novus as a supportive move. Synda was not going there to live but to keep an eye on things in Novus and report any information she had acquired to those in Kenosis.

Kai would not let one of his own go into Novus alone. He decided to offer his protection services to Amaury and Lady Verleah. No one in Novus had ever met Kai so he would not be suspected of being affiliated with Kenosis. He wandered upon Lady Verleah and her army two months before Synda planned to enter Kenosis and offered his services as protector. Kai hoped to make his way underground into Novus. The plan worked perfectly. Kai earned Lady Verleah's trust and soon was appointed the Keeper of Novus.

Kai and Synda found ways to communicate secretly. Kai soon learned that only those with special ranking were permitted to leave the underground of Novus. One of Kai's jobs was to make sure that no one left Novus, but no one ever wanted to. No one except Phillip, the old Supply Appointed.

"Did you kill Phillip?" I asked.

"No," Kai said. I was relieved to hear that. Kai took out his knife, pushing hard against the base of the handle and sliding it open. A small round blinking device about the size of a pill slid into his palm. "I have had this tracking device with me since I first left Kenosis for Novus. I was only to activate it if it was absolutely necessary. If there was a need for assistance and a situation I could not handle alone. I didn't have a reason to use it until today," Kai said. This explained why Lace and the others showed up to help outside of Novus.

"Why send us to Lady Verleah that day?" Alecander asked Concora.

"To be honest, I sent you as a false gesture of friendship and to earn trust from the Lady. She would see sending her more possible inhabitants as a step in her favor. I will never forgive myself for the loss of Synda, Roberto, and Addison. I regret that decision and will have to bear their loss until my own death," Concora said with sorrow-laden eyes.

The room was silent for a moment.

"Do you have any idea who attacked Lady Verleah's train? I believe they were the same people who attacked Gavaron," I questioned.

"Yes. The Truce," Kai said.

"What?" I said flabbergasted.

"You must be mistaken! The purpose of The Truce is to protect our rights and freedom," Famous said.

"Yes, and it will fight for them at any cost. The Truce also bombed the Market that day," Kai said.

"Vhat?" Zira shouted. Her face paled and her knees began to buckle. Alecander rushed over and took her arm.

"The Truce wanted to stop the creation of our kind. What better way than by causing us to look like unpredictable killers? Why create more of those who could destroy you?" Alecander explained. I was beginning to understand.

"Why did they attack Gavaron?" I questioned.

"Gavaron was attacked for extra measure. The general public would not support the creation of more Cresecrens if they saw the devastation the attack caused. It was the ultimate sacrifice by The Truce to help ensure they got what they wanted," Kai said. I could not believe what I was hearing but I knew what he said was true.

"Why attack Lady Verleah's train? The Truce was helping to create Novus."

"Did you actually see any attack?"

"Yes, we watched it on the screens!"

"So you did not actually see it in person?"

"Well, no," I admitted.

"There was no attack. It was Lady Verleah's way of getting you into Novus and showing you how much she wanted to protect you. Her main objective was to earn your trust. She would protect Novus and its inhabitants at all costs," Kai said.

"What about the man who fell off the train and died?" I said.

"Killed by his own," Kai said.

"The Truce's true enemy is The Truce itself," I said.

I sat down with the realization that my people had been used as pawns in some fanatical organization's game to get what they wanted. They deluded themselves into thinking they were doing what was best for Cresecren people. Novus was just a futile attempt to create a utopia. I shook my head. Human nature was something I could never understand. Sooner or later, Amaury and Lady Verleah would figure out what was going on and they would come looking for us. We were loose ends they needed to tie up.

That evening we sat around the living area. Famous was unusually silent. I thought about how close I would have come to feeling the same way if I had not pulled Mercy's trigger and saved Linnayah's life. Linnayah was sitting on the floor with Bonjú, playing ball with Elza. Alecander talked quietly with Kai. Bentum asked Zira if she could feel the babies yet. Zira said she had felt them for the first time that very day. She took Bentum's hand and placed it on her belly. Bentum smiled with the anticipation of feeling the life that was to come.

I could not help smiling too. I wandered around the room, looking at each of my friends. I realized they were more than that, they were my family. I felt what it really meant to care, what it really meant to love. I also knew there were more battles ahead of us but I now knew I would not have to face them alone.

Award-winning author **Crystal Marcos** lives on the Kitsap Peninsula in Washington State with her husband and their daughter Kaylee. *Novus*, her third book and first Young Adult novel, is book one of The Cresecren Chronicles.

Please visit her at:
> http://www.crystalmarcos.com/

Find her on Twitter:
> https://twitter.com/CrystalMarcos

Get updates on Facebook:
> https://www.facebook.com/CrystalMarcos

Made in the USA
Middletown, DE
19 August 2015